Days of Purgatory

Days of Purgatory

Ken R. Abell

RESOURCE *Publications* · Eugene, Oregon

DAYS OF PURGATORY

Resource Publications
An Imprint of Wipf and Stock Publishers
199 W. 8th Ave., Suite 3
Eugene, OR 97401
www.wipfandstock.com

ISBN 13: 978-1-62032-285-7
Manufactured in the U.S.A.

Scripture taken from the HOLY BIBLE, KING JAMES VERSION, Public Domain.

For Mom and Dad, who put the wanderlust in my soul by teaching me
the value of a story well told and well lived.

&

For Anita Irene, who gleans gems in brokenness.
She remains a bottomless well of inspiration and encouragement.

&

For our sons and grandchildren. May they always know the wonder
of adventure, the importance of obstacles, and the power of hope.

&

For friends and family at Navajo BIC Mission
where most of this tale was written.

Contents

Acknowledgment

A SPECIAL EXPRESSION OF gratitude to my friend Christie Lewis—she willingly read the manuscript and had many kind words to say about the storytelling. Some free advice for sunflowerbucky: Keep smiling, keep pressing on, and don't let the motards get you down

chapter one

No Escape

"Therefore thus saith the LORD, Behold, I will bring evil upon them, which they shall not be able to escape; and though they shall cry unto me, I will not hearken unto them."

~JEREMIAH~

WHEN THE MAN WALKED out of the badlands, he was an emaciated wreck. Half-mad and hollow-eyed, he moved like a staggering drunk, keeping to a wobbly but steady pace.

A raging fever burned through his veins. The throb of his heartbeat thumped against his eardrums. Crusty dirty, with tracts of dried blood matted on his forearms, he resembled a crazed shaman returning from rites of seclusion and sacrifice.

Death stalked him. It was about a step and a half away, its work almost complete. A run of bad luck was demanding its final payment. All used up, he was nearly ready to drop in his tracks and not get up, but compulsion compelled him to keep straining forward. Grimness settled in him, a combination of comfort and determination.

"She won't feed a dirty ragamuffin," he said aloud. The rasping words filled the expanse of the sky. A tiny smile creased his blistered lips as he cinched the remnant of belt a little tighter around his sunken waistline.

He beheld himself and remarked, "I won't be getting fed because I'm a dirty ragamuffin." His trousers were tattered and alkali stained, his shirt a raggedy mess that barely covered his torso, and the soles of his boots flapped like wagging tongues with each stammering step he took.

A grimy beard crawled up his cheeks like a gone to rot patch of weeds. The only thing protecting his skull from the shimmering waves of heat was a tangled crop of thick black hair. His hat had been blown away by a bullet in the getaway that'd started the string of misfortune that put him here. He stiffened and stood straight, a tall and rangy scarecrow of a man with oversized shoulders that looked awkward on his bony frame.

A week ago he'd been surprised by a renegade band of Utes. He proved a worthy quarry. He made them adapt tactics and gave them fits. He held them off until there were no more ruses to be exploited. He surrendered with honor.

They'd held him captive to beat and make sport of for days. Their punishment and knife-blade trickery extracted ounces of flesh in frustration for all the lies and broken treaties. He became the altar on which they poured out their contempt and scorn for the Great White Father in Washington.

Their games and torment came to a conclusion when they staked him out in an excruciating spread-eagle position, then abandoned him to be slowly cooked. By the time he writhed and wrestled free of the rawhide thongs, his wrists were bloody and shredded. It was a night and a day before he recovered enough to travel, and then, only for short stretches.

Three months earlier, an incident from his past filed a claim on his future. With a mercenary posse barreling down on him, the man took off on his big appaloosa gelding. That was when his headgear went soaring, and whatever remained of his life took a precipitous detour.

The horse had grit and stamina. For a solid week, with little food or water, and intervals of rest only when necessity demanded, he rode as though the spawn of Satan were licking at his heels. He applied every ploy he'd learned in all his wanderings, but his pursuers wouldn't be shaken loose.

He and the appaloosa had been through gullies and over mountains together, but now, in this desperate dash, a rare symbiosis took place. The beast never shied away from the adversity and deprivations forced upon it. With nary a flinch, it demonstrated toughness equal to its rider, and when its end came, there was no glory, but much respect. On a dodge down a steep and narrow mountain trail, the horse broke a leg.

Moisture came to the man's eyes. He hugged its neck, holding on stubbornly as tears blurred his vision. With a swift and adept slash, he slit the animal's throat to put it out of its misery, but not before tenderly whispering its name and saying kind remarks of appreciation and fondness.

Time was a swirling lunatic. The well-paid lynch mob, led by a full-time hired gunman sometime bounty hunter, was mere hours behind him. He partially skinned the gelding and carved as much meat as he could backpack. He shouldered his saddlebags and hoofed it out of there to disappear in the vast wildness.

Holed up in a sliver of a cave as a wanted man, he'd schemed and hoodwinked the scallywags chasing him. It was a number of weeks before he could be sure they'd given up on ferreting him out. When he knew the way was clear, he cautiously kept to a low profile routine of scratching out a survival.

Nights were cold, days hot. Hunger and thirst became constant companions. It might have been a foolish peculiarity in him, but he hadn't carried a rifle since the war. The only weaponry he had was a large hunting knife and a Smith & Wesson, for which there was precious little ammunition.

That mattered not for he had to avoid any gratuitous attention. Even if he possessed unlimited boxes of bullets he couldn't gamble using the pistol because in the high desert the bang of a gunshot would carry for many miles.

He was in a deep cut canyon that had a rock-strewn arroyo as its centerpiece. He studied it for several miles, then chose a spot based on a grove of vegetation—clumps of grass, pinyon pines, and scrub cedars. Using his knife, a make-do shovel whittled from a piece of dead wood, and his hands, he dug a rounded out basin, packed it hard around the sides, and waited.

It took many long hours, but enough water seeped from the apparent dry ground for him to fill his canteen. He wove a cedar branch lid to shield the makeshift well and keep it protected. Even as he did so, he knew that the seep-hole could become nothing but a dustbowl without notice.

He rationed the water carefully. A mouthful or two each day was all he allowed himself. Whenever needed, mostly under the cover of darkness, he'd returned to refill the canteen. If any water remained, he'd slurp and suck it all up.

For food he employed every method and tactic that his imagination, experience, and circumstance could devise. Each kill was to be cherished and hoarded. He parceled out the meat with a miserly touch. He snared jackrabbits and kangaroo rats from time to time, had the delicacy of rattlesnake twice, and once dined for weeks on a large turkey.

The days were growing shorter when he'd made a decision. Pangs of regret over a woman came out of nowhere to disturb his conscience. The unexpectedness of the vivid imagery confounded him. It came hurtling at him—he could see her face and hear her voice. He had been less than chivalrous, but years were gone and opportunities lost.

He knew that mending bygone yesterdays was impossible, and it made little sense, but nonetheless, remorse was a pestle of guilt grinding at his core. He eased out of his hideout with the intention of at least attempting to right a wrong. There was a letter in his saddlebags that needed to be posted, but then he had crossed paths with those marauding Utes.

Now, death was so close he could feel its coppery sickness breathing on the nape of his neck. The sun was an ugly gash of blazing yellow torturing him. He regarded it from time to time while muttering disjointed snippets of nonsensical phrases that long ago and faraway had meant something to him. Some thought that there was magic in the words he spoke, but he knew better.

Silence was everywhere. It closed in around him out of the emptiness. The desert landscape was endless, populated by unrelenting thickets of sagebrush and hedges of creosote bush.

A colossal mesa dominated his line of sight. He glowered at it. In the chaos of near-dementia flaming through his mind, it was an ancient jester mocking him. He wanted to spew cusswords at it, but then reason prevailed, and he saved his strength.

A dusky outline passed over him. He cringed and reached up to defend himself against it, his right hand fisted. Another sliver of grayness skulked ever so slowly past, then another came and lingered. He clawed at the shadows.

Everything began to stretch and spin. His life was ebbing away, yet he refused to accept the inevitable. A vigorous will to endure and overcome churned inside him.

"Lawrence . . ." There wasn't even a ripple in the air, yet the wind sang out to him. He *heard* it. "Lawrence . . ."

Sudden-like, he cocked his head to a curious angle. His feet lifted and dropped as he slowly marched in place. He laboriously made a full turn, his eyes squinting into slits. His bearings were skewed, and for the first time since that bullet sent his hat sailing, a creeper of panic weaseled through him.

Entirely disoriented, he had no idea where he was—in his delirium he could have been going in circles for hours, for days. He thought he heard a noise; a familiar, hopeful noise.

A monstrous hurt hammered through his head. His face twisted into a distorted grimace as he attempted to listen above the agony of bones grating his brains to smithereens. The sound in the still air was a dog. He was sure of it. His mouth worked in a broken-hinged way, but regardless of how much effort he put forth, he could force no cry or call from his parched throat.

A dog was barking somewhere, and it was nearby. For one fragile moment, the tiniest fragment of hope fluttered in his heart, but then was snatched away as darkness rushed out of the bright sunshine and knocked him down. He was falling and flailing in blackness for a long while until the deadweight of unconsciousness crushed him.

None of the next happenings would ever grace his memory.

The dog, a brawny redbone hound, belonged to Caleb Weitzel. He watched as it ranged ahead of him, baying as it frolicked with carefree abandon. He also kept an eye on three buzzards circling off in the direction of Angel Peak.

Fourteen years old and already as sturdy as a brick wall, Caleb had been doing a man's job for a couple years. His father didn't entertain lollygagging, his mother even less so. Idle hands led to trouble so each day was filled with chores and a to-do list that was neverending.

Blond and blue-eyed like his parents, he sat easy on the buckboard chatting to the mules while keeping his eyes peeled. He was returning home with supplies. The visit to the little outpost of a town was a long haul back and forth, but he enjoyed the responsibility. Along with taking delivery of a load of dry goods, on this particular trip he'd completed a bargain struck with a handshake six months ago.

A brand new Spencer rifle was at his side. He was as proud as he could be about it for he'd earned the firearm with honest sweat. It had cost him much hard work, labor over and above his regular duties. He'd paid for it with a string of saddle-ready horses, wild mustangs he'd captured and broken.

Rainy bawled loudly. Caleb gave a hard look. The hound was a hundred yards ahead, standing on the edge of a rise near where the buzzards were dipping low in the sky. It was doing an antsy dance, glancing back at its master as though seeking permission to follow its instincts.

Caleb spoke to the mules and urged a bit more speed. The animals complied, ears twitching and tails swishing. Rainy darted out of his line of sight. A moment later the dog let loose a wailing yawp that sent a chill down Caleb's spine. A man comes to know the timbre and notes of his hound's voice.

This wasn't the joyous song of the chase. There was no antelope or any other potential meat for the smokehouse scrambling over the rocks ahead of Rainy. The full-throated bellows were an alarm that trouble or danger, or both were lurking ahead.

The mules were excited and worried by the dramatic shift in the mood. Caleb let them have full rein. He saw that the buzzards were rapidly ascending in a tight spiral. He also heard a change in the redbone's vocalizing. It was a screechy moan that stretched into a howl and then became a constant whine.

Though he couldn't see, Caleb could tell that Rainy had stopped running. He slowed the mules at the crest of the ridge, but almost immediately started them down the slope with great urgency. The animals hee-hawed in protest, but obeyed.

What he saw made him search the surrounding area with a wariness that had been fostered in him. A man in rags was sprawled on his back, his legs akimbo. Rainy was standing over the man, whimpering and licking his face.

The buckboard lurched to a stop nearby. Rainy pawed the ground and began yapping incessantly as though giving orders and instructions on what needed to be done. Caleb leapt down, his Spencer in hand. He crouched low and studied the man's wounds. He'd seen death before, plenty of it, up close.

"Put a cork in it, Rainy," Caleb said sternly. The dog gave a final extended growl, then plopped down on its buttocks to watch, its head tilting and its eyes expressive and mournful.

The man was a blood-stained, dehydrated ruin. His skin was raw, his chest and back crisscrossed by multiple gashes scorched and puckered in ugly folds. Caleb touched the man's brow and felt his neck for a pulse. He pressed an ear against his chest. If there was a heartbeat, it was thin, thready, and barely discernible.

Rainy murmured a noise as Caleb scrambled to action. He raced to the buckboard and returned his rifle to its spot alongside the seat. He rearranged the barrels and boxes to clear a space on one side of the bed. Then he heaved and hoisted the man over a shoulder and half-carried, half-dragged him. It took tremendous effort, but he managed to wrestle him into place.

The mules stood docile, paying no attention to the events behind them. Caleb clapped once and pointed at the buckboard. Rainy made a small circle and jumped up. The dog thoroughly sniffed the man and curled up at his feet, laying its head across his shins. Caleb gave an approving nod. He took a quick glance at the sky.

It was a fading blue, speckled by wispy clouds and long gray fingers reaching out of the west. Daylight would soon be a scarce commodity. He could certainly make his way home by the stars, but preferred not to, so he spoke to the mules and demanded the best they had left in them.

A slew of dust devils swirled in the wagon's wake.

Eliza Weitzel sat on the front porch snapping beans. It'd been a busy day of canning, and now she was going to rest for a bit and watch the sunset. She appreciated this time of day, especially when she was happy with what'd been accomplished, and she was so just now. There was nothing more enjoyable in the evening than the satisfaction of a job well done.

A cool breeze was stirring out of the north. There was a remarkable amount of snow already showing on the La Plata Mountains to the northeast, while to the northwest Sleeping Ute Mountain was capped by its own wreath of white.

The last vestiges of autumn would soon be overtaken by winter. It was coming about a mite early, but she liked the way the changing seasons felt; the smell of the air tickled her nostrils. Life was good, and gratitude swelled in her.

The sun was sinking slowly, a beautiful orange ball perched above the rim of the world. Soon it would begin to ooze a glorious array of colors as it appeared to melt across the horizon. Sunsets were good for her soul. The simple rhythm of sunrise and sunset kept her tuned up like a fine violin.

A slaughtering bloodletting had brought the Weitzels to this hard land. It'd been an arduous journey, and there had been several harrowing difficulties which tested their mettle, but the triumphs outweighed the defeats.

They'd persisted in pressing onward until her husband saw up close what was so clear in his mind's eye. A spring-fed creek watered rolling swatches of pasture, but mostly it was lonesome terrain that required nurturing foresight to survive and rise above the challenges. Much more than surviving in the hardscrabble environment, they'd flourished here and were building a future on the edge of solitude.

The ranch, if that's what it could be called, was a work in progress. It was a jack of all trades enterprise, with sheep and goats penned alongside the barn and a few milk cows in it. Now that Caleb had developed skill with horses, plans were afoot to include them in the mix. A sturdy corral was in the process of being built to replace the temporary one Caleb had erected.

The four years on site had been marked by the completion of one project after another. All their exertion and industry resulted in a cozy house constructed of stones and ponderosa pine logs, a large barn with a blacksmith shop attached to its backside, a butchering shed and smokehouse, a small shack that'd been used by a hired hand before Caleb grew big and strong enough to work side by side with his father.

Behind the house was a dug-out root cellar where they'd spent their first year. Now it was stocked with preserves, dried meat, and bins of vegetables. When the shipment of staples Caleb was bringing from the trading post was added, there'd be stores enough for the winter ahead.

Of course, a respectable distance from the house was also a fit and proper outhouse nestled in front of a copse of ash trees. Its location hadn't been a slipshod choice based only on need, but rather, it was intended to be in harmony with the other structures and came as a result of extensive observation and consideration of airstream patterns.

The positioning of each building was practical and integrated into the landscape because Hans Weitzel had an exacting vision for how he wanted *Freiheit* to be built. He'd spent countless hours sketching and perfecting plans.

Hans had an artistic engineer's knack that was surprisingly accurate in its assessments. He was a careful craftsman who never stopped learning or tinkering. He could see how things would look when he was finished doing all that had to be done. He possessed the brains and stubborn will to transform drawings and notes on paper into reality.

Freiheit had been bred in his heart. It was what he named the homestead; the letters were emblazoned on wood plaques of various sizes situated at three key spots. There was one on the front door of the house, another above the big swinging doors of the barn, and an ornately decorated one framed in the large arch over the laneway entrance.

The iron and wooden arch was ostentatious and strangely out of place, but Hans wanted what he wanted, and by all that boiled within, if he could fabricate it, he'd have it. *Freiheit* was about the only word that remained of his native tongue. It was what he'd been searching for when he left Germany.

Freiheit meant freedom. The notion of it was a living thing inside him, fueling his choices and perspective. Hans Weitzel had looked for freedom in Pennsylvania, but the brand he desired got swallowed by turmoil and strife, so he packed up family and possessions and moved westward.

The wide open spaces of New Mexico had been good to them, though upon arrival they'd witnessed ugliness at its worst. It had bitten at their resolve and placed them smack-dab in the middle between justice and injustice. It also put them at odds with a contingent of the U.S. Cavalry.

In the spring of 1864 the campaign to round up and march the Navajo to Fort Sumner on the Pecos River was in full swing. A mere twenty miles east of the destination that would become *Freiheit*, the Weitzels came upon a dozen Indians in distress.

They'd been stripped of all nobility and were played out, finally prepared to surrender and accept whatever further abuse and indignities lay ahead. Three old men were leading five women and four children, a ragtag group wrapped in filthy blankets and shuffling along, vacant-eyed and vanquished. They'd been deprived of basic necessities and kept on the run, and were slowly starving to death. The sight of the refugees was sickening.

"Lord, have mercy!" Eliza gasped, her voice rising sharply. She jumped off the seat of the Conestoga before Hans even had the wagon stopped.

The oxen grunted a complaint. Caleb patted and whispered to them. He'd been walking alongside, with a young redbone hound pup cradled in an arm. He was wide-eyed and curious, watching his mother busily make introductions and communicate with sweeping gestures. Her hand signals turned out to be unnecessary because one of the men had a fair handle on English, and he animatedly translated for the others.

"Caleb," his father said, standing beside him. "Put Rainy in the basket. Get a fire started over there." He pointed to a place amongst a cluster of rocks. "We'll set up camp here for a while and see what we can do to help these people."

Caleb nodded. "Sure thing, Pa."

Hans surveyed the situation and surmised what needed to be done. "Eliza," he said, already moving. "Share what we must. I'll go scare up some fresh meat." He grabbed his Henry rifle and checked it over. He untied one of the mules trailing the wagon. He mounted it bareback and was sidling away when his wife caught his eye.

A blush of anger colored her cheeks as she approached him. "It never ends, does it?" she queried, the pretty lines of her face wrinkled into scars of sorrow. She was tall and willowy, her slender body highlighted by wide hips with the kind of pleasant curves which couldn't be easily hidden.

"No, I'm afraid not. There's no escape," he replied, reaching out to touch her shoulder. "Care for them."

"Care for yourself," she said, much authority in her tone. He pursed his lips and wagged a finger at her, then wheeled about and trotted away.

Midway through the next morning, Hans returned with a deer and a couple turkeys draped over his lap and the mule's neck. Everyone was spread around the fire munching on biscuits and dried beef. At the sight of the game, the men and women became cheerful and immediately went to work. It wasn't long before a feast of sorts was being roasted.

Hours later, when bellies were full and dusk was beginning its lazy descent, trouble came calling. They saw the dust rising before they heard the thunder of hoofs. The Navajo were resigned to their impending doom, yet stood tall and proud when the troopers rode into camp. There were six of them, all dirty and scruffy looking.

The leader, Jackson Scully, was an officious sort with a bulbous nose and bulgy eyes. He dismounted and gave orders for the other soldiers to do likewise and take charge of the prisoners. He moved with a distinctive limp in his gait, hitching his left leg with each step as though it had been attached as an afterthought.

"Thank you for your service," he said to no one in particular. "You did well capturing them. We'll handle the varmints from here. You folks can pull out in the morning."

Hans Weitzel shook his head with slow firmness. "We'll be staying with our friends. At least for a while."

Jackson Scully reacted gleefully. "Friends? Did you hear that, boys?" He tilted back on his heels, flipped up the flap on the holster, withdrew his sidearm, and pointed it menacingly.

A contagion of chuckles leapfrogged from one man to the next. They each had firearms angled on the Navajo, who held their posture stiff and erect. Eliza stood with them. Caleb was at her side, his chin thrust forward as he clutched his mother's skirt with one hand and cuddled the pup in the other.

Hans had his hands on his hips. A broad, muscular man thick in the chest and shoulders with a stump of a neck, he had a bold certainty in his demeanor that oft-times set-off fear or anxiety in others. "Why'd you pull a gun on me?" he asked, eyes flashing and a terse mockery in his tone.

Scully kept the pistol aimed at him. "I'm in command here representing the U.S. government," he answered flatly. "You'll pack up your gear now and be on your way. There'll be no waiting till morning."

"Well, I won't fight the U.S. government," Hans said, "but I'd be pleased to give you a lesson in manners. Why don't you put that handgun away so we can take care of this man to man?"

Jackson Scully pulled the trigger twice. The pistol bucked and roared, and clumps of dirt splattered up and danced on either side of Hans Weitzel, within inches of his feet. "The next bullet will be a dead-center gut-shot. While you're bleeding out, I'll burn your wagon and supplies, butcher the oxen, and confiscate the mules. I may even appropriate your woman. She seems like a lively one. What's it going to be, sir?"

Weitzel's hands hadn't strayed from his hips, but now they were fisted. Reason demanded that he stand down, but his blood was on the rise. He felt like a useless capon, and he despised the feeling. His teeth were grinding as his head bobbed ever so slightly. Every sense told him that Jackson Scully was fully capable of doing all that he said; not only would he carry out his threats, he'd do so with eager satisfaction.

"Hans!" Eliza called urgently. He glanced in her direction, and what he saw amazed him. An Indian man, the one who spoke English and was known as Gray Eyes, had sauntered away from the group and was strolling toward the showdown.

A soldier shouted at him and fired a warning shot, but Gray Eyes ignored it and kept moving with casual ease. Another bullet scratched the air over his head. Scully held up a hand to halt any further action against the old man.

Gray Eyes carried himself ramrod straight. No one could guess what he was doing, but it seemed apparent to all that he was on a mission for which he was prepared to die. His lean face, with its creased wrinkles, had a peaceful glow.

The wispy strands of his thin white hair hung loose, and his footsteps were light and carefree. It was as though long-ago drums and flutes were playing a ceremonial song just for him, and he was moving in sync with its refrain. In those moments, he reclaimed dignity.

Not the frayed and colorless blanket tied around his shoulders, the bitterness of loss and affliction, nor even the immense sadness in his eyes could diminish his presence. An ancient ancestral pride swelled within, and his frail frame took on a powerful and distinguished bearing.

He stopped in front of Hans. They regarded each other for a short while. Gray Eyes reached out to take hold of his wrists. Hans opened his mouth to say something, but Gray Eyes hushed him. Hans felt something warm and strange come over him. His fists unclenched, and they took hold of each other's hands.

"You are my friend," Gray Eyes said softly. "I will not forget you. Your kindness to my people will be remembered and spoken of in the times to come." He began swaying to the inner music. "Three, perhaps four days west and south from here there are meadows and good water. When you see it, you will know that it is the place for you." His eyes squeezed shut, and he began chanting a melody, which went on and on and on, mesmerizing and mysterious. Everyone's attention was riveted on him.

Hans Weitzel wasn't much on religion. It was there and it was real, but the practice of it was for others. He respected Eliza's hardboiled piety, but his dealings with the Almighty were tenuous and riddled with skepticism. Despite her tempering influence he remained coarse-grained and dubious. Even so, as goosepimples crawled over his skin, he realized he was in the midst of a holy moment.

When the singing came to its end, Gray Eyes smiled broadly. "I bless you, Hans Weitzel. Go now in peace. West and south. When you see the place, you will know."

Less than an hour later, the Weitzel family were on the trail. The sky was high and clear. A silence was heavy on them as they slowly rolled across the moonlit plateau.

Hans was troubled. Deeply disturbed and brooding, he kept his counsel locked away and endeavored to make sense of the old Indian's actions and words. The groaning of the wagon wheels expressed the emotions turning over and over in his mind, unspoken questions that had no answers to satisfy him.

Now, sometimes at night when coldness got into the air, Hans could become agitated by the memory. The experience had gotten under his skin. He still wondered about the meaning of that blessing prayed over him.

There was a cold wind easing out of the mountains this evening, and he was uptight. When he emerged from the barn, a sheen of sweat on his forehead instantaneously dried.

Halfway across the yard to the house he stopped. A feeling unbidden and unwanted came over him. It prickled the hair on the back of his neck. He looked to the west, intently searching for any sign of Caleb's return. There was no telltale dust rising that he could see.

The sun was halfway down, dripping its colors over the distant mountains. His eyes bent toward his wife. She was a pretty picture in the twilight, watching the curtain close on daylight. He came up on the porch and kissed her lightly on the cheek as he sat on the bench beside her.

"The boy's late," he said gruffly.

"He'll be along." Her hands remained busy. The beans were done; the bowl was on a sideboard in the kitchen, and now she was knitting a sweater from homegrown wool. "He's not much of a boy anymore," she reminded, the soft click-click of the needles sounding lyrical and happy.

"True enough." He folded his arms over his chest and leaned back a bit, which she read as a sure sign that he had something on his mind. She smiled in a knowing way, prompting him with a gentle bob of her head. His eyes narrowed as tension tightened the lines of his face.

She grew curious. "What is it, Hans?"

"Eliza," he began, looking off in the distance. "Do you ever think about what happened to Gray Eyes and the others?"

She stiffened. A twinkle flared in her eyes. "Hans Weitzel, you're an exasperating, stubborn old coot! It's been four years, and in all that time you've never said a word . . ."

"I'm saying a word now," he cut in, giving her a lame shrug. They stared at each other for a long while, a hard and familiar tenderness passing back and forth between them.

"Yes," she said softly. "I've thought about them often."

Hans kept his focus fixed on the sunset. "Those words he sang over me stick in my craw. I worry on them time to time."

"Why worry on them? That was a gift."

"I don't understand, Eliza."

"Neither do I, Hans." She reached over and took hold of one of his hands. "Sometimes all we can do is accept what someone gives us, whether good or bad, and move on. My guess is that those words Gray Eyes gave you were precious to him."

"Precious? How can that be? They were just words."

Eliza laughed. "Words have meaning in whatever language they're spoken. Don't be a pigheaded sour kraut."

He grinned. "I am a sour kraut. Being pigheaded is my charm." He gave her knee an affectionate squeeze, but then a frown darkened his brow. He tilted forward and suddenly stood. "He's coming too fast."

Eliza followed his gaze. It was exactly what they'd been waiting and looking for—a fog of dust seethed in the dusk, streaming into the reddish-orange hues blending along the horizon. They watched together as the buckboard came into view. It was rocking at a rapid, dangerous speed.

"He knows better," Hans said irritably.

"Yes, he does." She put her knitting down on the bench. "Something's wrong," she said in a whisper. She hitched up her skirts and ran several steps into the yard. He followed.

Caleb was shouting and Rainy howling when the buckboard clattered under the arch and seesawed to a stop. The mules were sweating, chests heaving up and down. Hans couldn't tolerate an animal being ill-used, and there was anger in him. That stewed for a hot moment, but promptly became compassion when he saw the brutalized man laid out beside the barrels.

Eliza winced at the sight that slammed her. "Oh, dear God."

"Who is he?" Hans asked, looking to his son.

"Dunno, Pa. Found him near the Angel Peak badlands."

A wordless dialog darted between the three of them. It was speedy and thorough. Then, with fixed purpose, they scrambled into action, each finding a task that needed doing.

Eliza Weitzel sat stone-faced. The enormity of the man's wounds stunned her. His breathing was shallow, his heartbeat faint and delicate. She washed his bruised and battered body, while Hans assisted.

It took two full tubs of water to clean away the grime and blood. Her hands worked with prayerful efficiency. All the while she racked her brain to recall every scrap of knowledge and experience of learning she had about caring for wounds.

When she was satisfied he was sufficiently scrubbed, she dressed the freshest gashes and gouges with a greasy salve saturated with medicinal herbs. He was burning up and near comatose. She did what she could to make him as comfortable as possible. Every few minutes she sponged cool water laced with a healing concoction into his mouth.

Each time she did so, she supposed that perhaps it was too late. It kept coming to her that he was too far gone to be nursed back from the brink. She refused those thoughts.

It was nighttime, and she was alone with her patient. The man was on a cot in the hired hand's shack. She was nearby, but far away. The flicker of an oil lamp glinted in her eyes as she remembered other men who'd fallen under her care, when their farm on the outskirts of Gettysburg was commandeered and converted into a hospital.

For three horrid days the battle tore apart the countryside as generals issued orders and armies clashed. The smoke and booming of artillery transformed pastoral stillness into pandemonium that resulted in nothing except savagery and misery. The air was thick and steaming with humidity as both sides maneuvered for victory, though in her mind there could never be any winners.

The bloodshed and mutilation was incomprehensible. Her bravery and boldness was constantly on display. She accepted her new role as nurse and surgical assistant. She'd held men down on her kitchen table as surgeons hacked off an arm or leg and casually tossed the limb aside. Her hands had been inside soldier's bellies. She'd packed gaping wounds with gauze and pinched veins to lessen the bleeding.

Many of those Eliza had bathed or helped to stitch together were not far removed from boyhood. To see their youthful bodies ripped apart made her sick. The anguish in their eyes begged her to rescue them, to stave off the grim reaper, but all too often, the herculean efforts were useless.

The dying was always detestable. Each death put its mark on her. When she got to two dozen, she'd ceased to number the men whose tears she wiped or hands she held as life withered away. She'd been sworn at in one breath, blessed in the next. Curses were spat out as prayers. She'd heard heartfelt confessions and pleading requests to do something to stop the agony.

The screaming of those writhing in pain was unending. The sound of it was a torment that got inside her head. When she could get her hands on it, she'd spooned laudanum into mouths or poured it down throats, depending on the maimed man's condition.

Hans had served in ways that fit his practical manner. He'd lifted and moved things to rearrange rooms. True to the fire within, he'd refused to be put under the thumb of blue-coated authority figures for he was predisposed to see all governmental agents as strutting gasbags needing to be knocked down a peg. Those inclinations could never smother the tenderness encased in his callous-encrusted heart.

He'd thrown himself into tasks that alleviated suffering, tending the wounded and feeding the hungry. When not engaged elsewhere his hands had kept busy tidying up the bloody mess, which had proven to be a perpetual venture.

Hans hadn't shirked any chore, no matter how distasteful or gruesome. He'd carried out the dead and laid them in the shade of a big maple tree in their yard or loaded them onto flatbed wagons. He had even joined the detail of soldiers who'd been assigned the duty of disposing of the pile of discarded limbs.

Shocked and morbidly fascinated, nine-year-old Caleb had watched it all, big-eyed and determined to heed the example set by his parents. He'd kept out of the way of the military personnel, but made it his mission to care for his mother.

Three or four times each day he'd slip into the surgical ward that had been their sitting room with a bite of food or a glass of fresh water for her. Few words had passed between them. Eliza would simply give his shoulder a squeeze or ruffle his hair. He'd respond with a tight smile.

Anxiety filled her. It bordered on bitter anger at the wrongness of it all. Each time Caleb arrived, she'd felt a sense of helplessness. It was as though he was aging before her eyes. The long hours of the exhausting days were like years piled on top of him. She'd never been a worrywart, but in the midst of those tribulations, she'd brooded about the ghastly furrows plowed in her son's soul.

After the last shots were fired at Gettysburg, the troops regrouped to be dispatched elsewhere, but the Weitzel household remained as active as a beehive. It had taken a few weeks before all the patients were removed from their home.

Two days after the final ambulance pulled away, Hans returned from town and unceremoniously announced, "We go west. Now. I've sold out everything."

That was just over five years ago, and now, here she was once again called upon to be a nurse, attempting to coax health back into the body of a malnourished and ill-treated stranger. She doubted her skills and his capacity to rally and survive, but the man, whoever he was, wouldn't greet eternity because she failed to apply due diligence and try every possible remedy. There were tears on her cheeks as she squeezed moisture into his mouth; tears for him and for the lament that swelled within her bosom. She held a finger below his nostrils and could feel the slightest whisper of breath. She regarded him with tremendous sadness, wondering what gross barbarity of man's inhumanity had put him here.

"Ma," Caleb interrupted her thoughts. He was standing in the open doorway, a silhouette in the moonlight. She hadn't even heard the hinges creak. "The animals are cared for, and supplies are put away in the root cellar."

"Thank you," she replied, giving him a quick look. "You go get some sleep. That corral isn't going to finish itself."

"What about you?"

"I'll be fine."

"That's what Pa said you'd say."

She smiled tiredly. "Never you mind. Tell Hans I expect that corral to be ready for use by sundown tomorrow."

"Why the rush? We won't have horses until springtime."

"Are you convinced of that, son?" There was an undisguised challenge in her voice. "I say you'll capture at least a couple before the first snow."

Caleb worked on that notion for a spell. "I suppose if I got at it in the next few days I might be able to do so."

"What are you waiting for?" his mother asked sharply. "Sleep tonight. Finish the corral tomorrow and start tracking wild mustangs the next day."

"Sure thing, Ma."

"Caleb." Her eyes were shiny with pride. "You did real good today, son. If this man lives, he'll owe you his life."

He gave a nonchalant shrug. "Will he make it?"

"God willing."

"Who is he?"

"Someone who needs our help."

Caleb nodded knowingly. "Get some rest, Ma."

Eliza shooed him with a backhanded swipe. She got off the stool to watch him walk to the house. He carried himself with the same stiff-shouldered, self-assured gait as his father.

The night air was cool. She enjoyed it for a moment before closing the door. The oil lamp sat on a shelf near a potbelly stove. She checked its wick before returning to her perch beside the cot. Now that the initial burst of activity had passed, she had a chance to really study the lines of the man's face.

There was something about him that jarred her, something beyond the ailments of his body. She couldn't quite figure it, but of all things, she found herself focused on his hair. Her mind raced. Abruptly, her backbone straightened as she grasped at a memory that jumped to the forefront.

It was mid-summer when the posse had passed by *Freiheit*. She'd been on the back stoop stacking tanned elk hides in preparation to be stored in the root cellar. The whinny of a horse startled her, followed by a loud, booming voice.

"Hello, the house."

Eliza came around the corner to see five dust-covered riders sitting outside the archway. They'd obviously walked the horses for the last mile or so, otherwise she'd have heard them coming. She was wary. She glanced over a shoulder toward the barn, took a deep breath, and approached them directly.

"Are you lost?" she asked in a somewhat friendly manner. She came to a stop beneath the arch, with her hands tucked into the pockets of her homespun skirt.

"No, ma'am," a round-faced man said, removing his hat as he spoke. He sat relaxed on a superb chestnut. He was burly and had a wisp of a beard and thinning hair peppered with gray. "I'm Yance Rawlins. We're tracking a murderous outlaw. We got a warrant on him from Judge Thomas Thornton out of Santa Fe."

"Been no one come this way." She looked each rider over. All were toughened, hard bitten men with weary eyes, the kind who'd come out of the war pockmarked by desperation. Her breath got wedged in her throat. At the back of the detachment, sitting on a white-faced sorrel was the U.S. Calvary officer who'd taken two shots at her husband and threatened to kill him. His battered old army-issue hat was pulled low on his forehead. She leaned toward him, her mouth pursing sourly.

"He was mounted on an appaloosa, but no more," Rawlins said, eyeing her. "He goes by Deke or Coburn. He's a killer."

"No, sir. Haven't seen anyone."

"A tall fella, with shaggy black hair," he said, then took a pull on his canteen. "He does bad things to little girls. They're only Injun or Mexican, but just the same. What he does is sick. I cannot say more in mixed company, ma'am."

Eliza paused. That news instantly tied a knot in the pit of her stomach. She shook her head. "Can't help you. Wish I could."

Yance Rawlins shifted in the saddle, taking a look at the home-stead. "You've got yourself a fine spread here, ma'am. Could we trouble you for some grub?"

She didn't hesitate. "You keep poor company, Mr. Rawlins. I'll consider fixing a sack to go, but *that* man gets none."

Rawlins turned slightly to follow her gesture. "Who? Scully? He's harmless. A miserable cuss, but harmless."

Jackson Scully rubbed his unshaven chin. When he spoke there was smirking condescension in his tone. "Rawlins, I didn't sign on with an outfit of mollycoddlers, did I?" He yanked on the reins to move the horse up beside the leader. It sidestepped, skittish-like. "This here woman knows something, and she's a do-gooder. If Coburn came this way, he would have found help and gotten a fresh horse. Maybe even stayed put for a while. I say we search the place."

"You ain't in the army any more, Scully," Rawlins said flatly. "I apologize for Scully's way, ma'am. But he does make a fair point. It'd be wise for us to have a quick look-see."

"If it was only up to me, Mr. Rawlins, that'd be fine," Eliza said, bending her eyes toward the barn. "But my husband doesn't take kindly to uninvited trespassers. My guess is that he's in the loft with a Henry rifle aimed at your head."

Yance Rawlins had a twinge of caution. He squinted at the barn. Someone could easily be hidden in the deep shadows. "What do you know about these folks, Scully?"

"The man's got sand, but the boy's a whelp."

Eliza spat out a derisive laugh. "My son is more of a man than you'll ever be, Mr. Scully." She shaded her eyes and issued a no-nonsense challenge. "You came looking for a killer, Mr. Rawlins. I told you no one has been by this way. Are you going to sit there and call me a liar?"

"No, ma'am," Yance replied, dragging a hand through his hair before putting his hat back on. He tipped the brim to her, then said, "Thank you for your offer of grub, but we've troubled you enough. Give my kind regards to your husband."

With that, they'd left. She'd waited by the archway until all she could see were tiny plumes of dust raising. Her daring gambit had worked. She'd been alone; at the time Hans and Caleb were working in a distant field, with Rainy at their side.

In the lamplight she remembered. *A tall fella, with shaggy black hair.* The gangly man on the cot certainly fit that sketchy description. She stared at his curly black crown.

"Lord, have mercy," she murmured, wringing her hands on her lap. "Who are you? What have you done?"

The young girl was scared out of her wits. A monster was scratching at the dirt near her hiding place. It had gotten her before, but this time she was sure that the cave would protect her. She was scrunched behind a stack of loose rocks, her breath coming in tiny hitches.

Dirt was encrusted under her fingernails, as well as being streaked on her cheeks. The plain cotton smock she wore was torn and bloodstained.

The monster was grunting as it clawed the ground at the cave's entrance. It was making progress, getting closer and closer. She cringed to make herself smaller. It did no good. She could feel its eyes on her.

Worse than that, she could taste its rotting breath. It loomed over her, slobbering and smacking its lips. Her stomach turned over, sending a gush of bile up her throat. It burned and hurt, but she swallowed it. Her eyes were raw and sore from crying, and gaped open, staring at the beast.

It grinned, and she screamed. There were bits of human flesh hanging on its sharp teeth. It reached for her with its big muscular arms, and she screamed again, louder and louder, but no one could hear her. She jumped and ran. It snatched her garment; it tore away like paper.

She was naked, running through the forest, with her pursuer toying with her. It took sadistic delight in the chase, which really wasn't a chase at all. The girl had no chance. There'd be no escape. Once captured, there was never any escape, only a series of tricks and morbid games.

The darkness was complete and oppressive, with no glimmer of moonlight. Her legs were wobbly, but pumping hard. She darted past tall trees on a rock-strewn trail.

It was huffing and puffing gales of hideous laughter behind her. She wanted to die. She was a mere girl, and she wanted to die, to be free of the terror. That thought was constantly in her mind.

She knew that death would soon prevail, but the fiend wasn't finished with her yet. It had much more enjoyment planned. She wasn't its first. There had been others, many others. The monster had told her so, providing horrific details.

She stumbled, caught her balance, teetered for several steps and took a nasty tumble. Scrambling, she crawled and struggled to get her feet under her, with the monster standing over her. It cuffed her across the back of the head, slurping and chuckling gleefully.

"You're still fresh enough, girl," it growled, pressing a foot on the small of her back. She was face-down in the dirt, squirming to get away. The rustle of the brute's trousers caused her to whimper. She squeezed her eyes shut, clenched her teeth, and felt its weight upon her.

Pain ripped her apart. A high-pitched shriek issued from her lungs, louder and louder and louder. She faded into nothingness, allowing the blackness to smother her. The rutting beast finished, yet still the agonized sound scorched from her lungs. In long distorted syllables she heard someone calling her name.

Sally . . . Sally . . . Sally.

She came awake thrashing, her body soaked with cold sweat, her throat hurting from the screech wrenching out of her. Her arms flailed violently, her fists punching and fighting, but being held tight by strong hands.

"Sally . . . Sally . . . Sally. It's me. Consuelo."

The eleven year old went rigid. Her dark eyes darted to and fro as she reoriented with reality. Her breathing slowed. Tears were glistening on her cheeks. She collapsed back on the bed, letting loose a long gasp of a sigh.

Daniel Twosongs watched from the hallway, his throat clogged with emotion. When he was sure the girl was fully awake and that his wife didn't require his assistance, he returned to the kitchen. Sitting at the wooden table, he packed a pipe and lit it, taking long draws and letting the smoke waft over him.

He was a man of no country, but of many lands. An old soul, he'd been abandoned as a newborn on the doorsteps of a Franciscan mission near Albuquerque. A note attached provided relevant information, which was scandalous.

In a remorseless style, the mother, a white woman from a reputable missionary family, reported the baby was a half-breed, the product of her liaison with a Navajo brave. She'd kept the pregnancy secret until the last possible moments, and with the birth, was being shipped east to live with relatives. She wanted the boy to be called Daniel, out of the Bible.

The order billeted him in a local home, but when the time came for schooling, took charge of his education. He was inquisitive and quick, exhibiting an eager mind that absorbed knowledge. He became fluent in English and Spanish. He also had a fondness and affinity for music, acquiring proficiency on a pair of instruments, the violin and wooden flute.

When he learned of his dubious parentage, he was a serious and sensitive young man. The news didn't disturb him, but instead, spurred a latent curiosity. All through his growing up years whenever the question arose, it had been diverted or brushed over, then at fifteen, he pressed hard. He demanded answers, so finally a well-meaning Brother gave him the note found pinned to his swaddling blanket.

Daniel read it, smiled a thank you, then quietly packed his few belongings and made plans. While the dark of the moon provided concealment, without a word or warning to anyone, he disappeared from the countryside. He flew the coop to wander where the wind or impulse would take him, and in a burst of pride, added the surname of Twosongs, to remind him that the rhythms of two cultures flowed in his veins.

He made his way to a Navajo village, where he sought to gain familiarity with that portion of his heritage. There was solace in him as he introduced himself as Daniel Twosongs in Spanish and English. The name felt right rolling off his tongue in either language. It invoked a range of reactions from others. Some thought it pretentious, others murmured approval. He hung around the edges of the community for a long while biding his time and soaking up customs and practices.

A holy man watched him, intrigued by the respectful young man who asked question in a tone that reflected sharpness and humility. The old man's eyes were aged and glassy, but clearly saw the dissonance between the physical and spiritual orbs. He knew that life was about narrowing the separation between the two spheres and thereby achieving a degree of tranquility.

He befriended Daniel Twosongs and took him into his hogan. For three years Daniel lived with him day and night, serving the wizened healer as he acquired insights into folklore and garnered wisdom passed down from the ancients.

The training was grueling. As an apprentice, Daniel had to be immersed in the language and oral traditions of the Diné. He tackled the commitment with willingness and discipline, and didn't slack off until he had memorized a multitude of supplication chants in word-perfect precision.

There were taboos to be avoided, and ceremonies of cleansing if a prohibition was violated. The rituals and procedures were treasures that totally resonated. He noted with contentment that the common theme in them was to bring an individual back into alignment, to restore health and balance.

The Navajo concept, *Hozhó*, vibrated in him like a stringed instrument being plucked and strummed. He sought to know, feel and embrace every note of *Hozhó*, which roughly translated meant *being in harmony* or *walking in life with beauty.* `

The methods to achieve and maintain *Hozhó* were complex, the sacraments steeped in the mythologies of antiquity. Daniel found it fascinating, and his mind assimilated it all. He could identify various crossroads where the odds of Catholicism came into accord with the ends of Navajo spirituality. Those junctions would become the places where his interest would always be titillated and charmed.

When he departed, he did so with the medicine man's assent and clearance. Daniel Twosongs was a young man who had been tutored in the humanities of two civilizations, and now he was off to explore whatever else a windswept world had to offer.

Early on in his sojourn, near a place known as *Naayízí*, he encountered an elder named Gray Eyes, whose life had been spent on a tightrope between the white and Navajo world. There was an almost instantaneous kinship. From him, young Twosongs learned many more native invocations and also the value of extending charity to everyone, for that pleased the Creator.

In his six months with Gray Eyes, a unique bond developed, but ultimately Daniel Twosongs was a wandering loner. He had a need to see whatever was on the other side of wherever he happened to be. He traveled far and wide for twenty years before there was any inclination to have a home.

It came upon him like an abrupt thunderclap. He fell under Consuelo's spell at a festival on the hard-packed streets of Taos. She was the daughter of a prominent businessman. It wasn't long before they were married, and he sort of put down some roots to be at least partially domesticated.

They had an adobe dwelling on a secluded hillside west of town, where they kept a few sheep and grew a large garden. He hunted when and where he wanted, sometimes vanishing in the mountains or far off trails for weeks and months at time. She was independent and accepted his penchant for rambling.

There were no children from their union, which was sadness between them. The girl Sally was in their care as a result of an encounter Daniel had on one of his extended journeys. There had been nothing official, but they'd adopted her and taken responsibility for her upbringing. It was difficult. She was badly damaged; she'd been rescued from a living nightmare. No one could surmise how long she'd be affected by the despair of being trapped inside it.

Consuelo came into the kitchen, a whirlwind of swishing skirts. "She's sleeping. Fitfully," she said, sitting across from him. "Deke didn't do that poor girl any favor." She was up and moving again, ever bustling.

"What are you saying?"

"She's not right in the head, Daniel." She was rummaging at a cupboard for new candles. She stopped, evidently deciding that the room had enough light, and returned to her seat.

"Would you rather she be dead?"

"Of course not!" she snapped, giving him a blast of indignation, eyes narrowing into slits. She held that expression for a moment. As she looked upon the empathy wrinkling his deep cut crow's feet, she softened, releasing a heavy groan of air. "It feels hopeless. I'm afraid. It's been months."

Daniel was firm. "It may take years."

"Years?"

"You are so impatient," he said, adjusting the corncob pipe cupped in his right hand. The smoke rising from the bowl made wispy patterns in the candlelight. "The night terrors are less frequent. She's talking more. Getting downright chatty."

She pinched a smile at him. "I suppose you're right."

"She's learning to play the flute," he said, a bit of pride easing into his voice. "It's doing her good. I'm crafting a special one for her that'll have her name on it."

"Will she ever be right in the head?"

"Time and tenderness, Consuelo. Time and tenderness."

They sat in silence for a long while listening to the night.

In Santa Fe, Judge Thomas Thornton couldn't sleep. He was a man used to getting his way and having others bend to his will. He couldn't tolerate loose ends. There was one disconcerting strand in his plans that needed tying up, and he was awake and chafing over that matter.

It was the middle of the night, yet he was fully dressed as though it was midday. The custom cut broadcloth suit hung loose on his broad frame. At fifty, he carried some extra thickness in the midsection, but much muscle remained through the shoulders. He was a fastidious man, with an obsessive attention to appearances that could almost be described as prissy.

He sat at a marble-topped desk in his ornate office smoking a cigar and drinking finely aged bourbon provided by business partners in Kentucky. All the oil lamps were burning bright, casting the mahogany walled room in yellowish hues. He was waiting expectantly. Men were coming to deliver a report that he anticipated would give him a measure of satisfaction.

He fancied himself an important man with big connections. Perhaps that was so; maybe he did know influential men in high places, but they'd all scatter if the truth ever came to light. There were secrets in his life that he kept locked behind carefully constructed layers for he knew that all his ambitions for high office were dependent on his squeaky clean law and order image.

If the skeletons ever crawled out of the closet, all Judge Thornton's associations and aspirations would be trashed. That was never going to be an acceptable outcome, so he kept ever vigilant, obscuring details and eliminating problems. He used his wealth with cunning efficiency.

There was no chance that he'd allow a weakness or mistake to derail his career. As a young man he had been a bit lax and indulged deviant passions whenever the urge arose, but had put that irresponsible behavior behind him. He had his appetites fully under his thumb, which meant that he paid dearly to pamper himself, and for those confidences to remain hush-hush.

He refused negligence on his part. He stayed fully engaged in every situation until it was handled. Neither would he put up with a slapdash performance from underlings. When he gave an order, he expected it to be carried out without excuse or delay.

Thomas Thornton had scraped and badgered his way along, fueled by the age-old quest for power and control. He came west from Missouri during the war with Mexico to build a substantial financial base. He did so by bulling his way into the right circles, then biding his time to gather inside tidbits.

No information was ever wasted nor forgotten. He filed it all away to be used at junctures of his choosing. Relationships were stepping stones, nothing more. Every alliance or friendship served its purpose of advancing his position or it was set aside until if or when it would do so.

He'd been ruthlessly wise in commercial wheeling and dealing, making every penny earn its keep by diversifying investments and interests. He had banking, railroad, cattle, lumber, and mining holdings. All of which were foundational for his presence in the territorial politics of New Mexico.

There were also numerous shady, lucrative deals. Each of these ventures was concealed by a complex series of buffers. The income streams from liquor, brothel, and black-market enterprises couldn't be traced back to him unless a dozen links in the chain went wrong all at once. The chances of that happening were nil and none.

For Judge Thomas Thornton, life was reasonably good. A run for the governorship was an imminent probability. His standing was secure and his future still held promise, but a tragedy had befallen him, one that stabbed at his heart.

All his ambitions and empire building efforts were to forge a legacy to be passed along to his only son, but God or fate had robbed him of that possibility, and bitterness had found fallow ground in his soul.

From the outside looking in, Lucas Thornton had been an up and comer, groomed to follow his father's footsteps. Less than four months ago, under incredulous circumstances, he'd died. He had been traveling the high country alone, and now there was scuttlebutt swirling that sullied his memory and distressed his father. The Judge carried on as though political enemies were spinning innuendo regarding the death of his son. No quarter would be given until those rumors were squelched.

Thornton took a final puff, stubbed out his cigar, then stood and stretched. He was a stumpy man, who seldom moved quickly. Even as he paced, with a dervish of impatience at loose inside, each stride was slow, methodical, calculating. There was never any wasted movement. All energy was employed in his brain, which had no shut-off switch. He routinely kept issues turning over and over in his head, reasoning every eventual angle.

A knock-knock was followed by the door opening. Yance Rawlins entered the room, with Jackson Scully close behind. Both men were dusty and dirty, their expressions strained by tiredness. They had their hats in their hands.

"Glad you could make it, boys," the Judge said, taking a gander at his pocket watch. "I did expect you before midnight, but you're here now." He spoke in an easy, deliberate way that had a calming effect. He went to the sidebar, splashed a healthy amount of bourbon into two tall glasses and served them. He returned to behind the large desk, settling in the maroon leather chair. "What's the status?"

Yance Rawlins finished off his whiskey, swallowing hard. "I'm afraid it's not good," he said, placing the glass on the sidebar. He ambled over and stood directly in front of his employer, between a pair of matching high-back armchairs. "The trail's cold, dead cold. We paid off the others and sent them on their way." He teetered on the balls of his feet with a glibness that belied the sober nature of the conversation.

Thornton took the news evenly. "Is that so?"

Jackson Scully was sticking close to the door. "As far as it goes, that's the way the story went."

Thomas Thornton frowned, cracked a knuckle and waggled both hands at them. "I need to hear more."

"I'm sorry, Judge," Rawlins said, shrugging. He cast a hard look at his partner and proceeded to speak in a determined manner. "It's been three months since we flushed him in Taos. He got away by a whore's eyelash. We tracked him west and currycombed every nook and cranny, but the trail went frigid cold, boss. It's like he evaporated. The man's gone or dead."

Judge Thornton smiled. "Is that so? If he's gone, I want him found. If he's dead, show me the body. And what about Sanchez? That Mexican alluded to written evidence. I want it."

"I don't know what to tell you, boss," Yance said angrily. "My best guess is that Coburn's dancing in the clouds courtesy of a band of Utes on the warpath. They spooked us and we had a running battle with them that took us completely off his trail."

"I'm not interested in, nor am I paying you to guess," the Judge replied, low and casual. "I want Coburn dead. If some stirred-up Utes have done that for me, God bless them. That'd be cosmic justice at work, but I want to see the corpse."

Yance Rawlins stepped to the sidebar, poured a glass of bourbon and drank it down in one swig, then eyed Thornton narrowly. "I don't foresee that happening anytime soon, Judge. Coburn is singing hallelu-jahs and that's it."

Thornton chuckled. He slouched back and twined his fingers together just above his beltline. "I think not, Mr. Rawlins. If he's gone, it isn't to glory."

"Judge," Jackson Scully interjected. He took a couple gimpy steps away from the door, his left leg dragging. "Rawlins is forgetting a possible lead that you ought to decide on."

Yance Rawlins clenched his teeth and cursed. The mood in the room heated up perceptively as he glowered at the former cavalry trooper. He took a step toward him, with his right hand balling into a fist. Scully didn't flinch or waver. He met the glare head on and gave it back in spades.

Thornton remained cool and amiable. "Are you boys having some troubles getting along?" He grinned at both of them and quietly asked, "Which one's going to speak his piece?"

Rawlins swore again. He dropped into an armchair in front of the desk. "Scully can, since it's his hairball idea."

Jackson Scully hitched another few steps closer, tucked his hat under his left arm and spoke with a swaggering lilt in his voice. "There's a family of homesteaders south of the San Juan River, past the badlands, no more than a dozen or so miles from where those Injuns harassed us off his trail. I say Coburn holed up there for a spell. If not, they helped him for sure. Most likely provided another mount and supplies."

The Judge leaned forward, interested. He eyeballed Rawlins carefully. "Why'd you leave this information out?"

"There's nothing there, boss," Yance said, edgy and brusque. "Scully's holding a grudge against those folks, that's all there is to it. He's got his shorts all knotted up over nothing."

Jackson Scully grunted snidely. His posture stiffened. "That ain't quite right, Judge. We should have searched the place, but Rawlins went nursemaid and got all mushy."

"Is that so?" Judge Thornton stood slowly. He was silent for a long moment. When he spoke, it was sharp and precise. "My orders were clear, were they not, Rawlins? No stone unturned, no obstacles allowed, no one exempt from suspicion."

Rawlins released a hiss of breath. "It was my call, boss. My belly wasn't aching when we stopped in there, and you know how reliable my belly can be. It ain't ever failed me."

"With all due respect to your reliable belly," the Judge said, giving him a sideways smile. "Let's review. Coburn lives outside all boundaries. He's sick and twisted, and needs to be put out of his misery. His debauchery with young girls is despicable. I want him strung up; legal or lynch mob, it matters not." With intentional strides, he moved from behind the desk and situated himself in front of Rawlins. "Are you forgetting that my son is dead because of Coburn?"

"I'm sorry as hell about Tommyboy, boss."

Thornton's brow creased darkly. He took a deep breath and tossed a look in Scully's direction. His strong-minded intensity was unmistakable as he focused on some invisible spot in the lamplight. "The man killed my son Lucas. I want proof that Coburn's dead." His eyes glinted eerily. He blinked several times and forced a grim smile at Rawlins. "I want that homestead searched. You'll get a clue or pick up Coburn's trail there. That's what my gut is telling me, and since I'm the bankroll, it supersedes your instincts."

Rawlins balked. "Winter's in the air, boss. Soon the passes will be blocked up as stuck as a constipated hog."

"Not my problem, Mr. Rawlins." He rubbed his hands together. "Now get out of my sight," he said, dismissing them with the hint of a sneer bending the corners of his mouth.

Outside, the air was brisk and chilly. When they were in the side yard, well away from Judge Thornton's view, Yance Rawlins cold-cocked

Jackson Scully with a roundhouse right that packed all the strength and gusto he possessed. His weight shifted and his shoulders rolled into the punch. The crushing blow came out of nowhere, caught Scully flush on the chin, and sent him sprawling to his keister.

Rawlins towered over him. "How's that for mushy? Don't ever backstab me again," he said, fierce and testy. "You got it?"

Scully turned his head and spat a gob of bloody saliva, then managed a weak nod. "Message received."

"Good." Yance offered a hand and pulled him to his feet.

"What now?" Scully asked, scooping up his hat.

Rawlins filled his lungs, looked up at the ponderous clouds hiding the starlight. He exhaled loudly. When he answered, his voice was muted. "I got a snug cabin a fair stretch to the north and west of here. At first light I'm heading that way and will be hunkering down until springtime." He bent in close and gave him a toothy grin. "You be welcome to join me, as long as we understand each other. You ever cross me again, that little love tap will feel like caresses from a pretty whore."

Scully was agreeable. They cemented the plan with a mutual head bob. Then, side by side they sauntered toward the stable behind the house. A couple hours of shut-eye in the hayloft would do them good.

In southern Ohio the sky was clear. A faint sign of color showed in the east. Angela Langton stared out her bedroom window at the earliest hints of the sun's arrival. Her face, pale and drawn, was a scowling mask reflecting in the glass.

Sleep hadn't blessed her. Eddies from a fuming turmoil of emotions were still rippling in her. Hot, penetrating anger had been set loose, consuming the night. She had never experienced such a boiling flare-up.

First she walked to give vent to it. The floorboards had creaked beneath her feet for hours as she kept to a half-circle course from one side of her bed to the other. Back and forth, back and forth in tiny steps—the pace and pattern never varied.

When tiredness made her eyes weary and muscles jump, she stretched out on the mattress. Flat on her back, she glowered into the darkness demanding to be released from the distressed questions clamoring through her mind. There was no relief or answers forthcoming.

All through the night, she kept switching a tri-folded sheet of paper from one hand to the other.

She hadn't even read its contents. The man who'd given it to her had told her all that it included before and after he wrote it out in stark, drastic language. Her initial reaction was to refuse the shock of the news. Life had handed her the crud end of the stick more often than not, yet she always managed to clean it off and make-do. She would rise above this setback to go forward with an upbeat and positive outlook.

It was on the buggy ride from town that burning anger took root in the pit of her stomach. Aggressive and fast-growing, it was soon full-blown flames lapping at her resolve. Her jaw clenched so tight that the hinges ached, her blood pressure soared, her vision blurred.

She tapped and stomped the fury down. It was subdued before she turned the horse onto the laneway that led home. She had no choice but to do otherwise because of her determination to be buoyant and brave. She had to put up a false front because she had not yet come to terms with the information herself. She was in no way prepared to share it with her daughter. She kept the ire smothered until she retired for the night.

The physical result was a bout of gastritis. Throughout the afternoon and evening the bile of indigestion bubbled in her belly, sporadically mushrooming up her throat. She kept a cheery smile in place and chatted abstractly about cowboys and such, which lately had become Abbey's favorite topic. Her wide-eyed girl was fourteen years old imagining being twenty.

Now, fearful and alone, Angela sat at the window praying that the sunrise would bring hope and discernment. She didn't know what to do. Shock and anger had mutated into rabid denial. She was a widow woman, fretting anxiously for the young lady beginning to stir in the other bedroom.

Angela Langton decided she had time; not much, but just enough. It was October. She would wait until after Christmas for the telling of the news. With that settled, she began softly singing the comforting promises of an old hymn.

~~~

Eliza Weitzel was stump-shouldered on the stool. Her chin was resting on her chest. She was dozing in and out of that silvery area that isn't quite sleep, but neither is it being awake. A raspy gasp startled her. She jerked and almost fell.

She stood, placed her thumbs at her temples, and began rubbing in tiny circular motions. It momentarily relieved the tension. She took several deep breaths. She pushed the door open to let a blast of crisp air revive her.

Somewhere in the distance a coyote yapped a forlorn complaint at the heavy laden sky. Dawn was breaking, gray and bleak. She appreciated the coolness of the morning so left the door ajar a crack, then sat beside her patient.

She soaked the sponge and lifted it to his mouth. The water dribbled over his lips. As it did, his tongue moved sluggishly. That paltry sign of life surprised her. She nearly dropped the sponge. In grasping it, she squeezed it much too hard, causing water to splash over his face. His eyelids twitched.

"Oh, dear God," she muttered breathlessly. "Help him."

She wiped his face with the sponge. His head tilted back as his jaw gaped wide. A croaky noise originating deep in his throat wheezed out of him. She recognized it as the same raspy gasp that'd startled her earlier.

She went rigid and waited. Time became meaningless as seconds turned into minutes. Minutes stacked on top of each other, and still she waited, stiff and keyed-up. The muscles in her forearms started to hurt because her hands were clenched so intensely. She sighed and tried to relax.

The man's eyes opened ever so slightly. Glazed and vacant, they were unfocused, but looking straight in her direction. His head moved again. She hovered over him, bending close to whisper encouraging words of comfort in his ear.

His mouth began puckering open and shut like a beached fish suffocating in the sun. It was as though he was chewing on the air before taking it into his lungs. She angled back to give him room to breathe. She stared at his face.

Their gaze dovetailed together, which caused her an enormous amount of joy mixed with jittery apprehension. She saw life and hope glimmering in the dark, murky pools of his eyes. His mouth was still functioning in its weird way, and she came to realize he was attempting to speak.

His eyes closed. "She won't feed a dirty ragamuffin."

"What?"

"Letter. She won't feed a dirty ragamuffin. Saddlebags."

"Who are you?" She knelt beside the cot.

"Lawrence." He sat bolt upright. His head swiveled. Color mottled his face. His teeth clicked. His eyes rolled back like tumbling dice, and a convulsion shook his chest, then he flopped back, strained and spent.

She scrooched even closer. His mouth was doing its beached fish weirdness, his neck muscles swelling and sagging crazily. It took great effort, but then, in a discordant squawk, his voice box finally worked once more. She responded by holding a hand over her mouth. She felt her stomach contract.

It was hoarse and barely audible, but there could be no mistaking what she heard. He'd said, "Coburn." Before the quiver of his weak voice was gone from the one-room shack, he slumped back into unconsciousness.

Eliza was numb. She checked his vitals, and as she did so, was sincerely afraid. Confusion was rampant in her. The words spoken were a hodgepodge that set her mind spinning: *She won't feed a dirty ragamuffin. Letter? Saddlebags? Lawrence? Coburn?* What did it all portend? What did any of it mean?

On top of that there was the ominous echo of Yance Rawlins along a lonely inner corridor: *He goes by Deke or Coburn. He's a killer. A tall fella, with shaggy black hair.*

A tremble gripped her. What was going on here? What bad news had taken up residence on their land? A part of her wanted to cease nursing him, but before she could entertain that inkling, she knew that mercy would compel her to continue caring for him.

She went outside. The sunrise was a dull yellow haze cloaked behind leaden clouds. A cold breeze was sweeping in from the north, carrying the scent of snow, but something else made her heart shudder. There was sorrow rising on the wind.

chapter two

Wanted Man

"I have done judgment and justice: leave
me not to mine oppressors."

~DAVID~

DEKE COBURN HADN'T ALWAYS been a wanted man. The turns on the road that had taken him there were complex and serpentine. A whole other destiny had been prayed and planned for him by his earnestly devout mother.

He was born to plain and simple folk on a small farm near Conoy Creek in Lancaster County, Pennsylvania. His mother, a purposeful woman, delivered her firstborn at fifteen, sweating, smiling, and quoting Scripture as he came into the world.

His father, a tall and quiet man of peace, listened to the activity in the bedroom, waiting patiently to greet his child. Rebecca Seider had married outside the River Brethren community, which was almost unheard of at the time. What kept her from any kind of shunning was that Amos Coburn, a hard worker and astute thinker, had embraced the ways of obedience and piety.

On a gorgeous October Sunday in 1835, Amos and Rebecca Coburn dedicated their newborn to the Lord. They covenanted to raise the boy in the fear and admonition of God, according to the dictates and counsel of the brethren. As was customary amongst the River Brethren, the service was conducted in German.

Deke Coburn would become articulate in German and English, developing a soft-spoken fluency that allowed him to efficiently switch back and forth. His formal education was practical, with much emphasis placed on theology and Bible learning. His feet were firmly planted on the paths of righteousness, but that was miles and years ago. A just cause had diverted him.

He had been a precocious child, fully capable of playing well with others, but much preferred to be by himself. That was seldom easy to do because his parents kept busy stoking the heat in the matrimonial bed. By the time Rebecca was twenty-five, he had four siblings, two sisters and two brothers.

Deke fulfilled all the requirements placed upon the eldest child, whilst delving into introspection to feed a burgeoning inquisitiveness. He was inclined to the lonely places, at one with nature. His free thinking sense of independence was a constant challenge to his parents. They encouraged a healthy respect for learning, but soon discovered that his curiosity could never be sated.

Creation held his imagination in its palm, never failing to fascinate him. He saw the wonder of God in every aspect of the natural world. He took to the forest and hunting, shooting and skinning his first buck just after turning ten. That rite of passage milestone ignited a latent passion within, setting him on a course that would ultimately betray him. He became an exceptional marksman and skilled woodsman, learning to track and read sign better than any of the adults in his circle.

The annual family excursion to Philadelphia did much to instill in him a healthy dislike of cities. There was always too much noise, too much bustle, too much running to and fro, and too little sanctuary from the uproar. As far as he could tell, the only good thing to be found in a city was the bookstores.

He read incessantly, omnivorously. The Bible provided the foundational base and he remained enthralled by its stories, rereading them over and over again. He committed whole sections of it to memory, reciting passages with a dramatic flourish that captivated or challenged others.

By his early teens, it was evident that God had given him a gift. He could speak Bible truths in dynamic ways. The River Brethren tapped him on the shoulder. He was to be instructed and trained to be a preacher. The apprenticeship would take years of faithful service and walking alongside church leaders, but there was never any question of having a choice. To do otherwise would be disobedience.

Amos and Rebecca were ecstatic. This was the prayers and plans of his mother coming to fruition. He reluctantly accepted the role, not quite sure how to balance expectations with an ever-expanding exploration of knowledge. There were so many more books to enjoy. He studied all that he could, and in little incremental stages, whether it was discernible or not, he drifted beyond the realm of parental influence and outside the restraints of the River Brethren.

There wasn't a topic or style that could put him off. He had difficulty keeping ahead of the reading curve. His greatest pleasure and reward was to sneak away to the woods for a week or so with nothing more than a knapsack of books, his squirrel rifle, hunting knife, and canteen.

One day in 1850 after all the planting was finished, a trip to Philadelphia filled his head with horrors. While mingling amongst rows of books at a favorite used bookstore, he came upon an autobiography that would affect his perspective and have long-term repercussions. *Narrative of the Life of Frederick Douglass, an American Slave* captured his attention.

He examined the copy, turning it over in his hands. It was thin and had obviously been well-read, for its binding was cracked and creased. He made a trade for it. As soon as the opportunity came, he devoured it in one sitting. The atrocious cruelty described triggered a gut-level response that began to bend him in a certain direction.

He read it a second time, which only served to solidify his mindset. He began considering himself an anti-slavery advocate, discreetly gathering all the abolitionist pamphlets and fliers that he could find. He immersed himself in the issue. More and more he'd make time to duck away to a favorite haunt in the forest for privacy to be shaped by his reading material.

As his eighteenth birthday beckoned, Harriet Beecher Stowe's novel *Uncle Tom's Cabin* came into his possession. The escape narrative inspired him. He was outraged and inflamed, and sought to be involved, to do something to help those ensnared in the evil of slavery.

An idea blossomed in his heart. He resisted it, but it wouldn't go away. The details of it would require him to move to Philadelphia, and he so despised the hurly-burly commotion of city living that he kept rejecting it, but the longer he opposed the thought, the stronger it seemed to become.

Days of Purgatory

In a wrestling bout of self-examination, he realized his reservations were rooted in selfishness, which annoyed him, for it went against the grain of what'd been nourished in him. He prayed, which soon settled it. He put together a plan and made preparations. He would go to Philadelphia and join a chapter of the *American Anti-Slavery Society* to do whatever he could and all things necessary to further its work.

There was much angst and displeasure in the Coburn household on an autumn evening in November 1853. The meal and devotions were over, and clean-up was happening when Deke spoke up, and in a concise manner made his announcement.

"No," his mother said, with certainty. "You cannot turn your back on your calling." She was still at the table with Amos. They exchanged a glance. She motioned for their firstborn to join them. He did so, as the rest of the brood continued their tasks, hushed and puzzled.

Amos was firm and formal. "You are a man. You will be held accountable for your choices. This is a mistake. I will not say otherwise. You will regret taking this path."

"Perhaps, but I must follow my conscience, Father."

"You have not thoroughly considered the consequences," Amos said, his head wagging side to side, slow and steady.

"Forgive me, but you are mistaken, Father." His voice was low-pitched, but there was fortitude in the tone. "What will the consequences be if I choose to ignore the cries for justice?"

Amos observed him closely as he scratched his chin-whiskers. "You were planted here. Justice for you is here in this place."

"I must go, Father. It's in my heart."

Rebecca harrumphed her disapproval. "I know what is in your heart. I sowed those seeds there and watered them with tears and much prayer." She kept her focus fixed on him. "We named you Deacon in faith, believing you would grow strong and take on the mantle of leadership. Many scoffed, but we remained firm because the Lord gave us the name. From the day you were born your father and I knew that God's hand was upon you."

"This is my burden, Mother."

"Is your mind set?" Amos asked gently.

"Yes. I have prayed through on it."

Amos winced and sighed. Sadness collected in his eyes. "Then there will be no more discussion of the matter." He looked sternly at his wife. "The Lord's will be done."

Rebecca pursed her lips and bowed her head for a moment. Then, eyeing her husband carefully, she made a request. "May I please have your indulgence to caution and advise him?"

Amos smiled sourly, considering. There was nothing else to say. His word was to be final. A tense silence filled the room for a long while until he finally came to a decision. "You may do so if you are brief, Rebecca."

She nodded in gratitude. She reached across the table to touch her son's arm. They stared at each other, both determined and steely-eyed, their expressions packed with emotion. "I do not approve of your intentions, Deacon. You are a man and I surely respect that, but you are treading on perilous ground, tempting the Lord. I will pray for you to find the way God has laid before you. This place is your home. There will be no breach in relationship."

She paused to give her husband a stony look, her mouth cast in an adamant manner. Amos responded with a modest gesture, misty-eyed in agreement.

Rebecca's lips tightened into a straight line as tears spilled down her cheeks. "You are always welcome here, Deacon."

The next morning, with all his worldly possessions in a backpack, he cast his life upon the waters of fortune, fate, faith, or destiny. It was frosty and crisp, with the trees ablaze with colors. He hiked at a determined gait, his trusty squirrel rifle in hand, and twelve dollars in his pocket.

Late in the afternoon of the third day he arrived in Philadelphia, stopping in at Dutch's Livery, the stables his parents always used. The owner, a gruff and greasy man with squinty eyes and a streak of larceny, recognized him.

After exchanging pleasantries, they negotiated a deal and sealed it with a hearty handshake. Deke could fix himself sleeping quarters in the loft in exchange for him mucking out the stalls morning and evening.

It was a beginning. He wasted no time the next day. With the dozen stalls cleaner than they'd been in years, he was on his way while the sun was still rising. He made the rounds of coffeehouses and grog

shops. He had a two-fold purpose. He wanted to learn where abolitionists gathered to discuss and organize, and also find a place to have his
meals.

The vibrancy of the city was now seen through a different prism.
Instead of detesting the hubbub, he found himself anxious to get into
the flow of the whys and wherefores of it. He walked the streets, striking
up conversations here and there, always being intentional about listening, watching, discovering.

One connection would provide information to take him a little
farther along. He filed all tidbits and gleanings away to contemplate
and process. The day was half over before he realized he was enjoying
himself immensely.

When that awareness struck him, he also concluded that he had
to focus on the immediate need for food. His stomach was growling
empty. He had stopped and visited so many places and engaged in so
many fascinating dialogs that he'd been sidetracked from the task at
hand.

Now he got down to business. All indicators led him to a popu-
lar tavern on the riverfront, just on the edge of the brawling district of
dives and roughhouses where, night and day, all manner of immoral
transactions occurred.

Gallagher's Cove was a busy joint. When he entered he had to push
his way past clusters of patrons exiting. He paused just inside the door.
It was a large and open space, dimly-lit and smoky. A wide staircase at
one end led to a second floor, which accommodated bed chambers and
living quarters. A spacious balcony overlooking the main room served
as a meeting place.

He moved past tables, both round polished ones and those which
were coarse planks hammered together. Conversations were buzzing,
and he made his way directly to the bar. In a soft but authoritative tone,
which more and more was becoming his natural pattern of speech, he
stated his case to the swarthy man seated on a high stool behind it.

The lean man listened, and as he did so, a glint grew bright and
shiny in his eyes. He had kinky salt and pepper hair, and gnarly eyebrows that came together above his broad nose. His left sleeve was
empty, pinned up at the shoulder. His right sleeve was rolled above the
elbow revealing a sinewy forearm colorfully decorated by a Union Jack
tattoo.

When Deke finished speaking, the man smiled and stood. He was tall and extremely skinny. "I be Blackjack. This be my place," he said, his voice raw and gravelly. "You're looking to find where abolitionists come a-calling, you say? See that buxom lass over there?" He pointed to a table where a raven-haired woman was conversing animatedly to those assembled around her.

"Alice will skin you alive if you express anti-abolitionist leanings within earshot of her. And I'll cut your gizzard out if you ever cross or hurt her. She's brackish and full of brine, but she be my only child. Her Ma is gone to wherever it is dead people go, but she'll come back and slice me sideways if I don't protect her little girl."

Deke shrugged. He didn't know what to say.

Blackjack grunted and studied him hard. "You're a strong, strapping lad. Just off the farm, are you?"

"Yes, sir."

Blackjack chuckled agreeably. "Wipe down the tables and sweep the floor once a day after the noontime meal and I'll feed you that often."

"Fair enough," Deke said, nodding.

"Then get to it."

Just over an hour later, Deke was sitting at a corner table with a steaming bowl of a tasty fish stew, chewy biscuits, and a tankard of hot apple cider. He munched slowly, savoring each morsel. His mind was jumping from one notion to the next. He was much involved with all the wondrous happenings of the day, considering each aspect of it afresh and anew.

Blackjack's daughter came and sat across from him, which caught him by surprise. While he'd been busy cleaning up, she'd seemed to ignore him. "Alice Gallagher," she said tersely. "Papa tells me you're interested in helping the Cause."

Deke gave her a quizzical look, saying nothing.

"Are you or aren't you?"

"Cause?"

"Yes, the Cause." She laughed distinctively, loud and brash, without any hint of self-consciousness. She tossed back her wavy black hair, and it came to rest curled up on her shoulders as she fixed him with an unwavering stare. "Abolition, stupid." She was nicely shaped and round-faced, with rosy cheeks and friendly eyes.

"Ah-huh. I'm interested."

"Upstairs tonight at eight we'll be setting strategy."

"The *American Anti-Slavery Society*?" Deke asked, eyeing her over the tankard as he took a swallow of cider. It was biting and sweet, laced with cloves and ground cinnamon.

"Not officially, but our group has the same goals," she answered, leaning closer and lowering her voice to say, "We're more action-oriented. If all you want to do is talk, don't bother coming. We already have enough yakking going on."

Deke was uncomfortable because of her nearness. "I'll be there," he managed, glancing away. He had a severe case of wandering eyes, which he was endeavoring to conceal. There was no denying he was entirely undone by the swell at the top of her loose-fitting blouse. Having been raised in the plain garb realm of caped dresses, her attire, which allowed for an occasional fleeting glimpse of skin, was tremendously distracting.

Alice noticed his dilemma. Several years older than he, she appeared to be quite amused by his obviously awkward reaction. She pressed forward, beaming a smile. "See you later this evening," she said, then got up and sashayed away.

He furtively watched and felt embarrassed. He finished his meal, took his dishes to the kitchen, and placed them in the washtub, then went outside.

Worry was in him. There was no way to know if meeting up with Blackjack Gallagher was a godsend or if his provocative daughter would be trouble of a formidable kind.

Deke Coburn filled his lungs. There were stirrings in his loins and shameful feelings churning into whitecaps of guilt. He cleared his head and determinedly muttered a proverb of Solomon under his breath, *"And why wilt thou, my son, be ravished with a strange woman, and embrace the bosom of a stranger? For the ways of man are before the eyes of the Lord, and he pondereth all his goings."*

The misgivings dissipated as he centered himself. He decided that he was thoroughly pleased with his progress. For six or so hours of manual labor per day he had the basic necessities of housing and food covered. He figured it was two miles from Dutch's Livery to Gallagher's Cove. If he had to, he could cover the distance in ten minutes.

Now the Cause had his undivided attention.

~~~

Five years later, as a seasoned crusader for the abolitionist gospel, Deke Coburn was hiding out, settled on his haunches, with ears pricked and eyes agile. He kept watch, ever wary. A horse was tethered nearby, next to a sturdy soddy obscured and almost hidden by a massive oak tree.

Angry voices shouted in the distance, then silence. He didn't move. The night was hot and humid, with nary a whiff of a breeze. He waited. More hollering—an unfettered bevy of curses stained the inky sky. Silence returned, disturbed now only by the cheerful chirping of crickets.

A bleached moon was above the treeline of the dense woods somewhere along the Virginia-Maryland border. There were a couple passengers soon expected, and by the sound of it, bad news was nipping at their heels. In his dealings, it'd never been this tight before, but he wasn't unsettled.

Instead, there was calmness in him. He was no Pollyanna. He fully understood that the potential for danger and the risk of discovery was neverending, but he was breathing evenly because none of the hazards mattered to him. His zeal to participate in justice being done was ofttimes overwhelming.

The milk of human kindness nourished and sustained him, prodding him to always do more. He was forever counting the cost and praying that there was no price he would be unwilling to pay in the pursuit of righting wrongs.

He heard the clip-clop, clip-clop of hoofbeats on the hard packed roadway to the south. They were a ways off, but coming steadily closer, though it seemed to be a slow, easy gait. At least four riders and the animals weren't being pushed.

Coburn shifted his weight in anticipation of having to move quickly. His clothes were stiff and grungy, having been sweated and dried several times on the journey. He'd brought supplies to stock the soddy, a way station along the Underground Railroad. The network was loosely interconnected, with information about routes and hideouts passed along by word of mouth. He was an experienced conductor, having made numerous safe passages.

The clip-clops, clip-clops were approaching, closer and closer. Then there was the sound of footfalls moving fast through the forest. A man and woman ran into the clearing, stumbling and shaking.

Coburn stood, hands held up and spread in welcome. He hurried to them. They were scared, soaked in perspiration, and despite the muggy heat, shivering. Their breathing was ragged and strained, their chests heaving up and down.

"Are we freedom?" the man asked, pleading and desperate.

"Not quite," Deke said, flinching. Exhaustion was evident in both of them, but the woman's condition was startling.

"I'm Saul. This be Maggie."

Deke hitched in a wince of breath, shaking his head. Maggie was pregnant, her belly swollen and protruding, with one arm cupped around the bulge. He stared unbelievingly at her, and stated the obvious. "You're going to have a baby."

"I sorry."

He gave her a weak smile. He grabbed their wrists to lead them to the horse picketed beside the soddy. He would put Maggie in the saddle to guide them through the remote wilderness over a series of hidden trails.

When Coburn was helping her mount the animal, she let out a low protest. He felt a spasm go through her body. There was a gush of fluid as her water broke, some of it splattering on him. He held her firmly.

"Oh, sweet Jesus," she whispered, and almost simultaneously, multiple gunshots shattered the stillness of the night.

"Light it up," a voice roared, and suddenly torches flamed and four horsemen came thundering out of the woods, slamming to a stop around them. The men were all armed with rifles. One of them dismounted and speared his torch into the ground. The others rode in close and crowded around them.

"We got them, Harvey," one of the riders said, smirking.

Harvey paced back and forth, his gun held waist high. He was a big-bellied man, but he moved light on his feet. "You niggers got lucky back there a piece, but luck's gone bye-bye."

Coburn was positioned in front of Saul and Maggie, who were squeezed against the horse. "You'd be wise to leave us be," Deke said, clear and direct.

Harvey guffawed. He had a mat of rusty red hair atop a squarish face that'd lost its battle to contain a wild crop of freckles. "These nigger monkeys belong to me. They're my servants. You best not interfere. After all, I'm just trying to learn them what the Good Book says."

Harvey paused, recalled the quote, and stepped closer. "*Servants, obey in all things your masters according to the flesh; not with eyeservice, as menpleasers; but in singleness of heart, fearing God.*"

Deke Coburn gave him a thin smile. He had his own Scripture to share. "*Masters, give unto your servants that which is just and equal; knowing that ye also have a Master in heaven.*"

One of the slave catchers on horseback snickered and gave a hoot. "I think the nigger lover got you there, Harvey. Are we going to jawbone all night or get down to business?"

"Get the rope ready," Harvey ordered, giving the runaways a snide look. "You want to pick out the tree for yourself, Saul?"

"Master Harvey, please!" Maggie squealed, her voice stressed and high-pitched. "I'm gonna be having your baby!"

"No, you ain't," Harvey said angrily. "No seed of mine is coming into this world a mongrel."

Maggie slumped to her knees. "Master Harvey, please!"

"You'd be wise to leave us be," Deke repeated, stern and even-tempered. "The wrath of God will hunt you down."

"Get out of the way."

Deke stood tall and strong. "No."

Harvey took the Lord's name in vain loudly. "Then I'll move you." He angled the rifle and pulled the trigger. The flash from the muzzle flared brightly.

The bullet struck Coburn high on the right side. He gasped, felt the burn, spun around, and landed on his hands and knees. He immediately started to get up, but then the butt of Harvey's gun came crashing down on the back of his skull. He went face-first into the dirt, stayed motionless for just a moment, then pulled up and crawled a couple steps. Harvey loomed over him, chuckling gleefully. He lined him up, waggled the rifle and struck another mighty blow that landed in precisely the same spot as previously.

Deke Coburn floundered bonelessly, his limbs twitching, his body convulsing. The last thing he heard before swirling blackness swallowed him whole was Maggie begging, screaming.

Unconsciousness treated him kindly. It prevented him from being an eyewitness to bloodthirsty debauchery. When it began to release him from its bowels, sunlight was stabbing at his eyes and an abrasive wetness was lathering his face.

45

He came to at a maddeningly slow pace. Pain accompanied even the slightest movement. His eyes flickered open and shimmering agony filled his head. His hands came up to clamp around the sides of his head, and as they did so, he brushed against something bent over him.

Salty wet breath caressed him. Through thin, blurry slits he saw the horse licking him. He patted and stroked its head, then gave it an affectionate push as it whinnied and blew. It sidled off to the end of its tether.

Deke gathered himself up in stages. He sat and found his equilibrium. He wobbled to his feet. His head spun. He took a half-dozen stutter-steps, tripped over a log or something, and plummeted to the ground, his hands landing in a gooey mess. His eyes were shocked into focus.

A shriek mushroomed from somewhere deep in his guts. It scorched upwards, but he fiercely strangled it and clenched his mouth. All that emerged was a guttural groaning that gained intensity as sickness cramped through him. He crawled to one side and vomited a geyser. He wrenched and jerked in great hurling grunts until there was nothing remaining but bile.

He spat the last of it out as he collapsed onto his buttocks. He had to willfully force himself to survey the gory scene. The assault on his senses was visceral. He'd taken a tumble over Maggie's legs, which were gruesomely spread apart.

A desecration had been done to her abdomen. More of her innards were scattered around the grass than remained in the cavity. In a grotesque act of overkill, her throat had been slit ear to ear. Hopelessness marred her blank-eyed stare. Her head drooped absurdly, attached by the thinnest of tissue.

Deke tried to keep his breathing level, but self-discipline betrayed him. His chest would swell with air and stay expanded for a full minute. There'd be a whistling hiss as he exhaled through gritted teeth. That pattern continued as he kept mentally cataloging the murderous savagery.

When he'd fallen, his hands had come to rest on the corpse of the baby. Now as he studied the innocent victim, his stomach somersaulted, but there was nothing left for it to spew up. The child had been battered, slashed, and mutilated so badly he couldn't even tell if it'd been a boy or girl. Huge, hot tears streaked down his cheeks.

He hung his head. When he did so, he saw a blotchy stain on his right shoulder. He touched it gingerly. It was blood, and the homespun material was soggy. He frowned and blinked several times, then remembered getting shot. His shirt was ripped at the edge of the collar. He peeled it back to examine the damage. He instantly realized his good fortune.

As best as he could determine, the bullet had gone cleanly through a thick knot of muscle, ricocheted off bone, and left a jagged gash that was still seeping blood. He scrambled to his feet, intending to find some moss to pack in and over the wound.

He looked around for a likely tree to provide the necessary material. It was then that he saw Saul swinging from a branch above where the soddy had been. The rabble had ransacked and demolished it. Saul's tongue bulged from his mouth. He was stripped naked. His genitals had been hacked off.

Anger surged and roiled through Deke Coburn. It was bleak, cheerless, foreboding; a seething gall that coiled and slithered like a living thing inside him. He let it have its way. He entertained and fed it, and it took up residence in a gray, murky lair in his soul.

He moved around numbly. His head ached. His body hurt. Draped in gloom, he got busy. He cut Saul down and tidied up the dead as best he could.

As he dug a shallow grave and collected rocks to enclose it, he made a vow that if he ever crossed paths with Master Harvey again, retribution would be furious and exacting. He considered the solemn promise coldly. He reiterated it aloud.

When he was finished, dogged satisfaction mollified him. Saul and Maggie were beside each other, with the child between them beneath a mound of rocks. A crude cross had been lashed together as a marker and put in place.

Then, covered in dirt and blood, with fatigue and frayed emotions toying with him, Deke Coburn took his Bible out of the saddlebags and read over them. He did so by rote, not really needing the text in front of him.

Some of the old familiar words were only for him. He spoke them with certain resolve, but in those mournful moments, he didn't really believe them anymore. *"Yea, though I walk through the valley of the shadow of death, I will fear no evil: for thou art with me; thy rod and thy staff they comfort me."*

He rode away with an immense sadness festering within.

"John Brown is a righteous man," Blackjack Gallagher declared, slapping the newspaper down. "I'd follow him through hellfire. We should've been at Harpers Ferry." He paused to tuck a chaw of tobacco in his mouth. He rolled it around and adjusted it to a cheek, while wagging a bent finger at Deke Coburn. "You should have ridden with him."

Coburn sat grim-faced and sullen. The sensational headlines excited his sense of justice, but also disturbed him: *Extensive Negro Conspiracy in Virginia and Maryland—Seizure of the United States Arsenal by the Insurrectionists.*

"That's right," Alice remarked, focused hard on him. "A man with your nerves could have made all the difference."

Blackjack agreed. "I ain't ever seen anyone with a sharper, straighter eye for shooting. It be a gift, lad."

Coburn let out a deep sigh. He had a room upstairs, and if he could do so without offending his adopted family, he'd head there because he was broody and morose. He recognized that a day was fast arising when he'd be called upon to participate in the use of force on behalf of the Cause. Until now, being true to his upbringing, he had avoided that option.

It was October, 1859. The last boisterous customer had departed the tavern long ago. A half-dozen candles and the same number of oil lamps were still burning on various tables throughout the room. The wee-hours of the morning were creeping up, but the three of them remained, reading newspaper accounts and discussing the astounding events.

Hysteria was galloping across the country. John Brown advocated and practiced armed insurrection in the pursuit of abolishing slavery once and for all. He was either demonized as a lawless fanatic or lionized as a saint; a red-tailed devil with pointy horns or a zealous Old Testament prophet calling the nation to repentance.

Northerners and Southerners alike were stunned by his raid and seizure of the federal armory at Harpers Ferry, Virginia. The event was becoming a rallying call to action for the radical extremists in the abolitionist movement.

Alice Gallagher acted thrilled by the possibility of slaves mobilizing against their oppressors. She made no secret of her allegiances. Just now, she tapped on the table before topping off their tankards from a pitcher of spiced rum.

"Thank you," Deke said quietly.

"Hey, Papa. He speaks." Alice laughed, eyes jesting him.

Blackjack grinned crookedly. "I hear."

"What's wrong? You've been muzzled all night."

"I apologize, Alice," Deke answered, giving his friends a halfway shrug. "War is now inevitable. It's only a question of when and where it starts, and once that nightmare is loosened on the land . . ." He stopped to think for a moment, then, "*I am for peace: but when I speak, they are for war.*"

"There's a lot of war and bloodshed in that there Bible you're so fond of quoting," Blackjack said sternly. "You'd best remember what's at stake. Human freedom, dignity, common decency. Doing unto others." He spat a runner of tobacco juice into a tin can he kept close for just such a purpose. "War is the only solution here. Slavers are vile creatures. I know of what I speak." His forehead furrowed so that the clumpy thatch of hair over his eyes became even more pronounced.

Alice's countenance grew forlorn. "Tell him, Papa."

Blackjack ignored her, his eyes fixed on a lamp flickering on another table. "The only good slaver is a dead slaver."

"Papa." She reached across the table and patted his left shoulder. "Tell him," she said insistently. "All of it."

"Ah, lass."

"Papa, don't skip over any detail." She glared at him, her big brown eyes assertive, yet moist with tenderness.

Deke Coburn observed and listened to this byplay between father and daughter with abundant interest. He felt like a kind of intruder being given a glimpse of an intimate matter.

Blackjack cleared his throat. He glowered at Coburn, his face wrinkly with heartache. "Other than me, only two people in the world know the whole story," he began, punctuating the words with a gruff blast of air. "And one of those is dead. Been just over ten years since we buried my precious wife. No man was ever loved by a better woman."

He flicked a glance at his daughter. "The other one is the vinegary lass at this table with us." He chuckled and shook his head. "You really want me to tell it?"

"Every word, Papa."

Blackjack deposited his chew in the can, palmed his mouth, and leaned forward. "My father was a slaver. He raped my mother, which is how I came into being. They called me Enoch. It was on a plantation in Georgia or Tennessee, I really ain't rightly sure where exactly. She was light-skinned and worked in the big house, so he had easy access to her." His voice was flat and dispassionate. "When I was ten or so, I walked in on him getting nasty with her in the kitchen. He made me watch, telling me if I moved, he'd kill us both. Her shame was unbearable. He finished his business and left my mother sobbing on the floor. It was the last time I ever saw her. The master called for the overseer, took me to the woodshed, tied me down, and chopped off my arm." His right hand grasped the stump.

Alice was crying, her face marred by anger.

Coburn sat stiff, listening attentively.

"Taught me a lesson, he did," Blackjack continued, calm and matter-of-fact. "They cauterized it, and Ole Pappy nursed and doctored me with all kinds of herbs and medicines. Ole Pappy must've been a hundred years old or more. He knew all there was to know about healing and caring for folks. It was him who told me the master sold my mother off. He said that was just the way it be, so I should get over it, 'cause I had life to live. Ole Pappy taught me how to read maps, both the kind on parchment and the one in the sky. A couple years after I was healed up, when the time was ripe, he gave me final instructions and helped me escape. I don't know whatever happened to Ole Pappy. I pray to God he died of natural causes." He lifted his tankard and had a look inside it. He took a long swig.

"I was fortunate," he said, nodding. "I had angels watching over me. There were several dicey circumstances, but I came through all the briars just fine. I made it to Savannah and kept low. I picked a likely vessel, flying one of these." He flexed his forearm, showing off the Union Jack tattoo. "One night, I swam out to it, climbed aboard, and stowed away. When we were out to sea, I fell in with the crew swabbing the deck, intent on hiding in plain sight, which lasted about half a minute."

He quit talking and stretched. "It's getting almighty late. We best pick this up on the other side of the morning."

"No, no, no, Blackjack," Deke said urgently.

Alice burst out laughing. "He's full of crud, Deke. Quit joshing, Papa. Get to it. You're past the bad stuff."

"That I be," her father agreed. A wistful look came into his eyes as he recalled the memory. "I got hauled in front of the First Mate, a fun-loving joker of an Irishman named Gallagher. For reasons I've never known, he took a shine to me. Maybe he figured my story and took pity on me, I can't surely say, but he acted like he'd hired me and what was all the fuss about? Right off he started calling me Blackjack, which stuck like molasses on cornbread. *Where you been hiding, Blackjack?* he sez, all cheeky and bull-throated. *I got work for you to be doing.* And just like that I was a sailor." He took another swallow of rum.

"In the beginning I was nothing more than First Mate Gallagher's attendant, running and fetching for his every whim, and believe you me, he was full of whimsy." He made a muffled humming noise and shook his head. "It weren't slavery, and I didn't mind because he was the first white man to treat me with a measure of respect." He raked his hand through his gray spackled hair as a smile crawled up his face and made his eyes twinkle. "First Mate Gallagher told me I was Black Irish, which resulted in lots of hee-haws, but it became my story. Enoch ceased to be, deep sixed forever to Poseidon's realm. It weren't long before Gallagher's boy Blackjack got to be known as Blackjack Gallagher, and I think I done fine putting grizzle on the moniker. I spent fifteen years at sea, doing every possible job there is to do on a merchant vessel. That be the end of it."

"Finish it, Papa. Tell the best part."

"Oh, for the sake of blue blazes!" he exclaimed, eyes narrowing. "You be the most irascible, stubborn, unyielding child a man ever did have. You just want to see waterworks."

Deke inched closer to the table and settled his elbows on it. "If there's a best part, I dearly wish to hear it."

"I took shore leave," Blackjack said, head wagging. "I expected to spend a few weeks drinking and carousing before shipping out again. I had a nice nest egg stashed away 'cause I never spent my earnings on anything beyond basic needs. When I got off the boat I planned to cut loose and then get right back to it, but I came in here." He took notice of his daughter, a film of tears forming. "A spunky Italian girl who looked like my little girl there served up my meal with a smile and style that sliced my heart wide open. I was instantly smitten. She was the sassiest, smartest, sharpest woman God ever did create. I started living at one of these tables. Well, the birds and the bees were hard at it." He exhaled a whisper of breath, thumbing the corners of his eyes. "I despise being weepy."

Deke directed a sincere look at him. "Ma taught me that a man who doesn't have the courage to cry isn't much of a man."

"Mayhap she be right," the old seaman allowed. "We married, acquired this joint, rechristened it, and had a helluva good life together. And that really does be the end of it." He placed his hand palm down on the table. "It be my tale, Deke. I want it kept that way. It's not public stuff. Swear to me."

"Oh, Papa. If we can't trust Deke, we're in sorry shape."

Coburn spoke soberly. "You have my solemn word, Blackjack. I'll treasure the privilege of knowing your story, but it'll stay here." He patted his chest.

"You're a good man, Deke Coburn." Blackjack's eyes were sparkly as he cast them in his daughter's direction. "I always reckoned you and that hellcat of mine would find each other."

"I tried once, Blackjack. She put the boots to me."

Alice gave Coburn a good-natured jab in the ribs. "I'm not the marrying kind, that's all there is to it." She bellied up to the table and said, "The matter at hand is war. I wanted you to hear Papa's journey through the past because his experience with slavery gives credence you ought to heed."

"You make a wrong assumption, Alice," Deke said, his voice taking on a subtle edge. "I carefully weigh your father's words. It's just that I pray for an end to slavery without war."

Blackjack gave a dismissive wave. "That prayer is destined for the ash heap, lad. I've been young and now I'm old, and I can say with certainty that freedom demands spilt blood."

"Peace is a better way," Deke asserted, with conviction.

"Better, yes. Seldom possible though," Alice said dryly.

Blackjack Gallagher stood. "I've been to the four corners of the world and this I know, a bully only understands force or the threat of force. And slavers are nothing more or less than the worst type of bullies.

You get a bully's attention with a smack in the mouth or, better yet, a swift kick in the crotch. Slavers need to be thoroughly crotch kicked." He sidled toward the stairs. "If there's nothing else, I'm going to bed."

When he was gone, Alice shifted in her chair to scrutinize Coburn. "When war comes, what's your answer going to be, Deke?"

He mulled it over for a long while before finally giving her an indecisive bob of his head. He had no other reply to give her. He rose to his feet and started blowing out the candles and oil lamps. He was tired; weary, even. The question vexed him, *when war comes, what's your answer going to be?*

In the spring of 1861 Deke Coburn returned to Conoy Creek for the first time since leaving in the autumn of 1853. He was almost exactly at the midpoint mark of his twenty-sixth year. In the early stages of his new life in Philadelphia he had connected with his parents and various siblings when they came to the city early each summer, but it'd been five years since he'd seen anyone from home.

Rawboned and leathery tough, he carried one hundred and seventy pounds on a six-two frame. He had tree-branch shoulders, which were oddly straight. That, plus his ramrod posture, gave him a military bearing, as if he were perpetually at attention. His curly black hair was longish, hanging in ringlets. Though he had coarse whiskers, he was clean-shaven except for a fashionable moustache which he kept neatly trimmed.

As he walked the final mile to the farmstead, it occurred to him that the countryside was unchanged. Everything looked exactly how he remembered it. There were many good memories slip-sliding through his mind, but he couldn't lock any single one down. He stopped in the shade of an ancient oak tree.

The sunlight was cheery, the sky clear. Instead of taking the laneway, he decided to cut across the field, loop around and try to sneak up to the house. It was peaceful and quiet. From a fair distance he recognized his mother. She was working in the garden, which appeared to be as large as ever. He crept close, removed the backpack, and asked a question.

"Where is everyone?"

Rebecca Coburn was startled. She spun around, saw who it was, and smiled. The sun was at his back. She shaded her eyes and said, "Father will be back bye and bye. He had a pick-up at the feed store." She dusted her hands together, then wiped them on the bottom half of the drab colored bib apron. "Your brothers and sisters are scattered here, there, and everywhere. Married off and some are growing families of their own. I'm a grandmother, don't you know." She walked over and stood near him. "You should have wrote you were coming, Deacon."

He surveyed her face, somewhat surprised by the deep creases gathering like a net around her eyes. "I wasn't planning on it. A few days ago I decided to go for a long walk out of the city and the road brought me here."

"I'm glad it did, son. You look fine." She took his hand and led him into the house. In the privacy provided by four walls, she fussed over him a bit, attempting to arrange his unruly hair. After several tries, she abandoned the undertaking, sat him down at the table and hurried around. She served him a glass of buttermilk and a generous slice of crusty bread.

Deke took a sip and smacked his lips. "Thank you, Mother."

"Just enjoy," she said, taking a seat beside him. "You look distinguished, but Father will not approve of the moustache."

"If that's all he objects to, I'll be pleased," Deke said, breaking off a piece of bread. He soaked it in the buttermilk and ate it without dribbling a drop.

"How long can you stay?"

"A week or so, if I'm welcome."

"You are welcome, Deacon. Always."

"We'll see."

"Why do you say that?" she asked sharply. "What made you decide to go for a long walk? Is there trouble in the city?"

Deke finished off his buttermilk. "It's the city, Mother. There's always trouble of one kind or another."

"Is something bad following you here?"

"No, ma'am. I had to get away to think."

She rose, refilled his glass and cut him another thick slice of bread. He put up a clumsy protest, but she would hear none of it. She returned to her chair and queried, "Are you attending Sunday Meetings?"

"Quite regularly, yes," he answered quickly. "I even do a moderate amount of speaking in various churches."

"Well, praise be to God," she exclaimed, enthused and happy. "My heart is thrilled to hear that you are preaching."

Deke sighed, wondering how to explain or whether he ought to even make the effort. After a rapid inner debate, he chose to be as forthright as possible. "It's not exactly preaching as the River Brethren would see it. There's some of that involved, I suppose, but mostly I tell the abolitionist story. I speak of experiences, successes, and failures. I present challenges and opportunities, and attempt to raise funds and support."

As he spoke, Rebecca's disapproval became evident in the stiff set of her jaw. "Sounds worldly and sacrilegious."

"Maybe so, but it's what I do."

"You were taught better," she said, harshness in her tone. "At least tell me that you still read your Bible."

Deke produced a broad smile. "Every day, Mother."

"Mind your attitude," she cautioned, eyes tense. "*Pride goeth before destruction, and a haughty spirit before a fall.*"

"Tread lightly, Mother." He winked. "I take no pride in reading the Good Book. It humbles and cuts me to the quick."

"As it does all who read it with eyes to see."

When Amos Coburn returned from town, his eldest son went to the barn to greet him. The reunion was chilly and reserved. At once there was uneasiness between them. It was much more severe and concentrated than Deke had anticipated. He sensed a palpable discontent in his father.

They worked together in strained silence, unloading the wagon. The simple action took Deke backwards, and for a fleeting instant he was twelve years old engaged in the routine and rhythm of farm life. There was no stress, no worries, no breach in relationships, no haunting memories of Maggie and Saul, no guilt over failing them and the unborn child, no confusion, no vow, no ambiguity, no shades of gray, no pressure, no anger lurking in his soul, no slavery, no Cause. He wanted to cling to those sentiments, but the impression faded and was gone.

The last sack of seed was stacked. Amos moved to the workbench and brusquely motioned for him to follow.

"Father, will you speak with me?"

Amos sat on a stool. "Why have you come back?"

"It was a mistake."

"That answers not the question."

"I reckon not." Deke squatted on his heels. "It's far too compli-cated, Father. I wish it wasn't, but it is."

Amos considered this, then said, "Perhaps the complications are merely weeds that need plucked and put on the burn pile."

"If it was only that easy, Father."

"Nothing worth doing is ever easy." Amos chafed his hands to-gether. "Mother still prays and cries for you. Her travails are great. Her heart aches. You have broken it."

Deke swallowed dryly. "That grieves me."

"As it should."

"Father." He got up and moved around some. Frustration was in him. He didn't want to be disrespectful or strident. He was searching for guidance, direction, or insights; something, anything, that would help him come to terms with the conflict stirring and straining him. "I should not have come."

"That is a correct assessment."

Deke pulled up a stool and settled directly in front of him. "I'm right here, Father. Do you wish me to leave?"

"When war comes, will you fight?"

"Father, I've seen horrors—*blackhearted* horrors."

"That answers not the question."

Deke flinched, his mouth puckering as he bit his tongue. He wanted to yell. He wanted to reach over and shake his father. Instead, in an exceptionally placid manner, he said, "Father, you live in isolation. There's inhumanity happening which ought not to be ignored by those who follow Christ. I won't apologize for the choices I've made in pursu-ing justice. I have worked to help those who are helpless."

Amos smiled sourly. "I will not be lectured by an outsider."

"An outsider?"

"Indeed," Amos said, eyes cast downward. "Years ago. You were disciplined and disfellowshipped. The shunning has been a burden and stain on the family. Out of affection for my wife, I consented to her wishes for you not to be notified."

Deke mulled the news over. "As I said, I do not apologize for my life, but there's much remorse in me because you choose to view me in displeasure and condemnation."

Amos was inflexible. "When war comes, will you fight?"

"I have seen *blackhearted* horrors, unspeakable abominations visited upon innocents." He stood, grasped his hands behind his back, paced, and kicked at an occasional bit of straw. In that ordinary moment, surrounded by the trappings of childhood, he made his final decision. "Yes. When President Lincoln calls for volunteers I'll report for duty."

"Shame, shame, shame!" Amos snapped, incredulous.

"It'll be my consequences to pay, Father."

"It is not the way of peace, sir."

Deke Coburn rolled his eyes. "Then somebody ought to tell God the way of peace isn't doing too well for those in bondage."

"You dare to blaspheme?"

"Blaspheme, Father?" His voice rose ever so gently. "Slavery is an infinite blasphemy for the times in which we live. What slavers do to fellow human beings is abhorrent, despicable."

Amos stood, abrupt and hastily. "You will leave."

"No!" Rebecca shouted, suddenly storming into the barn. She moved rapidly, coming to stop scant steps in front of her husband. "Deacon will not leave. He is our son, Amos."

"Woman," Amos said, voice buzzing as though hornets were nesting in his throat. "How long have you been eavesdropping?"

"Eavesdropping?" Her eyes bulged. "I'll grant you that characterization by telling you that I have been openly in the doorway long enough to hear you violate your promise to me. Deacon was never to be informed of the shunning."

"It's for the best that I leave, Mother." Deke reached out to touch her. "The shunning matters not to me."

Her cheeks were crimson, her eyes flaring angrily. "When a husband gives his word to his wife in the seclusion of their bedchamber, it does matter."

Amos recoiled. "Thee shames thyself."

Rebecca leaned close and tilted her chin upward as she glared at him. "Husband, you have emphatically disappointed me."

Amos seemed to wither under the intensity of her outrage. He sagged onto the stool. He tried to say something, but couldn't put together the emotions or words. He held his hands up in a gesture of surrender as he stood. He started to exit, and his son side-stepped swiftly to block him. "Please excuse me. There is no further dialog necessary."

"Fare thee well, Father," Deke said amiably. "I bear no grudges and have no thorns in my heart for you." He thrust out his right hand and kept his gaze intent. Face to face, father and son resembled mirror statues, rigid and stiff. Amos quite definitively refused the offered handshake. He turned away and left the barn.

"Amos!" Rebecca called, her voice cracking.

Deke went to her. Her body was trembling. He wrapped his arms around her, held her tight, and whispered tenderness. She disregarded propriety and stoical expectations. She wept against his chest as his tears darkened the brim of her bonnet.

When they were both cried out, they prayed for each other. Before she went into the house to have words and make peace with her husband, she gave her firstborn her blessing. He received it with thanksgiving. Afterwards he lightly bussed his mother's cheek. He retrieved his backpack and as twilight encroached, he departed.

His footsteps were dragging along the laneway. As he came to its end, he turned and took a gander at the house he had grown up in. It sat in the granite colors of dusk. A hitch caught in his throat. He had a premonition that he'd never see his parents again. He pondered it, released it, and moved on.

One week later, on the twelfth of April, Fort Sumter, a Federal fortification in the harbor of Charleston, South Carolina was bombarded by Confederate batteries. In response to the rebellion, which appeared to be small enough to contain, President Abraham Lincoln called for 75,000 volunteers for ninety days.

One of the first to answer the call was an abolitionist and skilled rifleman from Lancaster County, Pennsylvania. Deke Coburn arrived in Washington on a morning in late April, all business and commitment, ready to do his part to obliterate the beastly evil of slavery.

His enthusiasm for the Cause was buoyed up when he found himself wallowing in a restless sea of chaos. Thousands of newly minted soldiers were camped out and getting billeted everywhere. The city was a clamorous muddle of adventurers and patriots. As the early days of organizing passed, Coburn's superior ability with a rifle was duly noted by those in command.

Meanwhile, in the southwest, far away from the furors tearing the east apart, lines were being crossed. A young man was descending into madness. Dark voices were beckoning him. He heard their coaxing call and was creepy scared.

The voices were seductive scratches that clawed at his brain. He understood every word, every syllable. The whispers were accompanied by blaring pain that droned through his cranium. He touched his private parts when they spoke. That pleased them, but also caused them to grow louder and louder.

He resisted. He *wanted* to reject them, but he was weak and they were strong. They urged him, pushed him, goaded him, prodded him past genteel boundaries.

Oh how he longed to oppose them, but each instance spurred him deeper down a crevice in his soul where mildew-covered stones buried forbidden tales and enchantments.

The voices bellowed at him, high and thin and irresistible. His facility to hold up against the intoxicating shrillness was wilting. The directive was a demand for him to sort through those stones. He yelled and refused to disregard boundaries, but a wheedling hunger was set loose within which was insistent and thriving. The hunger enjoyed the voices and wanted to explore the puzzle beneath the stones.

The voices and hunger combined to form an invincible fascination too strong, too pleasing, too beguiling for him to withstand. He dug his fingers into the dirt-encrusted cracks around the stones and began prying them up.

Excitement thrilled through him as one by one the stones came free to unmask a shimmering blackness that engulfed him. It was ugly, enticing, beautiful, powerful. It took hold of him, surging and shattering.

Now he craved more. He *wanted* to listen, he *wanted* to follow instructions and do what he was told. When he capitulated to the voices and fed the hunger, there was an invigorating physical euphoria that was exquisite and addictive. He yearned to experience it again and again. And again.

As he heeded the incessant murmuring and fed the voracious appetite, a monster crawled out from under the moldy stones and, with a wondrous burst of enlightenment, he guessed that it was indestructible, and that he, in fact, was the monster. That knowledge and vitality was delectable, and he savored it.

The little Mexican girl didn't have a chance. She was eight years old, in the wrong place at the wrong time, separated from her mother at a busy marketplace. She would be the monster's initial conquest. The monster-man snuck up, snatched her, chloroformed her and carted her away to a special place.

The voices had told him where to find the hideout. They also gave implicit details on how to prepare it and enhance the naturally obscure entrance. He'd been dutifully obedient.

He held her captive. He experimented on her. He tortured her. He used her. She screamed. She cried. She bled. She died. When the line between sadistic rapist and cold-blooded murderer no longer existed, the monster-man was delighted. It had all been so easy, so exalting, so pleasurable.

The voices were gratified, the appetite appeased, at least for now. He was just a man again. He missed the power of the monster and longed for the murmuring and hunger to return. He waited. When the ravenous call came again, he'd be ready.

On the evening of the second day at Gettysburg, Deke Coburn checked out. From its formation, he'd been attached to the Army of the Potomac as a marksman and sniper. He'd tasted bloodshed and carnage, and seen plenty of action, had been in the thick of it at Fredericksburg and Chancellorsville.

When he went mad, he was in a company of sharpshooters manning a brigade on the extreme left of III Corps at Devil's Den. Brigadier General J. H. Hobart Ward, surreptitiously known as John Henry to his men, was in command. The ferocity of the fighting was relentless, an avalanche of assaults.

It was rocky, broken ground. Sweaty and parched, with the blood of others streaking his face, Coburn was crouched behind a grisly barricade. The bodies of the dead, blue and gray, were piled high, a flesh and blood breastworks. The attacks and counterattacks were cyclones of confusion.

On the second Confederate wave, it was hand to hand combat. A gray-clad soldier, with bayonet fixed, came over the top out of the smoke and turbulence, yelling and thrusting at Deke Coburn. What happened next was slow motion surreal.

Coburn parried the attempt and came eyeball to eyeball with his assailant. He was just a boy. As firing and slashing went on all around them, they stared at each other. There was unfettered fear in the rebel's eyes, which Coburn mercilessly snuffed out. With sickening calmness, he squeezed the trigger of his rifle.

At point-blank range, the bullet entered below the chin on an upward angle. The terrified boy's head exploded, a mist of blood and bone fragments spraying the gunsmoke-saturated air. He collapsed against his killer. In an involuntary reflex, Coburn latched onto him and found himself gaping into a gory, shredded cavity where seconds earlier a grimacing face had been.

It was then that a switch inside Deke Coburn flickered and flashed. This fundamentally decent man was in crisis. The wiring in his brain sputtered. It was sizzled and frayed, beyond its capacity to cope and process. His charred conscience went haywire, sending urgent messages that were electric in him, sounding like the frenzied beeps generated by a hyper, drunken telegraph operator. His mind went blank.

Deke Coburn, a tenderhearted man with a tough exterior, lost himself. He dropped the body in his arms. He laid down his rifle and gave it a quizzical look, as though it was a poisonous snake—what on earth had it been doing in his hands?

A shell blasted the ground nearby, which pelted him with a shower of dirt, but he hardly even noticed it. He stood there unarmed and unprotected. His head tilted skyward, then swiveled in incremental stages as he surveyed the battlefield, wondering what he was doing there.

For a crazed instant, he was stalking a twelve-point whitetail on a mountainside. The acrid gunpowder haze burning his eyes brought him back to the blood and guts. He was merely a talented hunter from the woods of Pennsylvania who'd succumbed to inner pressures and deceptions.

What had his ability to accurately aim and shoot a rifle accomplished? How many men had he killed? How many husbands and fathers had he dispatched to graves? How many wives and mothers grieved because of his handiwork?

The afternoon was ablaze and growing old. While the warfare raged all around him, he walked blindly, and though he was never aware of it, he wasn't alone. There were others traumatized and distressed, wandering or running away from the slaughter. His weaving, wayfaring venture out of the danger zone to a spot of relative safety was miraculous bordering on mystical.

The grand sweeping movement of runners, troops, medics, and supplies was a bewildering riot. It was helter-skelter upheaval in all directions. The booming noise was continuous. Artillery and gunfire blended with shouts and choked shrieks.

There was aimlessness in him. He zigzagged roughly eastward. An ambulance wagon clattered past, loaded to overflowing with the wounded and dying. He followed it for a ways. When it veered north, he paused to consider his choices. He decided to keep bearing to the east because a grove of spreading oak trees caught his eye.

He headed there. As he got closer, his nostrils prickled with the scent of water. There were other stragglers, in various degrees of physical and mental health, gathered at a stream beneath the branches. Some were clustered together, while others kept to themselves. He avoided everyone.

He went to a vacant section of the riverbank, bent low, and drank deeply. The water was cool and soothing. He buried his face in it and gulped until he could hold no more. Upon rising, he had a cursory look around, picked an isolated nook, and moved numbly toward it.

Behind him the battleground came alive with a renewed thunderous roll of bedlam. He was oblivious to it. He curled up in a sheltered hollow near Rock Creek, and despite the raucous din, was sound asleep in minutes.

When he awoke, it was nighttime. He listened. The stillness was wrapped in a jittery tension. There was hushed, intermittent chatter. He stayed motionless, pretending he was still asleep. He picked up bits and pieces of data, but none of it was helpful. He couldn't remember anything. He didn't know who he was, where he was, or what he was supposed to be doing.

Apprehension crawled all over him. It felt like ants, prickling and nipping at his skin. He was spooked and addled. His brain wasn't functioning properly. There was much senseless clutter inside his head. He couldn't pigeonhole any of it so that it'd have value or significance.

It came to him that those who were quietly conversing at the water's edge were aligned against him. He sat up gradually. He decided they were definitely talking about him, saying vile things and conspiring to do him harm. He scrutinized them suspiciously. They were incredibly ignorant, giving him no notice as they bartered for tobacco and coffee.

The paranoia pushed at him. It had muscle and vigor. It disagreed with him, and he wanted to be free of it. Overwrought and shivery, he grasped at the jumbled fuzz fogging up his brain, and endeavored to think precisely.

No matter how much effort he exerted, it was impossible to garner any clarity. He muddled through it. All he came up with was that wherever he was, he had no hankering to be there anymore. He wanted to hightail it and drop off the map.

Instinct kicked in and served him well. He was operating under the pretense that those conspirators huddled nearby were out to get him, so he instantly went into stealth mode and kept that mindset alive and active. He slipped away and stayed on a path of least resistance.

The darkness was broken by hundreds of campfires encircling him. He skulked along, assiduously steering clear of human contact. Everyone he saw had the same garb as those men beside Rock Creek, scoundrels in blue or gray determined to get him.

Comprehension riffled in his mind. He realized that he was camouflaged. He had on blue garments, the perfect disguise to breakout and take flight. He would shed and discard them when deliverance was assured, but for now he had the appearance of those he perceived to be in cahoots to get him. He crept warily and stuck close to the river, moving generally south, then north and west, lying low whenever necessary.

From the beginning, he established a pattern. He traveled at night, and when the sun was a pinkish glow sketched on the eastern horizon, found a suitable hidey-hole, settled in and slept. He lived off the land, grubbing for berries, crab apples, edible plant stems, wild leeks, onions, mustard greens, along with whatever he could scrounge, or on occasion, steal.

One night and day led to another. He wasn't in any kind of hurry, maintaining a comfortable pace. At some juncture, he started moving slowly and steadily westward, with no particular destination in mind. He just kept walking and enduring.

When he slept, he dreamed. They weren't pretty dreams with happy endings, but rather, in them, he was hideous and attempting to conceal his disfigurement. A blood-drenched horror was racing to punish him.

It was always the same, always bothersome and taxing. He believed his imagination reflected reality. His past only went back to when he woke up and heard those plotters beside Rock Creek. He couldn't be sure if whatever or whoever was after him had given up, so he remained ever alert and vigilant. He never spoke to anyone. He wouldn't even get close enough to do so.

A month passed before he came to a semblance of his senses. He still had no name or history to link to it, but he knew that he had been a soldier and was now a deserter. He had no concept of country or state. What side he'd been on and the reason for fighting was an unsolvable riddle.

Adding to the conundrum was a blank page in the geography department. He was completely befuddled as to where he was or where he was going. All he really understood was that he had to stay ahead of those who were behind him, so each night he put his shoe leather to work.

On a drizzling wet morning, while seeking a place to make his bed, he came upon an isolated farmhouse and barn, way off the beaten track. He stayed in the shade of the woods and studied it for a bit. It wasn't quite to the ramshackle state, but it was in dire need of repairs.

Grass was growing almost waist high all around it. Shutters dangled at two of the windows, the roof was shabby, needing patches in a half-dozen spots he could see, and the flooring of the front porch was drooping. A section of the pole corral beside the barn was completely missing.

He wondered if it was abandoned. If so, the foraging could be rewarding. He would scour it later for whatever prizes might be available. He found a place to nest and slept fitfully.

It was just past midday when he stirred awake. The sun was shining through the cover of trees, and steam was rising off his wet clothes. He felt clammy and crusty. He rubbed his eyes.

Not too far away, a snort startled him. Caution reared up. He inched to the edge of the woodland. Halfway between his location and the rundown farmhouse, a pair of cows grazed in the high grass. His mouth watered as he started thinking about fresh beef steak and dried jerky.

It was then that he heard singing. A sweet alto voice carried to him before he saw the woman walking from the barn to the house. She had a bucket in each hand, and her gait appeared harried and a little disheveled, but she hit the notes of *Rock of Ages* beautifully. He didn't know why, but the melody and words made him warm and placid inside.

He watched until she went into the house. He was tired, hungry, grungy, and in need of doing something to earn a measure of good fortune. He considered his options, thought over an introductory phrase or two, and decided to take a risk. He stood and walked stiff and tall toward the farmhouse. He patted one of the cows on the rump. It mooed a protest.

The door opened when he was twenty yards away. "Stop where you are, please and thank you." He complied as she came into view. Slim and tall, she wore a flowery long-sleeve dress and a matching sunbonnet that obscured her facial features. "We don't get many visitors here, mister. If you'd be so kind as to stay put until we know each other better." In one hand she held a pistol; the other was draped over the shoulder of a spunky looking blonde girl with pigtails and rosy red cheeks.

He nodded a greeting. "Ma'am, if there are any tools around here, I'd like to do some fixing in exchange for a meal. I could get those shutters in shape mighty quick."

She read him as best she could. "Have you mustered out?"

"Ma'am?"

She gestured with the gun. "The uniform."

"Oh," he grunted and shrugged. "Yeah, yeah. That's right."

She gave him a thorough look-over. "There's a workshop in the front part of the barn. Not sure you'll find everything needed, but that's where the tools are kept. Supper's when I call you, and when I do, I expect you to be cleaned up some. I won't have a dirty ragamuffin putting his feet under my table." She spoke in an assertive cadence, clipping each sentence off with a crisp verbal twitch. "You'll find the pump beside the barn. There's likely an old razor round here somewhere. I'll leave it at the water trough. Use it."

"Yes, ma'am."

"I'm Angela Langton. I do not tolerate any shenanigans," she said, wagging the gun. "This spitfire is my daughter Abbey."

His mouth opened, but then he realized he didn't have a name to tell her. He groped around in gawky silence before finally managing to say, "Thank you, ma'am." He took a few steps toward the barn, but paused to look up at the sky. He turned back to her. "Excuse me, ma'am. Could you tell me where I am?"

She laughed. "Ohio. The town of Xenia is north of here."

His brow wrinkled in acknowledgement, though the information did nothing to enlighten him. He remained out of sorts.

The tools were of high quality and someone had cared for them. They were clean and arranged in logical order. He got down to it in short order. The shutters were an easy-breezy job. He tightened the hinges and reset them in place. After testing them several times, he was satisfied. He returned the screwdriver, hammer, and ladder to where he found them.

Checking the sun's position, he calculated he had time to get started on another chore. There was a scythe in the workshop, its blade wrapped in oilcloth. It wasn't as sharp as it could be, but it would do.

He picked it up and gave it a couple practice swings as he went outside. It felt good in his hands. He couldn't remember the last time he'd used one, which wasn't all that surprising since his memory wasn't much more than a month old.

It took just a few passes to get into a productive rhythm. Everything else disappeared as he worked his way down a length of grass, then without slowing, came back. Side to side he went, the scythe acting like an extension of his arms. He had a wide swatch cut when a shrill voice struck his ears.

"Hey, mister!"

He halted and looked up, appreciating the perspiration pouring out of him. Abbey wasn't more than ten feet away, with a petulant expression on her face. He had no inkling as to how long she'd been there. "What can I do for you, little miss?"

"Mom says you got ten minutes until supper," she said, with a stink-eyed glare. "She won't feed a dirty ragamuffin." She spun and ran to the house, her pigtails flopping.

He wiped the scythe down before putting it away. He went to the water trough. On a stool beside it were a towel, soap, and a straight-razor.

He peeled off his army issue shirt, unbuttoned the one-piece undergarment, and squirmed out of it, letting it fall around his waist.

It took some doing, but he put the soap and razor to good use. He washed up first. Then, he attacked the beard. His face was a scratched up mess by the time he scraped its thick whiskers off to be entirely clean-shaven. Even the moustache had been stolen by the blade. He lathered up once more, rinsed off, toweled down, shook out his grimy shirt and redressed. He finger combed his dripping hair as best he could. There was no tin or mirror to check, but he deemed himself presentable.

He entered the house tentatively. "Evening, ma'am." The inside was immaculate, cozy, and nicely decorated. It wasn't yet dusk, but there were candles burning and situated all around the kitchen and dining area.

Angela never gave him a glance. She simply pointed to a chair at the head of the well-set table. "That's your seat." She was a beanstalk with charming top and bottom curves. Her face was pinched and delicate, with lean cheekbones, accented by pale eyes. Her auburn hair was snugly tied in an unattractive bun.

"What's your name, mister?" Abbey asked, watching him close.

"Well," he said, sitting down. "I can't rightly say."

Angela scowled at him. "I beg your pardon?"

He held his hands up. "Something happened. My head is a mishmash. I cannot remember anything about myself."

Angela gave him a doubtful look. She kept it on him for several minutes, with the silence growing taut and vexing. She exhaled loudly, making her lips flutter. She passed judgment. "You cast an honest impression, I'll give you that," she said, sitting beside her daughter. "We have to call you something other than mister. I had a brother named Lawrence." Her voice softened. "He died in an accident when he was just a boy. Would it be alright if we called you Lawrence?"

He consented with a halfway grin. Abbey said grace. Angela dished up bowls of chicken stew with fluffy dumplings. The aroma was strong and pleasant. He noted that the serving placed in front of him was to the brim. He was tempted to dig in and devour it lickety-split, but instead, partook with meticulous slowness, relishing every bite.

As they ate, they eased into conversation. It was tentative in the beginning, but after stumbling past polite chitchat they struck a relaxed ebb and flow. Since he had little to tell, he engaged in asking questions.

In doing so, he discovered that she was anxious to talk, and she learned that he was a better than average listener. Once primed, her story came quickly.

"George and I, that'd be Abbey's father, bought this place dirt cheap the day before our wedding," she said wistfully. "We spent our first night together here. Abbey's nine, so that was ten years ago. It was in disrepair, and there was lots of work that needed done, but we were young and strong, and we were going to get to it quick. George was a carpenter and handyman. He treasured his tools. There was nothing he couldn't do, but then he got sick and took fever." She held a spoonful of stew to her mouth, and sipped it. She returned the spoon to the bowl. "He died on a Saturday. Abbey came along four days later."

"Pa got buried in the morning, Mr. Lawrence. I was born in the afternoon," Abbey said, frank and innocent.

He tended to his tongue and kept it caged because he had nothing helpful to say. He tried on an encouraging smile, but the emotions set loose in the room caused it to slide away.

Angela sighed. "As you can see, I'm not much for doing the outside fixing up. I manage a fine garden, but the tinkering chores, no. I tried, but I just couldn't keep up and it all got away from me. I do just dandy inside." She pushed her bowl aside, and folded her hands on the table. "If you're of a mind and can stick around for a spell, I'll trade you three squares and a cot for your labor. There's a room in the barn you can arrange for your own and much work to earn your keep."

The man now known as Lawrence appraised the offer. He finished off his meal, and gave them a genuine smile that stuck. "That's almighty kind of you, ma'am." He stood. "If it's all the same to you, I'll go get my quarters set, and then be at it bright and early." There were no objections, so he stepped to the door and went outside.

True to his word, he was cutting and stacking grass at sunrise. For the next while, he stayed busy from dark to dark. He only ever stopped long enough to thoroughly wash up, so he could put his feet under Angela Langton's table morning, noon, and evening.

In all his efforts, he never wasted movement nor allowed Miss Abbey to distract him, though she was always hovering close by. Nosey and impetuous, she wanted to inspect or take charge of each task, but he put up a bantering defense that she couldn't penetrate. The place was starting to exhibit practical signs of his sweat and toil, which pleased him.

On the third day when he came in for breakfast, there was a set of clothes sitting on the counter. He noticed them right off and responded with a tilted head frown.

"Those are old, but not worn," Angela said, giving him a hesitant, feeble smile. "They belonged to George. I took a chance you might want to be rid of those army rags. I had to do some guessing as to your size and make a few adjustments, but I think you'll find they fit. If not, let me know."

"Thank you, ma'am."

"You're welcome, Lawrence."

The three of them settled into a routine. The days grew shorter, nights longer. Summer faded into autumn, but before the leaves were off the trees, the roof was repaired and had no leaks. The pole corral was complete and functional once again, and the front porch had lost its droop. He had to shore up the foundation and replace a portion of its floor.

Then winter came. Sometimes in the evenings after supper, they'd play cards or board games around the kitchen table. Or Angela and Abbey would sing harmonious duets that were sweet and sensitive. He tried to chime in once or twice, but his singing voice was lame and he couldn't carry a tune worth a penny.

Or, while Abbey busied herself with a craft project or scrapbook, he'd just visit with Angela. There was warmth and a like-minded give and take between them. They chatted about everything, and he became awfully fond of their conversations and discussions, but no topic ever jogged his memory.

He got to thinking that this had always been his life, but then those thoughts would disperse. Each time he retired to his room, he raked through his mind, frantic to remember his past. The dream hadn't released its hold on him; the blood-drenched horror chasing him haunted his hours of slumber.

One bitter cold February night, after a spirited tic-tac-toe tournament, Angela asked him to wait while she tucked in Abbey and read her a Bible story. She'd never made such a request, and he considered it strange. He sat at the table, marking up the play sheet with a random X here, an O there. It was fifteen minutes before she came back.

She slid a chair close to him and sat down. "I'm not looking for forever," she said, boldly placing a hand on his shoulder. It was the first time they'd ever touched. "I promised that once. It lasted less than a year."

His face reddened. "I don't even know who I am, Angela."

"You're Lawrence. That's enough for me." She loosened the knotted bun and shook her head. Her hair was thick and wavy, a jumble of auburn that came to rest on slender shoulders. "I'm not the prettiest woman, but I'm not ugly, am I?"

"Pretty," he whispered, dry and tense. She took his hand and led him to her bedroom. He followed, wordlessly. Broken in ways neither could fathom, they were vulnerable, patient, and gentle. There was respect as they breathlessly reached for each other—lonesome souls searching for meaning, and settling for the tenderness of making love.

When she woke up, she was alone. The space where he'd slept, where she'd held him, was empty and cold. A small murmur caught in her throat, which birthed a bittersweet smile. She knew; she didn't have to check his room in the barn. He was gone.

In the dream the man had no conception of who he was or why he existed. He'd been on this terrain before, many times. It was a dumbfounding place, stark and gloomy. Dangers and fearful traps taunted him at every turn. Tall black towers encircled, akin to a craggy picket fence to keep him penned in.

Something was behind him. A big, strong, repulsive *thing* had him in its sights, a shrieking crimson nightmare with glowing jaundiced eyes. Its mouth was a twisted slash, its breath skanky and rancid, souring the air with its stench. It smelled like lots of tiny animals had crawled up inside it and died, and were constantly decaying in its belly.

The man was running. All he knew about himself was that he was hideous, an appalling wretch ashamed of his obnoxious appearance. There was a malignant ugliness in him that leaked out into the open for all to see. He hated it with a living hatred that consumed him. He wanted to tear off his skin. He was a ghastly creature, and he couldn't bear it.

Harder and harder he ran. His muscles were straining, his heartbeat rapid and heavy. He moved with dynamic, fluid strides, but never made any progress. The ground beneath his feet was soft and spongy. The surroundings flickered and flashed all around him, but he never got anywhere.

The *thing* behind him was relentless, coming fast. It had never gotten this close before. In previous incarnations, the blood-drenched horror had only moved stealthily around the edges, muttering accusations and threats, its voice a clattering of bones. Now it was within reach of him, and he was afraid, *very* afraid. It had long arms and barbed talons for hands.

 Closer and closer it got. Faster and faster he pumped his legs and arms, but he went nowhere. He had no traction. The softness of the earth was pulling him. He was snared in the middle of quicksand. He kept running and running, sinking deeper and deeper. Tentacles writhed around his ankles, yanking him down and down. The swampy quagmire would soon be his grave.

A gasp wrenched from his mouth. He thought that this was the end of him, but then oppressive weight clamped on his shoulders and snatched him up. Sharp pain grabbed at his upper arms, his legs were thrashing and flailing in midair. The *thing* had him in its grip, and now he was sure he was a goner.

He screamed in silent, anguished terror. It railed out of him in a rush. His body went limp. The crimson nightmare set him down on solid soil and held him there at arm's length. Their gaze locked together; its sickly, freakish yellow eyes pierced him remorselessly. It was then that the sound screeching out of him swelled to heretofore uncharted decibels.

Everything came spinning, surging, snaking into focus. His past was a kaleidoscope slashing away the murk. He convulsed wickedly. He began hyperventilating. He couldn't breathe. He was suffocating in the revelations. The substance of awareness was too putridly nauseating to be real, but here it was staring him in the face. He *was* the blood-drenched horror.

He woke up, jerked into a sitting position, and groaned. It wheezed out of him in asthmatic spasms as he clutched at the air and shadow-boxed to ward off an invisible bogeyman. In fits and starts, his brain cleared. He slumped back onto his elbows.

The sun was hot on his face. Its brightness stabbed his eyes. His breathing slowly normalized. The sound and scent of water was everywhere around him. He was on a flatbed riverboat. It took a few minutes to recall that he'd booked passage south on *Fiddler's Ghost* in exchange for a regular shift on the pole or rudder. He was on the Mississippi River, drifting toward the Confederacy. His companions were unprincipled bootleggers heading to a black-market hub near Vicksburg.

The captain claimed to be an experienced blockade runner, though that appeared dubious. He commanded a crew of six, fugitive scalawags to a man.

"Lawrrrrence," a voice called, mocking. It belonged to Edgar, a gap-toothed ne'er do well squatting ten feet away from him. "Lawrrrrence," he said again, singsonging it and smirking.

For unknown reasons Edgar found the name particularly amusing to pronounce by lengthening it with a lilting lisp. He had taken much joy in doing so from the first introductions.

The man, who until mere seconds ago thought of himself as Lawrence, sat up. He had accepted that moniker a year ago, but now, with a riveting abruptness, he knew better. It'd been six months since he'd abandoned an opportunity for love and a decent life by pulling a predawn vanishing act; six months since he'd vacated Angela Langton's bed with nary a word.

"You was twitching like a hummingbird, Lawrrrrence."

"Back off, Edgar." His tone was low and harsh. He shifted and leaned against the half-wall. His interior landscape was a pockmarked wasteland in the throes of deconstruction. His brain whirled with questions: How many murders had he committed? Could the lives he destroyed even be counted? How much blood was on his hands? Would there be cleansing or redemption for him?

"Need some whiskey, Lawrrrrence?"

"Leave me be. I'm a killer."

"What?"

"I'm rotting, fetid garbage." Guilt, regret, shame, sorrow erupted in volcanic fury. He slackened and sank into himself, then without warning, he uncoiled and leapt at Edgar in a singular motion. He took him by the scruff of the neck and seat of the britches and in a one-hop hurl tossed him overboard. While the humungous splash sloshed the deck and Edgar plunged below the surface, he returned to his spot and calmly sat down. He pulled his knees up and wrapped his arms around them. His face was blank, his eyes frigid. Disgust, revulsion, and self-loathing galloped within. He diligently stoked it and took solace in the hoofbeats.

The swiftness and severity of the onslaught had caught everyone off guard. Shouted oaths and curses streamed like a litany. The captain and others scrambled to throw Edgar a rope. When they pulled him to safety, he was cursing and spitting mad, but smart enough to stay away from his shaggy-haired assailant.

Fiddler's Ghost became graveyard quiet. Everyone onboard gave the straight-shouldered man a wide berth. Not too long afterwards, the riverboat tied up on the western bank so a few crew members could hunt fresh meat.

It was then that Deke Coburn, a man whose inner balance was precariously off-kilter, departed to be on his own. He returned to walking or, if the mood struck, running. He got separation from the Mississippi River, then trekked south and west.

"How much for the big gelding?"

"Which one? The dapple gray or the appaloosa?" Big Bull Wallace asked, pushing his hat up his forehead. He was a hardboiled rancher in east Texas who, at six inches over six feet, was a walking mountain of a man.

Deke Coburn took a better look. There were a dozen trail tough and well cared for horses in the corral. "The appaloosa. I hadn't even noticed the dapple gray. That appaloosa has heart and smarts, and is plenty nimble for its size and strength."

"Well, now," Big Bull drawled, a twinkle coming into his eyes. "Sounds to me like you're smitten and ripe for the picking. If I set the price to the sky-lights, maybe you won't quit my outfit. I hate to see you go, Deke."

Coburn removed his hat, grimacing a grin. "Come on, Bull. We covered this territory. I've been here far too long, almost two years." In his time on the *Double B*, Deke had gone through a metamorphosis from raw greenhorn to seasoned cowpuncher, proving himself to be a quick study who rapidly mastered each skill. He learned by doing, and there had been lots to do. He worked harder and longer than ever.

There was always another job waiting. He had done everything there was to do on a cattle ranch—branded calves, rode the grub-line, cleared out water holes, cut posts and mended fences, tracked and trapped wolves, had run-ins with brambles, briars, and mossy-horned steers during spring round-up.

He had a natural affinity for the work and affection for being in the saddle for hours on a savvy horse. He developed a kinship with the wild, wide-open country. The loneliness of being on the range particularly appealed to him.

Big Bull Wallace lounged against the top rail of the corral. "You're a solid lead hand, fast and steady, Deke."

"I appreciate that, Bull." Coburn pressed a smile at him. "The *Double B* was prosperous long before I came along, and I got a mind that I'll be dust and it'll still be here shipping beef." He hooked his thumbs in his gun belt, adjusting its weight. He'd become quite proficient with a six-shooter. He was no flash of leather gunslinger, but neither was he a slouch.

"Maybe I'm getting to be a sentimental old fool . . ." Wallace paused, and rubbing his jawline, said, "A Bible-reading foreman with character will be hard boots to fill."

"That's nice of you, Bull."

"I've got plenty of work for you. Stay put!"

Coburn's lips pursed tensely. "Something's behind me."

"So what?" Bull queried sharply. "Something was stalking me when I rode into this country twenty years ago. I put my stakes down and let it be known. Here I am. Come get me."

"We're different men, Bull."

"That'd be a true statement." Bull spat, eyeing him. "But you're going to have to face down your past, and let me tell you flat-out, sooner is much better than later."

"Maybe so," Deke allowed, taking a look at the horizon. "There are places to see before trouble catches up."

"Make your stand here, Deke. I'll back you."

"It ain't that kind, Bull."

"I don't have a clue what that means. You got a frigging habit of talking cryptic, you know that?" Wallace wagged his head and spat again. "Well, pardon me, but I ain't got any words left to persuade you." He spat once more. "Never let it be said I stood in a good man's way. If you're determined to ride on, have the appaloosa and take my best wishes, too."

"Your best wishes, I'll take, but I can't . . ."

Big Bull cut him off. "You can and you will."

They shook on it. That was the end of the transaction. Deke Coburn scooped a handful of oats from the feed-bucket, climbed through the middle rungs of the corral, and strolled toward the appaloosa. He slipped past a couple mares seeking his attention, then spoke to the gelding in a soft-hearted murmur. The horse whinnied and shook its mane proudly.

As it fed from the palm of his hand, he nuzzled its ear and whispered, "The Lord will not hearken to my voice, so you're Kadesh, and will be for many days." The mottled horse responded by pawing the ground and giving its mane another shake.

Deke took some time and gave his companion a thorough brushing and rubdown. He then busied himself in preparation for leaving. He drew his final wages, packed up and said his goodbyes in the bunkhouse. He tied his gear in place.

When he was sitting easy in the saddle, he took one last look around the *Double B*. It had been rich, rewarding, and healthy for him to ride its range. He tipped his hat to the cowhands gathered in the yard to see him off and was about to give Kadesh a nudge when he spotted Big Bull Wallace as he came down the steps of the porch of the main house. The rancher had his trusty Winchester in his hands, and he headed toward him.

"Where you bound for, Deke?"

"Can't rightly say. Just staying ahead of it, you know?"

Wallace was tentative. "We're square?"

"Better than square, Bull."

Big Bull aimed his eyes at the ground, uncharacteristically hesitant and at a loss for words. He grunted and unloaded a gob of saliva while looking up at him. "You'll be covering some hard-bitten country," he said, offering him the weapon. "I want you to have this Winchester. It shoots straight and sharp, and it'd mean a lot to me if you'd take it."

Deke was firm. "Thanks but no thanks, Bull. Can't do it."

"Why on earth not?"

"I laid my rifle down," Deke answered, dry and emphatic. "If I come up against it and need something more than my knife or pistol, I'll have to rely on my trust in God."

"You telling me it's *vaya con Dios* or nothing?" Wallace swore beneath his breath. "Only a crazy man would ride out of here without a rifle." He took a step back and cursed out loud before blasting him. "If I hear tell that you got scalped, skinned, or killed in a shootout where this Winchester would've made a difference, I'll ferret out your burying place and put up a plaque that says *Here Lies A Crazy Man*."

Coburn wrinkled his eyes. "That sounds about right."

Bull Wallace cradled the rifle. "You get back this way, stop in." He took a huge breath, exhaled loudly, and fixed him with a blunt stare. "If I catch news that you ever pass through here without visiting me, I'll hunt you down and shoot you myself. And I'll use this Winchester for good measure."

Deke chuckled. "That's only fair."

"You're crazy, you know that?"

"Yeah, I do, Big Bull," he said, deadly serious. "But most of the time I keep my crazy locked up."

Big Bull Wallace rolled his eyes. "Well, maybe God watches out special for crazy men." The two men shared a nod, a look, and a handshake, all of which were laced with respect.

Deke Coburn pulled his hat low over his eyes, pointed Kadesh north, and let the gelding have the rein. The sun was on his left, midway across a sky gathering a fortress of clouds. He had no worries. He was on a good horse riding free. If a rainstorm rolled in, the new friends would handle it together.

"Don't you know I'm the devil, little girl?"

The girl—bruised, battered, bleeding—cowered near the campfire in the squalid cave. She was quivering from the latest assault. He had been especially vicious. Her lips were swollen, and she was fingering grainy dirt from her mouth. Her face had been jammed into the filthy floor of the cavern.

She watched him, scared and hurting all over, waiting for a chance. Her strength was zapped, but her will had fiber and resolve. She was ready to take advantage of even the most piddling opportunity to escape. Her faculties remained bright and alert. She was fourteen, slightly older than his usual victims, but had received the same brutal treatment.

She had learned she was merely disposable trash to be used and discarded, like the other Mexican or Navajo girls the monster-man had imprisoned. And he was finished with her. She was no longer fresh enough for him. The only joy left for her to provide him was dying, which he explained had to be accomplished according to certain specifications.

He moved like a cat, keeping an eye on her as he yammered on and on. He liked to talk. All the while that he tormented her, he chatted. He told her what he was going to do to her next, what he'd done to the others.

He showed her the stinking pit that contained the remains of previous conquests, which was where she'd be dumped after he pleasured himself in killing her. He breathed threats and carried each one out with finicky exactitude. He did what he said he was going to do and bragged of his prowess.

When he wasn't running off at the mouth, he listened, but not to her. *Something* spoke to him, but she wasn't allowed to speak at all. Any sound, even a whimper from her, earned a beating. She'd learned that lesson before he raped her the first time. He'd placed her in a chloroform induced fog and almost tore her tongue out with a pair of pliers.

Now she kept an eye on him. He was crouched on a boulder across from her, his head tilted cockeyed, his mouth opening and closing. He appeared to be staring off into space, unfocused on her, but she knew that wasn't so. Even in an almost trance-like frame of mind, tuned into voices no one else could hear, by painful experience, she'd discovered he stayed riveted on her.

"Strangle her?" His head craned even more awry as the words wrenched from his mouth. "Strangle her. Bash her face in. Yes, yes." The monster-man stood. He grinned at her, licking his lips as he approached, his hands flexing and eyes blinking furiously.

She cringed, crab-stepping away from him. "Who are you?"

He looped a fist that smashed her backwards. He loomed over her, slobbering and panting menacing laughter. "Don't you know I'm the devil, little girl?"

She was crumpled on her hands and knees. The phrase stung her ears. It wasn't new to her—he'd gloated, chiming it in a mantra-like modulation whenever he ended molesting her.

He circled her now, smug noises babbling in his throat, low and gravelly. There was lots of peacock in him. He strutted and preened with self-aggrandizing audacity. He was dependent on her being terrified, debilitated, emotionally crippled, and completely under his thumb. He had mastered control. He was unprepared for what transpired next.

As he reached for her with both hands, he took a misstep, turned an ankle, and momentarily wobbled. She reacted in a frenzy. She mule-kicked him between the legs with every ounce of force she could muster, but her aim was skewed. Her heel didn't strike squarely, but rather, it was a glancing blow.

Nonetheless, he recoiled. He squealed and blabbered as he clutched at himself. She scooted past him. She could see a faded wedge of light streaming in from outside. It wasn't bright sunlight, but even a swatch of gray gave her hope. There was something beyond the craggy walls of her prison. She scrambled toward it while he gave chase, hip-hopping along.

She banged a knee against an outcropping of rock. She let out a sobbing gasp. He came down on her, throwing himself through the air and tackling her. They thudded to the stony ground. She writhed, but he pinned her down and immediately started pounding her with both fists. He kidney-punched her a half-dozen times, then with a near merry gusto, he hammered away at the back of her head.

She went limp. He grabbed handfuls of hair and dragged her back to the campfire. He stretched her out beside it as he proceeded to be compliant to orders.

He strangled her, his forearms vibrating as he choked life out and crushed her larynx. He giggled when he felt the flabby cartilage squishing. He then seized a rock with both hands and pummeled her face until there was nothing left of it. The voices were gratified, the appetite appeased once more.

He sighed contentedly. He picked up the corpse and, limping on the sprained ankle, carried it down a narrow ravine at the back of the cave. The steep-walled passageway ended in a deep pit. He carefully counted the steps because of the gloomy darkness. When close enough, he pitched the body into the hole, disposing of it as he had all the others. He smiled at the muffled sound of it hitting bottom.

An hour later, the monster was just a man, cleaned up and relaxed. He was smallish with nondescript features. He wore a bowler hat and was a bit of a dandy. He carried an ivory-handled pistol on his left hip, with the butt turned forward. He imagined himself to be a crackerjack gunman, though he'd only ever drawn against empty tin cans and whiskey bottles.

He sat at a campsite less than fifty yards from his killing lair, chronicling his exploits by the light of a campfire. He enjoyed journaling, savoring each specific detail. He especially relished reading and rereading his notes.

Excessive gratification encased him. He lazed serenely, smoking a cigarette, sipping coffee, and watching the starlit sky. From all outward appearances he was above reproach, a man of some substance. And reckless boldness was swelling in him.

Daniel Twosongs had been married for all of six months before he got the itch to do some roaming. Consuelo understood. She'd known what she was getting into when she stood in front of the priest. His meandering ways and her easy acceptance set a pattern for the marriage. At least once every year he would get itchy feet, and the only tonic was to be on a trail.

On this jaunt, Daniel had already been away from Taos for a couple of months. He'd headed easterly to the Mississippi River, then west, approximately following the ever-shifting end of the tracks town of the Union Pacific. The monumental project of building a cross-country railroad fascinated him.

Curiosity had bitten him. Mostly he kept his distance from the always brawling tent city, but being a student of human nature, on occasion, he visited to study it close up. It always provided amusement of one variety or another.

Business flourished as entrepreneurs, both the legitimate and shady type, catered to the vast collection of workers. Ties were laid, rails set in place and spikes driven, and mile by mile the steel line was drawn across the continent.

The end of tracks town kept pace with the progress. It was a portable conglomerate of canvas pavilions and awnings, embroiled in all manner of enterprises. Every few weeks the population would pack up all paraphernalia and relocate to better serve, and in many cases, fleece the work force.

The whole shebang—merchants, traders, con artists, bartenders, prostitutes, gamblers, whiskey runners, charlatans, wannabe prospectors, cheats, stragglers, hangers on—would move and set up a little farther west.

The atmosphere was always rambunctious and lawless. Fist fights and gunplay were common. A homemade blend of whiskey flowed like water from a bottomless spring. Its ingredients were raw alcohol, chewing tobacco, and burnt sugar.

It had bite and kick. If the mix wasn't quite right, the drink could be pure poison, but it lubricated the games of chance and gave loose women an edge to ply their wares.

In December 1867, somewhere in the middle of Nebraska, Daniel Twosongs rode in to the current sprawl of shanties on the plains, found what passed for the livery, and stabled his horse. It was early evening, and first off, he was looking for a meal.

Turning up the collar of his sheepskin coat against the chill, he moved in a bow-legged amble. Squat and solidly put together, he had bronze skin and shiny black hair tucked under a flat-brimmed gray hat. His coal-colored eyes seldom missed reading signs in others correctly. He was ever mindful of the happenings around him.

He came to a big tent establishment billed *The Prairie's End* and went inside. He sensed stares on him immediately, but purposefully ignored them. He'd spent his life on a path where the white and Indian world routinely intersected, so he belonged wherever he chose to be. There was authority in his steps, and he had a way about him that exuded confidence.

It was rowdy, with several card games in action. All gaming tables were full, while plenty of spectators waited for a player to crap out or take a powder. The air was smoky. There were sparse bits of brown grass still clinging in places, but it was essentially a dirt floor sprinkled with a scattering of sawdust collected from railroad ties being cut.

He slipped past the bustle. He declined a busty brunette's explicit offer. He had to persistently push away a slim blonde who rubbed against him. He found a spot at a table, ordered food and coffee, then got down to the serious business of observing.

At the noisiest poker table a tubby man was holding court. He was a blowhard, which was amongst the easiest exercises in discernment that Daniel Twosongs had ever undertaken.

The man had a jacked up ego and a voice as shrill and brassy as the clanging of a cowbell. He regaled all with quips and stories having to do with where he'd been or what he'd done. His cheeks were rosy and speckled, seeming to be in permanent blush. He was balding, with a fringe of rusty hair.

Just now, he noticed the man in the flat-brimmed gray hat eyeing him. A smirk puckered his mouth. "Looky here. An Injun sitting pretty as he pleases with God-fearing white people." He made a jabbing gesture, and all of a sudden, many eyes were angled at the stump of a man waiting on his supper. An unnatural quietness settled over the room in anticipation of violence.

Daniel Twosongs was unruffled. He measured the man to be nothing but a bully. He directed the thinnest of smiles at him and spoke in a commanding tone, "Mister, if you truly fear God, demonstrate wisdom and be at peace with all men."

Someone in the room clapped three times, which set-off a roar of huzzahs and hollers. It built in momentum, which soon faded to a lull. Everyone started getting back to their doings, but the bulky man wanted to have the final word.

His eyes were bulging, and he shifted uncomfortably. "The war ruined this country," he stated flatly. "I had a string of niggers back in Virginia, and times were good because niggers and tomahawkers knew their place before the war."

"Shut up about the war!" someone shouted, which was greeted by a chorus of agreement. He lowered his eyes to his cards, examining them as though he was considering the odds. He acted as if nothing except the game had anything to do with him.

The madhouse clatter soon blossomed anew. When a plate of beef and beans were delivered, Daniel Twosongs removed his hat and closed his eyes for a moment. When he finished praying, he swept a hand through his longish hair and put the hat back on. As he ate, he continued surveying the room.

Two sharks at a corner table were bilking honest workers from their pay. They were courteous and gentlemanly, but it took Twosongs watching for ten minutes to know they were managing a tag team swindle. If the laborers didn't wise up soon, their pocketbooks were going to get lighter, and if the sharks kept up the pleasantries, the men would never realize they'd been systematically robbed in full view.

Directly across from him, a wide-shouldered man lit an oil lamp and situated it in front of a book. He took a sip of whiskey from a shot glass to his right. He swallowed slowly. He took a gulp of coffee from a mug on his left. He returned both vessels as he flipped a page. He folded his hands under his chin to form a support as he read.

Not far from him, the busty brunette Twosongs had spurned now had a paying customer. She was giddy and carrying on like a school girl. She flashed glimpses of her ample assets and wiggly jiggled a dance as he clutched at her. She led him behind a dusty blanket curtain to service him. It was so nonchalant and ordinary that no one paid any mind.

An ear-splitting hoot took hold of everyone's attention. It had torn out of the red-faced man's throat. "Looky here!" he bellowed, gleeful and banging a fist against the table. "You called? Are you kidding me? You want to see my cards?" He snapped them down one at a time, then tapping each one, he sang out in rhythmic laughter, "Ten, Jack, Queen, King, Ace. All spades. Look at the little nigger monkeys."

The man across the way sipping whiskey and washing it down with coffee jumped up so abruptly his chair tipped over. He promptly put it upright. He stood still for a moment, tall and as straight as a flagpole, as though he was a soldier in a bind with a superior officer.

He had a tangle of black hair and a woolly worm moustache. He closed the book he was reading, removed his gunbelt, and hung it on the back of the chair, then strolled toward the winner of the pot. "Excuse me," he said, his voice a barely audible rasp. "Your name wouldn't be Harvey, would it?"

"Who's asking?"

"Deke Coburn's asking. Is it *Master* Harvey?"

The man flinched. His face darkened to a deeper red, the mass of freckles seemingly blending together as though someone had connected all the dots. "I've been called that . . ."

"This is for Maggie." With a withering intensity, Coburn unleashed an untamed uppercut. The former slaver's teeth slammed shut with a shuddering clack as he went flying up and backwards. His arms grabbed fistfuls of air. The chair splintered into pieces as he crashed atop it, landing on the floor on his back with his legs rocking over his belly.

"This is for her baby." He rose up and stomped on his groin. "And this is for Saul." With a cool efficiency he brought his boot down in the middle of the man's squarish face. Blood splattered. Harvey was beaten. He was moaning and gasping.

It was over, but apparently Coburn wasn't persuaded. He didn't lose control. He behaved like a man who had much more punishment or retribution to extract. He agilely and almost effortlessly lambasted Master Harvey to a blubbering mass of mangled flesh and blood. As bystanders milled around, some gaping in disbelief, some cheering and egging him on, he unloaded with unfaltering, deliberate, intentional brutality

Eventually it was evident that a measure of fulfillment came over Coburn. He overshadowed the bleeding man. "*Vengeance is mine; I will repay, saith the Lord,*" he said, in a sinister tone as dreadful as death. He stepped over him to return to his table. He buckled his gunbelt in place, put his hat and heavy duster on, tossed off the whiskey, picked up his Bible, tucked it under an arm and walked out into the night.

Daniel Twosongs had watched it all. He'd never witnessed such a display. He'd seen an abundance of fisticuffs, had even been involved in a fracas here and there, but in all the years and miles, he'd never seen such a thrashing. This had been a mauling administered with an ordered methodology.

He was intrigued. He wanted to know the origins. He hurried after the man. When he got outside, he saw Coburn heading toward the livery. Daniel jogged, his footfalls crunching on a newly fallen layer of crisp snow. The man stopped and turned.

The half-breed slowed and approached cautiously, with his hands lifted halfway. "I come in peace, friend."

Coburn looked him over, and gave a noncommittal shrug. He continued on his way to the paddock where horses were billeted. Daniel followed at a respectful distance. He detected turmoil. It came off the man like stink on a dead skunk.

The night was cold and still, with clumpy clouds swaddling a bright moon. Their breath puffed in white plumes. In the straw-littered corral behind a canopy of drooping patchwork canvas they went about the business of saddling their horses.

They were side by side, and worked at an easygoing tempo. Daniel rode a mountain bred Indian pony, a grayish stallion that stepped sprightly. He took appreciative notice of the appaloosa.

"You know," Daniel said mildly. "For a Bible reader, you're carrying around a whole slew of violence."

Coburn grunted. "Just studying on the ambiguities."

"Any eye-openers?"

"Nope," Deke answered gruffly. "Teasers and mazes, mostly. Unravel one riddle only to find a puzzle."

"God does seem to have a harlequin streak."

Coburn took some moments to thoughtfully ruminate on the notion. He offered his assessment, which sounded dour, almost surly. "That'd be a fair reckoning."

Twosongs was finished. He edged away from his horse and guardedly remarked, "That man back there could die."

"It is appointed unto men once to die," Deke replied in a dull monotone. "Harvey will be a croaker when God rings the bell for him. If that's anytime soon, I won't lose any sleep."

"Been after him long?"

"I wasn't even looking for him," Deke said, giving the cinch a final quick tug. "It was destiny, fate, luck, or the sovereign hand of God that put us in the same joint tonight."

"Never put much stock in destiny, fate, or luck."

Coburn gave him a thorough look-over. "Me neither."

Twosongs stepped into the saddle. His pony snorted. "If you're of a mind, I'd like to trail along with you for a spell."

"It's your neck," Deke answered, laughing.

"Which way you heading?"

"West, maybe. South is a possibility. It could be north, I suppose, or maybe even east. I never know. I go where Kadesh takes me," Deke said, ruffling the horse's mane.

"Kadesh?" Daniel said, his voice rising. A smile crested on his lips as he rummaged through memories. He found what he was looking for, cleared his throat, then spoke somberly, "*And the children of Israel, even the whole congregation, journeyed from Kadesh, and came unto mount Hor.* Numbers 20:22."

Coburn gave a low whistle. "I'm impressed." He mounted and settled in the saddle. "You missed it, though. I was thinking on a different passage." He thumbed aside his thick moustache with a flicking motion. "*And ye returned and wept before the Lord; but the Lord would not hearken to your voice, nor give ear unto you. So ye abode in Kadesh many days, according unto the days that ye abode there.* Deuteronomy 1:45-46."

Daniel Twosongs rocked back in his saddle. "Franciscans," he said, patting his chest. "I was schooled by them."

"River Brethren did it for me."

"Ain't ever heard of them."

Deke arched an eyebrow, grinning. "Nobody has. Good folks back in Pennsylvania, though they outright disowned me."

Daniel grinned. "Did you earn that prestigious status?"

Deke Coburn pulled a pair of gloves on, then said, "Is it going to be chin-music all night or are we riding?"

With that, two loners formed a partnership of sorts. The moonlight was good. They poked along south and west. The mood between them was tranquil, both closemouthed and content with their interior wanderings. By daybreak, though few words had been spoken, the foundation for friendship had been built.

The men wintered together in the natural hollow of a bluff beside a tributary of the South Platte River. It was a rock-walled grotto that could be taken advantage of for their purposes. Over the years it had been used by others, though it hadn't been occupied for several seasons. Neglect had put it in need of an overhaul. There was an exceptional amount of debris and raw materials left behind by previous tenants.

The location was ideal. Timberlands were nearby for hunting, along with various areas where the horses could forage. They worked with hyperactive zeal, and within days they had crude stables, a secure and practical shelter, and a suitable supply of firewood. Keeping it stocked would be an everyday task.

A division of labor for the two major needs occurred with ease. Since Deke Coburn didn't own a rifle nor ever intended on carrying one, he took responsibility to keep the wood inventory up. Daniel Twosongs did all the hunting. They shared in the cooking, cleaning, and caring for the horses.

In the evenings, when all chores were completed, they'd sit around a campfire, chatting or more often than not, in silent reflection. It took many weeks for their stories to be parceled out in bits and pieces, but as they came to know each other, a unique kind of comprehension passed between them.

On one of these evenings, they came upon a topic that would galvanize their relationship and effectively make the bond tying them together a permanent knot. Outside, a mid-winter thaw was creeping across the countryside, while inside, the scent of cedar from the fire was acutely thick.

Daniel was sitting cross-legged, playing a wooden flute. It was a serene and evocative melody. Stretched out with his hands behind his head, Deke had his eyes closed, allowing the soothing music to wash over him.

He was thinking about Angela Langton. He did so frequently, for though he had deserted her, she'd never really left him. She popped into his mind at random intervals, always lingering long enough for his perspective to sour. He'd forsaken the possibility of love and the potential stability of family life.

There was untiring shame in him. It was interred beneath the skeletons of all the men he'd murdered, but it often crawled out from under the bones to convict him. He wondered if there was any way he could ever right the wrong he'd done her, then the song unexpectedly halted in mid-note, jarring him.

"A purification ceremony," Daniel said excitedly.

Deke rose up on his elbows. "Beg pardon?"

"We need cleansing." Daniel slipped his instrument in its deerskin sheath. He carefully set it aside. "I need cleansing. You need cleansing." He reached for his pipe and tobacco pouch, and spoke as he packed the bowl.

"My Navajo forefathers, or said better, my Naabeehó people the Diné, have a traditional cleansing rite that's practiced to be in harmony with the Creator." He lit the short-stemmed corncob pipe off a twig from the fire, smiling sedately as he fanned the smoke over his face. "Diné means *the people*. In the four sacred mountains of the Diné homeland, there's always the seeking for balance, health, and harmony. To be in balance with the Creator is the essential element of life."

Deke was much interested. "Sounds like Bible to me." He sat up, crossing his legs as he hobbled nearer to the flames.

"Most Christian missionaries would adamantly disagree with that assessment," Daniel replied, enjoying his smoke. "It's disgraceful. They have no respect, viewing the Naabeehó as godless pagans. What you've just said is close to truth." He shifted forward, a hand raised in prayer. "We'll build a sweat lodge, you and I. We will present ourselves to the Creator, and sweat out our troubles."

Deke's brow tensed quizzically. He tilted his head and made a hand gesture, indicating he wanted to hear more.

Daniel tapped the charred tobacco into the fire. "Catholics teach of purgatory, taken from the Latin *purgare*, which means to make clean, to purify. It's an afterlife state or condition of temporal punishment for those not quite good enough for heaven or for those who haven't fully paid restitution for their transgressions. There are impurities that must be purged."

"What of the blood of Christ?" Deke asked quietly.

Daniel Twosongs shrugged. "It's a good starter question. What of the blood of Christ? Are your sins forgiven and washed away by the blood?"

Deke Coburn scowled. The darkness of great sorrow marred his expression. "They were once upon a time, but no more."

Daniel clasped his hands together and laughed loudly. "You have a harsh judgment, my friend. For a man who was going to be a preacher, you have a poor image of God in your heart. Did you not study that part about his love being from everlasting to everlasting?" he asked, gently mocking. "One day you'll come to know that the Creator of all things, the Judge of humanity, is much kinder than you are to yourself."

"I hope you're right."

"Me, too," Daniel said wryly. "I'm banking my life on it." He sighed, and there was sadness in it. "Purgatory has kept me on my toes. It has consumed much of my thinking. Catholics are onto something with the doctrine, but I believe they're slightly mistaken. It isn't an after death experience." He repacked his pipe, but didn't light it, then continued.

"We're told that nothing unclean can enter the presence of God in heaven, but what of the blood of Christ?" He held his hands up and frowned dramatically. "Christ shed his blood for the remission of sin, but here we live, in a sinful place despoiled by the Serpent of old. We get sin on us and it sticks like pine tar. It gets in our pores and messes us up. To my way of thinking, on recurrent occasions we live through purgatory for we must be cleansed." He took a stick with a smoldering end, touched the tobacco, and puffed mightily.

"And," he added more gravely, as a wreath of smoke wrapped itself around his head, "there are sacraments and rituals where we participate in doing something tangible to be purified. We are personally responsible for the condition of our souls."

"No truer words were ever spoken," Deke said softly. "Unfortunately, my soul is wretched. I cannot give back life for death. In cold blood I shot a countless number of men, so by all my reckoning, I'm beyond the realm of purification, for I deceived myself. My purgatory has no end. All that remains for me is Judgment Day and the awful wrath of God."

"That's a lie." Daniel removed the pipe from his mouth, cupped whiffs of smoke to his face and said, "Judgment Day is now, every day. We choose life or death each day. The sunrise is a promise of hope and grace. So you and I will be humble before the Creator and sweat out all that ails us."

Deke was tentative. "Maybe we can do that sometime."

"If not now, when?" Daniel's retort was brusque and final. "If not here, where?" His manner was so uncompromising that there was no room for argument. He poked a finger at him. "From here on forward, everything we do will be undertaken in reverent gratitude, with awe and respect for the Giver of life. Cutting the saplings, building the lodge, gathering the rocks, making the fire—it must all be consecrated. We embark on a sacred pilgrimage, and we do everything to honor the Creator."

Deke Coburn agreed reluctantly. "I submit to your wisdom."

Daniel Twosongs raised his hands in a benedictory pose. "Tonight we sleep, inviting the Creator to sanctify our dreams. Tomorrow we prepare and begin the process of cleansing."

That was all. At first light they were in the woodland cutting willow saplings of various lengths for a wickiup. They worked without talking, which wasn't unusual for them, though for this task, Daniel had solemnly insisted on silence.

The day was warm and getting warmer. The horses grazed nearby in a meadow where swatches of green were showing in a white blanket. The forest was dripping as snow rapidly melted.

Along with the framework materials, Daniel selected a thick branch that, with a little carpentry, he could transform into an improvised pitchfork. It would be needed to carry hot rocks to the pit dug at the center of the lodge.

For the construction site they chose a level clearing located fifty yards from the front door of the renovated grotto. All the resources were organized. They walked the perimeter, stepping off the plans, while communicating in sign language accentuated by nods and shrugs. They labored until sundown, and were hard at it again at sunup.

By mid-afternoon, the wickiup was finished. Deer hides, from Daniel's many kills, had been stitched together, stretched over the dome and knotted tight. A bonfire was burning near the entrance, which was oriented to the east, for the sun returns as a herald of new beginnings. All preparations were finalized, and the two men hadn't spoken a word to each other.

They stripped down to be naked before the Creator. Deke entered with caution and sat cross-legged on a mat woven from evergreen boughs. Daniel brought loads of glowing rocks from the fire, the prongs of the make-do pitchfork smoldering.

When the central pit was full, he pulled a canvas cover down over the opening. He crept to a pine rug opposite the former sharpshooter. The darkness was complete, the air heavy and oppressive. Steam rose off the rocks.

Daniel Twosongs offered an invocation, "We call upon the One who holds all yesterdays and tomorrows in his strong hands. We humbly invite your presence to be made known to us. Hear our hearts cry out to you, our Creator, our God, our Father."

There was a short period of quietness full of an unnerving expectation, and then, in a low rumble, Daniel began chanting. It had a goosepimply cadence. It swelled and fell, sometimes tearing from his throat in a high-pitched wail, sometimes becoming a guttural moan.

Deke Coburn never understood a single phrase, yet an intrinsic sensitivity gave him perception and empathy. He *felt* the song. In a while he found himself humming the tune, then without consciously choosing to do so, he was mimicking it. He sang out the catchphrases in sync and agreement with Daniel. It was effortless and emotional, setting his spirit free in ways he'd never experienced. Euphoria took hold of him.

The singing and sweating went on for an hour or more. From time to time it was punctuated by heaving sobs that gushed from some inner black-hole depth of Deke Coburn's soul. The sounds were not at all melodious, but rather, hoarse and grating. It was the noise of poison leaking out of him in spurts, joining the freely flowing perspiration and tears.

When the song wound down to its end, silence rushed into the void. It held steady, filling in all the empty spaces. They were both breathing shallowly. The rocks had performed well, but were now cold. Darkness remained between them, but their eyes had long since adjusted to it. They gazed at each other caringly.

"I've seen the future, my friend." Daniel reached across and took hold of his shoulders. "You have hard traveling ahead, but on the other side, you'll find healing and goodwill."

"There's much for me to process, Daniel Twosongs."

"Most certainly."

Deke locked onto his forearms. "I, too, saw a forthcoming vision. It was mystifying—two divergent paths ahead, arriving at the same location. I couldn't grasp it all, for it got murky, dark, and scary in a place, but when it cleared, you were there and all was well. You were on both paths."

"Strange, preacher," Daniel said in a sigh. "For me I saw something that is impossible, but I know it to be real."

"Tell me."

Daniel wagged a finger side to side. "I cannot."

Deke nodded acceptance. "I am at peace. It's strange, as you say. There are many breaches to repair in my past, but for the first time that I can truly remember, I am at peace."

Barefoot and covered in bristly gooseflesh, they went outside to bluish shades of twilight and an inch deep cushion of snow. Large fluffy flakes were still falling down. The bonfire was now only a smoldering pile of cinders.

It took several hop-scotching steps for them to grab their boots and clothes. Gales of laughter echoed as, like boys inside of men's bodies, they scampered to the shelter.

When spring was bursting out all over, they rode south. They'd cleaned the campsite, packed up, left a brace of firewood for the next occupant, and headed for New Mexico. It was past time for Daniel Twosongs to get home to his wife.

On a glorious morning, with the sun shining on the Sangre de Cristo Mountains as though they were ablaze and touched by the finger of God, the partners sat on horseback, viewing the wonder. They were on the south side of Raton, sitting side by side, together but alone in the solitude of their thoughts.

Daniel cut into the silence. "Home for me is west."

"My trail is south."

"Consuelo will want to meet you, preacher."

"I'll get there," Deke promised, with a tug on his hat brim. "I have a letter to write to a woman, and I've never done such a thing. I need time alone for I suspect it'll take a while to get the words down on paper. I intend to post it in Santa Fe. Afterwards I'll swing north to Taos. I'll find your place in a few weeks."

They shook hands, holding the grasp for a long while.

Deke Coburn watched until his outline disappeared on the horizon. He spoke aloud to Kadesh in a mild tone. The appaloosa snorted and blew anxiously. He patted its neck and gave it a nudge. It snorted again and pranced, taking several high-steps before starting off at an easy canter.

A week later, the letter was completed, secured in his saddlebags. He'd eased along at a sluggish ten miles or so per day, meditating on the process. He had been on tenterhooks the whole while writing, struggling with every word. Years were gone, yet there was no nice way to acknowledge foolishness and stupidity. No sleight of hand or heart could ever justify his rude behavior.

He had devalued Angela Langton, cheapened her. His decision to steal away made a mockery of the love she gave without restraint, of the life she freely offered him. He didn't couch an apology in flowery language. He simply told the truth as best he could and asked for her forgiveness.

It was getting late in the afternoon. A thin ribbon of smoke rose off to the east in front of a serrated wall of mountain. Deke was tracking toward it to investigate. Kadesh was restless and anxious to stop for the night.

"Maybe we'll have some company." It was a mere murmur, but enough for the horse's head to tilt in response. The gelding was canny and trail-wise, seemingly able to move soundlessly through the forest when necessary. It did so now, ears perked forward as it stepped slow and sure.

The smoke was a campfire. Deke pulled up a careful distance away to study on it. Riding in unannounced on another's campsite had the potential to be a lethal mistake. He gave a hearty hail. After an extensive length of time, which agitated curiosity in him, he received an affable invite.

Deke walked Kadesh in and dismounted, taking in details as he introduced himself. There was a saddle and bedroll beside the fire, and a splendid chestnut stallion loafing disinterestedly nearby. Coburn immediately had a bad feeling. It was coldness that shivered along his spine. He also sensed unease in his horse. Kadesh pawed the ground and fidgeted.

"Lucas Thornton," the man said, overly friendly. He'd been drinking. Indeed still was—there was a half a bottle of whiskey in his left hand. He was clean-shaven and attired in the finery of a riverboat gambler. "Glad to meet you."

"Likewise," Deke muttered blandly.

"Will you be keeping company a while?" The man had all the eccentricities and conceits of a warped ego. He was a short statured twenty-something greenhorn masquerading as a wily desperado. He expected to be given a wide berth. He moved with a strut in his step, and prominently flaunted on his left hip was a fancy handgun, the ivory butt turned forward.

"Thank you, no." Deke noted the weapon's positioning. That pretention, plus the rakish angle at which he wore the bowler hat, made Coburn think of a bantam rooster. The coldness along his spine had tightened across his shoulders. He wanted to set a record for getting out of a bad situation. "I'm passing through. Stopped in to say hello, but I got business in Santa Fe."

"Santa Fe!" Lucas exclaimed, slapping a thigh. "Sit a spell and have a drink with me. My old man's a big-shot in Santa Fe. A real heavyweight, and I'm his pride and joy. I'm Tommyboy, the apple of his eye, the heir apparent, that's who I am."

Kadesh whinnied skittishly. It was then that Deke Coburn saw the girl. Disheveled and dirty, she was squatting on her heels in some bushes. Her eyes were wide, her arms folded over her chest. She was trembling.

She wore a threadbare buckskin shift, which was weirdly hitched up over her hips. She was staked out like one would picket a horse, with a rawhide tether entwined around an ankle. Beneath the grayish film of grime, she was a pretty child with a button-nose and long black hair.

"Don't mind my Sally," Lucas said, grinning. "She's mine, bought and paid for, but she's got to learn her place."

"Untie her. Now," Deke said, subdued and controlled.

"What? Why?" Lucas asked, exasperated.

"That wasn't a request."

Lucas Thornton barked a squeaky giggle. "Would you like a taste of my little squaw? She's tolerably fresh. I've only done her twice, so she's still nice and tight. Both holes."

Coburn was sick. His stomach did a queasy roll. "Mister, I appreciate your hospitality. I surely do, but I cannot abide your character, so we'll be parting company." He moved with care, taking strides to have the sun at his back. As subtly as possible he thumbed the thong off the hammer of his pistol, eyes attentive. "This is the way it's going to be. You're saddling up and riding out of here. The girl stays with me."

"Now see here!" Lucas shouted, stiffening his shoulders. He was already impaired and emboldened by the alcohol, and now he took another swig. "I told you! She's mine, bought and paid for, and this is my camp." He corked the whiskey and put the bottle down. "I'm Tommyboy Thornton! No riffraff drifter is going to sashay into my territory and take my squaw."

"I don't want to kill you, Tommyboy."

Lucas was incredulous. His chest expanded angrily as an ugly sneer took shape on his face, crinkling his eyes. "Kill me? I'm indestructible. Don't you know I'm the devil?"

"Then hell has a special place for you."

Lucas Thornton recklessly squared off with him. There was exaggerated bravado in his posture. His hands were flexing, his tongue flickering over his lips. Twitchy-eyed, he went for his gun. He fired it twice. He missed both times.

A wisp of gunsmoke floated from the barrel of Deke Coburn's Smith & Wesson. The revolver had been in his hand before the other man's first bullet hit dirt at his feet. With sheer will he'd waited until the second shot whizzed past his ear. He then pulled the trigger once. His reflexive aim was true.

The slug entered Lucas Thornton's upper torso just left of center, and his heart exploded as his body heaved and crumpled backwards. His eyes blinked rapidly. He flopped and convulsed in uncontrollable death throes. His final breath was a gasping rattle of bloody spray from his lungs.

Deke Coburn holstered his gun. He went to the girl and cut her free. She cringed and whimpered. There were shocking streaks of dried blood on her thighs and massive bruising on her arms. He reached out to hold her, but she screamed and flailed to get away. He stood and backed away.

Enormous helplessness paralyzed him. He took his hat off. Speaking gently, he told her his name and that he would take her to safety. He gave her one of his canteens. She drank her fill, then splashed some on her hands and started cleaning up.

He went to the body. He knelt and picked through Thornton's pockets. There was a jackknife, an embroidered handkerchief, an elegant gold timepiece, and an elaborately engraved billfold.

Deke opened the final item to find a couple hundred dollars in cash. He wrapped and tied up everything in the handkerchief, and tucked it in his saddlebags beside the letter.

He glanced at the girl. She had edged close to the fire and was following his every move with scared-eyes. He pushed a kind smile at her, and she returned it with a frightened puppy look that prompted melancholy in him.

When he searched through Lucas Thornton's bedroll he found a small flask of chloroform and a notebook. He riffled through the leather-bound pages, pausing to skim a paragraph here and there. What he read made his skin clammy. Bitter nausea burned in his belly, and he clapped the book shut. He placed the toxic drug and journal alongside the dead man's other possessions.

Dusk was descending. He got his spare shirt out. It was blue cotton and far too large, but he handed it to Sally. She refused it at first, frowning and shaking her head, but then took it. He pointed at the fire. She squinted and nodded.

He dragged the body away from the campsite. He arranged it under a cottonwood tree, wrapped it in the bedroll and fastened it tight with the tether that had kept the girl tied down. He busily gathered stones and rocks. It took much more than an hour before Lucas Thornton was sufficiently buried, with his boots on and his pistol belted around his waist.

By moonlight Deke Coburn spoke the ashes to ashes, dust to dust litany. He ended by quoting a portion of a Psalm: "*For a thousand years in thy sight are but as yesterday when it is past, and as a watch in the night. Thou carriest them away as with a flood; they are as a sleep: in the morning they are like grass which groweth up. In the morning it flourisheth, and groweth up; in the evening it is cut down, and withereth. For we are consumed by thine anger, and by thy wrath are we troubled. Thou hast set our iniquities before thee, our secret sins in the light of thy countenance. For all our days are passed away in thy wrath: we spend our years as a tale that is told.*"

When he returned to the campfire, he was pleased to see its flames were licking at new fuel. Off to the side there was also a pile of sticks and dead wood that Sally had collected.

She was standing, eyeing him. Her face had been scrubbed. There was color showing on her cheeks. She was wearing the shirt he'd given her. It was drawn around her and the sleeves were rolled up. It hung loosely past her knees, but at least it was clean. She had torn strips off the discarded buckskin shift and used them as a belt to bunch it together at the waist.

They had a meal of jerky and dry biscuits. He made a pot of strong coffee. He nursed each cup. He saw to it that she was fixed for the night in his bedroll, making sure she'd be warm enough. She slept sporadically, tossing back and forth, and moaning most of the night. He sat up, kept the fire banked, thought through the events of the day, considered what to do with the girl, and intermittently chatted with Kadesh.

The next morning they were riding north and west, following an old trail that weaved its way through the mountains. He had canceled his visit to Santa Fe. They were heading for Taos, simply because he didn't know what else to do. He was taking the terrorized girl to Daniel and Consuelo Twosongs.

Sally had yet to say a word to him. Her vacant expression was unnerving. She was mounted on the appaloosa ahead of him because Deke knew Kadesh could be trusted. The chestnut stallion had proved to be something of a malcontent. It had attempted to bite him twice and required a veteran hand. At the earliest opportunity he planned to be rid of it.

That fortuitous chance came on the morning of their second day. After camping beside a gully of a stream running fast with winter run-off, they got an early start. Before the sun reached its apex they came upon a small adobe ranch-house. It sat on the edge of a spacious mesa of sagebrush and scrub grass fringed by meadows in the lee of evergreens.

Sheep and goats announced their arrival, bleating noisily. Two donkeys and an old smoky-white mare perked up to watch from the corral. A man and woman were hoeing and planting a large fenced in garden. They put their tools down, dusting their hands as they moved to the porch of the fair and fine house.

"I'm Sanchez. My wife Maria." They were both built low to the ground, well rounded and durable, with lively and animated eyes. In their middle years, there was friendliness in them, but also an undercurrent of being on guard.

Coburn swung out of the saddle. "Deke," he said, offering his right hand, which was accepted vigorously. "This here's Sally. She's had a rough go of it." He removed his hat. "Ma'am, could you take Sally inside while I talk some business with your husband? If you filled her belly, I'd be obliged."

Sally had followed his lead. She stood beside Kadesh, her hair tousled and untidy on her shoulders. Her arms were locked in a fierce hug around her, eyes wide and distrustful.

"And," Deke added, "if you could set her up with some decent clothes she'd be mighty pleased."

Maria was all bubbly and cheerful. "Oh my, yes. Come, little one," she said, whirling. She took short, quick steps. Sally reluctantly fell in behind her.

When the door closed, Sanchez asked, "What's wrong with the little one? She's not right."

Deke Coburn picked up the reins of both horses. "That'll be one of the topics of our conversation," he assured, leading the animals toward the split-rail corral. "Are either one of those donkeys saddle-wise?"

"The jenny more so than the jack," Sanchez answered, rolling his eyes suspiciously. "Where is this going, senor?"

Deke gave him a wrinkly-eyed smile. At the corral, he began stripping the gear off the chestnut. "I want to trade this ornery stallion for that jenny, but not straight up. This saddle is part of the deal, and you also get a jackknife, handkerchief, timepiece, and billfold with a couple hundred dollars in it."

Sanchez's mouth tightened. "Why so generous?"

Coburn laid it out for him. "It all belonged to a bad hombre I killed. He was sick and contemptible. He held that little girl prisoner to rape and abuse her at will."

Sanchez held a hand over his mouth, his head shaking. His forehead creased as his eyes widened in shock. "The jenny is for the little one, yes? You take it. I want nothing for it."

Deke stopped. "Now you listen to me, Sanchez. For all I care you can bury the stuff and burn the money. A few days after we're gone, set the chestnut free. It's miserable enough to do well against coyotes or even a grizzly."

Sanchez thought it all over. "I will bury the possessions, but cash money is hard to come by. We'll use it careful like."

"Makes no difference to me," Deke said bluntly. "Anyone comes snooping around, tell them you dealt with Deke Coburn, but don't say anything about Sally. She needs no more troubles."

Sanchez nodded amiably. "You were riding alone when you passed by. I'll handle it. You get that poor child to safety."

"I got nothing to hide," Deke said, "and plenty of evidence against the dead man, in his own hand. You tell any meddlers that I have the goods, straightforward and no doubts. Point them in the direction of Taos." He led the stallion to the gate, took off the bridle and released it in the corral.

Sanchez gave him a peculiar smile. "That horseflesh isn't commonplace. Someone's going to come looking, senor. When they do, you really want me to send them to Taos?"

Coburn fingered aside his moustache. "There's no wrongdoing on my part, Sanchez. I have done judgment and justice."

Two hours later, a pleasant breeze was blowing. Deke and Sally were on their way, their appetites sated due to a torrent of hospitality which wasn't allowable to refuse. They had a meal of goat cheese, spicy mutton, and tortillas, all washed down by a cool and minty tea concoction that was tasty.

The jenny was even-tempered and eager. Sally was sitting pretty on an Indian saddle Sanchez had rigged for her. Maria had done well, too. The girl had bathed, soaped up, and rinsed clean. Her hair was shiny and silky, done in an intricately plaited braid that fell past the middle of her back.

She now wore a pair of trousers and a plaid shirt beneath a woven blanket cut and stitched as a poncho. The clothes were oversized, but not nearly as baggy as her previous garment. Maria had snipped and made alterations with quick hands.

The weather was warm, with a blue cloudless sky that extended to forever. Coburn realized that it was going to be slow going from here on. The donkey was frisky and sure-footed, but no match to go stride for stride with Kadesh. It would take extra time to get there, but that was hunky-dory with him.

It was new country, and the trail was trustworthy. He also prayed that the traveling would be beneficial for the girl. Night sweats and terrors made it ever apparent that her emotional well-being was balanced on a thin wire.

At about the same time that Deke Coburn and Sally bid farewell to Sanchez and Maria, Yance Rawlins was on their trail. The hired gun and his partner, a former cavalryman and scout, were reading signs of the chestnut stallion. They were in the high country, in the employ of a hardnosed magistrate anxious to uncover and prune a glitch before it blossomed on the vine.

Judge Thornton's son was the subject of their investigation. Always queer and idiosyncratic, Lucas Thornton's behavior had become increasingly sporadic in recent months, which put his father, the ever vigilant Thomas Thornton, on edge. The son, derogatorily known as Tommyboy, would vanish from Santa Fe for weeks at a time, purportedly on business ventures, but there were no records of any deals or contracts.

The territorial governorship was within the parameters of Judge Thomas Thornton's ambition. He was currently readying a campaign, so there was no room for sloppiness. When his son went missing this last time, he had waited longer than he deemed wise, then assigned his most effective operatives with orders to solve matters before a problem ripened.

Yance Rawlins and Jackson Scully came across the rock pile grave when it was only two days old. They removed just enough stones to identify the body as Judge Thomas Thornton's son, then canvased the area and did some figuring.

Agreement on what had likely happened came easy. Tommyboy Thornton had gotten into a shootout with a faster draw. The why of it was an open question, and presently, they were dead on the mark. The chestnut stallion was walking behind a big horse that in terms of weight, had next to nothing on its back.

"Post that letter!"

Deke Coburn grinned and waved his hat as he rode away, with those words from Consuelo Twosongs striking his ears. It had been a good two weeks with Daniel and Consuelo. He glanced over a shoulder and felt warm inside at what he saw.

It made a lovely picture. Daniel Twosongs was standing in front of the adobe, with Consuelo at his side and an eleven-year-old girl pressing between them. The goodbye scene put a bit of a clog in Deke's throat.

The childless couple had tenderly embraced the young girl, demonstrating an exuberance to raise her as their own. Late one evening, Daniel had taken Deke aside to make an astounding admission. His voice had a tremble as he confessed that the knowledge he and Consuelo were going to receive a daughter was what he had foreseen in the sweat lodge. Deke responded to the news with a smile. He also whispered a prayer of gratitude.

Sally hadn't said many words yet, but there were hopeful indications that a breakthrough was close. Smiles were coming more frequently, and sometimes the creased lips reached up and touched her dark eyes. There was one of those expressions on her face just now.

Deke turned away and spoke to Kadesh. He was going into Taos to do as Consuelo urged, then it'd be off in whichever of the four directions the big gelding chose. He was feeling fit and fine, intent on yielding to contemplations from the sweat lodge while on the search for new beginnings.

To that end, the flask of chloroform had been disposed of, and Lucas Thornton's journal was now in the safekeeping of Daniel Twosongs. They'd had an extensive discussion on how best to proceed with it. Their plan involved employing a lawyer to draft a certified affidavit, along

Days of Purgatory

with obtaining a safe deposit box. Daniel had the task of following up on the details.

As far as Deke was concerned, he was finished with the unfortunate incident. He had ridden unaware into another man's unraveling delusions. He'd done what was necessary to rescue a child from a monster. The killing of Lucas Thornton had been pure self-defense.

It was mid-day. The adobe lined main street in the village of Taos was busy. There was much activity, many people going here and there. He rode up to a hitching rail near where several folks were gathered and was about to get down when he stopped cold, his eyes flinching at the news that he was a wanted man.

Wanted: Dead or Alive. The poster, along with a broadsheet of community announcements, was on a bulletin board on the wall of the General Store that did double duty as a postal station. He saw his name in bold letters. He dismounted and stepped up onto the boardwalk. Without a word, he rudely pushed past those milling around to examine the handbill closer.

The sketched likeness wasn't even close, but the name was exact, and the physical description fit. Deke Coburn was wanted for murder. Those he'd crowded past were watching, whispering, and collectively moving away from him.

He took the poster down and folded it in half. He would get this straightened out quickly enough. He ambled onto the dusty street and was standing beside Kadesh, on the lookout for the jail. That was where he'd find the local lawman. He pushed his hat up his forehead, his mouth pursing in disgust.

Down the street a dog was barking nonstop. There was a commotion of shouts in which Coburn heard his name called out in the midst of curses. He looked. Thirty yards or so away, a man with a left-leaning gait was running toward a burly man. A scruffy sable collie was yapping at his heels. He was attempting to kick at it as he hop-ran, but it wouldn't be dissuaded.

Just then, the dog and man got tangled together. He was swearing a blue streak as he went skidding in the dirt. He rolled and, before he regained his feet had his pistol out. He calmly lined it up and shot the collie in the head. It yelped and dropped. A woman screamed, a child cried.

That was when the bottom fell out and mayhem ensued. People were hollering as they scrambled to get out of the way of the disturbance. The gimpy man had joined his partner, a husky fellow with a wispy beard. Others were falling in behind them, all with guns drawn and ready. Their attention was leveled straight at Deke Coburn.

Gunshots rang out. Bullets were scorching the air, wild and careless. One hunk of hot lead went through the crown of Coburn's hat and sent it skittering off the hitching rail onto the boardwalk. The gunmen were racing and knocking bystanders out of way, attempting to get a clean shot at him.

Deke Coburn didn't see tin stars on any of them. He was their target, and since they were all aiming at him, he reckoned it'd be best not to stick around to pleasantly philosophize with them. He leapt onto Kadesh and skedaddled.

The appaloosa had no qualms or hesitations. In three huge, loping bolts it was at full speed, galloping out of town, with its friend and master bent low in the saddle. There were lots of shots fired, but the bullets all flew harmlessly, and also, there was an infuriated stampede as Yance Rawlins and Jackson Scully organized their crew in pursuit.

Two miles out of town, Deke Coburn pulled up on a rise and surveyed his back trail. Five horsemen were coming hard, with the burly man riding point on the ill-mannered but impressive chestnut. Whether it was a legitimate posse duly sworn in or a half-drunken mob of rented thugs, he had no way of knowing.

Neither did he care. He concluded that he couldn't outgun them, but was fully confident that he and Kadesh could outrun and outlast the bastards. To that end, he headed for wild country, speeding breakneck into the sun.

chapter three

Homesteaders

*"Build ye houses, and dwell in them; and plant
gardens, and eat the fruit of them . . ."*

~JEREMIAH~

When Hans Weitzel got off the boat in Philadelphia in 1850 he
knew a dozen or so English words and some of those were obscenities.
His German was spoken sparingly, always gruff and croaky. Mostly he
listened to learn English, but it was a struggle. His brain seemed determined to reject it.

A butcher block of a man, he carried himself with a poise that
crept perilously close to arrogance. He was something of an enigma and
contradiction; an innate kindheartedness was hidden by a tendency to
be profane.

He was a twenty-five-year-old widower who was actively putting
the past behind him. Nothing was ever going to lessen the loss, but hard
work and moving on kept it neatly tucked away. As far as he was concerned there were no ties binding him to the old country. The plights
and intrigues in the state of Hessia were to be forgotten. He had no
intention of carrying any of it into the beginnings he was forging.

What he had was a satchel of belongings, a sack of gold coins, a
heart full of passion, and a dream to build a new life in a new land.
He was an artisan trained as a blacksmith. A true craftsman, no task
or job was outside the realm of his imagination. A problem existed to
be solved. In his mind a complication came only as an invitation for
creative thinking.

He surveyed the dock. Busyness was everywhere he looked. People were hurrying hither and yon. He moved past other passengers disembarking and stayed out of the way of stevedores stepping and fetching cargo.

The summertime sun was going down, its twilight colors shadowing the outline of the city's buildings. He was hungry. He wanted nothing more than a hearty meal. He headed up a long incline to the first street on the waterfront.

He looked both ways before heading in what would prove to be the wrong direction. It only took a moment or two for him to realize he was in a seedy district, but curiosity had to be satisfied. He kept going. There were men and women loitering in front of or spilling out of saloons that functioned as gambling dens and brothels. The farther he went the shabbier and more ramshackle the neighborhood got.

When he made an about face to head back in the direction he had come, four men straggled out of an alley across the street and tagged along behind him. Weitzel immediately took note of them, but didn't speed up nor vary his buoyant, self-confident stride in any manner.

A pair split off and scrambled to get past him. They spun around to face him, both grinning. Hans stopped. He backed up and turned slightly, adjusting his angle so that two were to his left and two on his right rather than in front and behind.

A smirk of a smile chased over Weitzel's lips. He pinched it off. He had no desire to give the impression that he was undaunted. On the contrary, he wanted to project fear to take advantage of their brazen audacity, which was their weapon of choice. Other than that, they were unarmed.

The obvious ringleader had a flat face and the rough-neck slinkiness of a whippet, trim and lanky. "What you got in that bag, boyo?" He jerked a thumb at it as he crept in close.

In response, Hans Weitzel put his satchel down and nudged it toward him. The leader of the antagonists gave him a slouchy-eyed stare that was difficult to take seriously because one eyelid was blinking like a defective shutter.

"Careful, McGuire," one of the gang urgently warned.

Weitzel had his hands spread in submission at half-mast, apparently resigned to the inevitable loss of his possessions. McGuire inched forward warily. When he bent to pick up the bag, the newly arrived immigrant coughed nonchalantly, which oddly froze McGuire and created a split-second opening.

With a startling cat-like quickness that took the would-be robbers by surprise, Hans Weitzel lunged at McGuire, whose fists came up, but not fast enough. The bearish German twisted him around and put him in a gigantic hug. McGuire's arms were locked at his side. His feet were in the air, kicking wildly. Weitzel's hands were gripped together over his breastbone, applying increasing pressure as he swayed back and forth.

There was a sickening snapping sound accompanied by a gasping scream as bones cracked in McGuire's ribcage. His body went limp. Then with an astonishing ease, Weitzel began whirling him around like a sack of dried leaves. The others rushed in to help just in time to receive their leader's boots to their heads or bodies.

All three scudded to the ground. They clambered to their feet, but kept their distance. They watched in gape-eyed wonder as Weitzel increased the speed of his spinning. His legs were pumping in herky-jerky motions as momentum built up. Exhaling a great guttural grunt, Hans leaned back and heaved, releasing McGuire. The flat-faced ruffian sailed brokenly, arms and legs flopping. He crash landed and bounced twice.

Two of his partners were already running away. The lone stayer was spitting mad and scared, grousing cusswords and never taking his eyes off their intended victim. He knelt beside McGuire, carefully helped him up, then shouldering him and shambling along, headed back from whence they came.

Hans Weitzel dusted off his hands. He picked up his satchel and went on his way. His breathing was level, his blood pressure just fine. He hadn't even whipped up a sweat.

A half-block or so past the juncture where he'd made the erroneous directional choice, he came upon a busy tavern. There was a large sign over the door. He stopped, sounding out the words to the best of his ability. While he was doing so, several customers came out, laughing and chattering pleasingly.

He took that as a good omen. He went inside, made his way across a large open room. There was a haze of smoke forming interesting patterns in the candlelight. Beneath the scent of tobacco an aromatic mixture of herbs and spices stirred up the juices in his stomach. He found a spot at a plank table and placed the satchel on the bench beside him as he sat.

A raven-haired woman with a full figure came over. She was loud and joyful, with apple-dumpling cheeks and eyes filled with mirth. She teased him good-naturedly as he communicated in hand gestures. He appreciated the sway of her backside as she went to the bar to give his order to a one-armed man.

She brought a tankard of ale. He almost finished it in one pull; it was cool and satisfying. Soon there was a steaming bowl of beef stew and a basket of bread in front of him. He dug in, but after a few gulping bites, slowed down.

The food tasted exceptionally good on an empty belly. As he ate contentedly, Hans Weitzel deliberated on what tomorrow held for him and how he would shape the days ahead to conform to all that he envisioned.

Anticipation was alive and well in him. The atmosphere of the joint was congenial and conducive to thoughtful planning. He had a second serving. He would never forget that his first meal in America was at a pub called Gallagher's Cove.

~~~

"Miss Pringle."

The slender woman looked up from marking papers, which she was doing without much enthusiasm. Her attention was elsewhere. The classroom was her domain, and she had an extraordinary gift for teaching, but lately she wanted more. She always seemed to be distracted as she was now.

"Miss Pringle." Samuel Beadle was standing beside his desk. He was a young whippersnapper who always had one more question to ask before being placated. "I've finished reading the assignment. May I please be excused? I promised Pa I'd try to get home early to help with preparations for tomorrow."

Beth Pringle glanced out the window. The day was indeed growing short. "Yes, Samuel. In fact, since I'm sure everyone is excited and has extra chores to do getting ready for Harvest Fair, class is dismissed," she said, rising to her feet. The one-room schoolhouse went over-the-top with hoots.

When the students were all gone, Beth Pringle gathered her books and files, and placed them in a quilted handbag. She made a thorough check to make sure all was tidy and locked up. She began the walk home. She, too, was anxious for the annual festivities celebrating the goodness reaped from the land.

It was a gorgeous autumn afternoon. She strolled along the familiar streets of the borough where she'd been born and raised. Souderton was solid and substantial, and had been fabulous to her parents and grandparents, but she could not imagine her future here. Discontent had taken root in her heart.

At twenty-two, she knew of the chitchat that whispered along the grapevine about her. She was already being referred to as an old maid. Gossip had it that her standards were too grand, her expectations too imposing. The busybody chatter said that she still lived in her father's house because she was too brittle and outspoken. There hadn't been any marriage proposals because she frightened away potential suitors.

For her to worry over such idle speculations was a waste of time and energy. She had no patience or inclination to do so, for she lived with purpose. Just now, there were decisions to be made regarding the culmination of the next day's proceedings, a box social community picnic.

Should she arrange a basket to be auctioned off to eligible bachelors? Or should she simply provide a dish in the mix to be shared by everyone? She was prone to the later simply because she expected that she knew those who would be bidding. Some had been quite persistent calling on her wanting to keep company.

She had no interest in any of them. They were either dull and ordinary, or pompous windbags who enjoyed hearing the sound of their own voice. She didn't want to encourage nor give anyone false hope. Neither was she predisposed to phony niceties nor playing silly games to meet societal presumptions.

Yet she was adventurous and open to be surprised. One could never be sure about what tomorrow would bring, and in fact, she routinely approached each sunrise with a keen sense of hope and expectation. However slim it might be, there was the possibility that newcomers or strangers would be present for Souderton's Harvest Fair of 1852. With that idea settled in her mind, the only question that remained was what she would prepare.

The next day was picturesque and beautiful. The hours eased away amid old friends visiting and children's laughter. By mid-afternoon, the competitions were almost over. The final heat of the three-legged race would signal time for the picnic to begin, which featured the auction as its showpiece. That happening always garnered much participation, with lots of back and forth jostling from competing men.

Beth Pringle was sitting on a blanket in the shade, relaxing and waiting. She was leaning back a bit, with her legs folded beneath her and off to the side. She had resigned herself to having her basket purchased by a resident gentleman who, though she had rebuffed him, kept making his aspirations for her known.

She thought of him as insipid and disagreeable, and the prospect of once again having to go through empty motions with him didn't rouse any optimism in her. Her options to divert the likelihood of that outcome were limited.

The idea of feigning illness toyed through her head, but ever positive, she made it scram before it took hold because she had conceived an improbable daydream scenario. Perhaps it was foolishness worthy of a vapid airhead or an unrealistic teenager, but she nurtured it as a diversion.

Earlier she'd met and had the briefest of conversations with a barrel-chested man who had the most intriguing style of speaking. He wore a tweed cap that rested high on his forehead. There hadn't been any great physical attraction, but rather, his accent tickled the funny bone of her curiosity. She searched the crowd for him now, but didn't see him anywhere.

The sale began with a clanging of a bell, along with a bellow from the auctioneer. There was ample enthusiasm and an exchange of bantering and catcalls. Several eager bidders were involved, which resulted in the first two box lunches bringing respected prices, six dollars and eight dollars.

Then it was Beth Pringle's basket that was lifted high. When her name was announced, she kept a pleasant expression on her face, though a part of her wished the ordeal was over. As it turned out, the bidding would be finished before it started.

The auctioneer began his sing-song. "Who'll give me . . ."

"Fifty dollars!" a loud voice responded convincingly. There was a wheezy gasp as though everyone in the gathering had swiftly inhaled all at once, then huzzahs and applause.

Beth felt flushed. She could feel color rising in her cheeks. She saw that it was the man she'd spoken to earlier. He completed the transaction. He moved in a self-assured gait as he strolled directly to her.

She heard chuckles and giggles, and there were pointing fingers. She was aware that everyone was following him, anxious to see her reaction. She didn't relish being the center of attention, but faced it head on. She casually adjusted her skirt, boldly eyeing the purchaser as he approached.

He sat down and placed the basket between them. "Miss Pringle," he said, taking off his cap. "I am Hans Weitzel."

She dipped her head and gave a hint of a smile. "Elizabeth, though I prefer Beth. Everyone calls me Beth."

"Eliza."

She frowned hard, not liking it at all. "Beth."

Hans ignored her. "Everyone watching, Eliza."

"Beth," she insisted, eyes flaring.

He shrugged. "Why everyone watching?" He spoke slowly, thoughtfully. There was a halting, hesitant roughness as though he was translating and reaching for each word, but he wasn't at all self-conscious or embarrassed. His brash certainty had an endearing quality that appealed to her.

She considered him. Unusual warmth stirred in her. "Fifty dollars is a lot of money, Mr. Weitzel."

"Yaw, it tis. I am Hans."

"I am Beth." There was steel in her tone.

"Yaw, I heard." The pitch of his voice matched hers to the note, his blue eyes glinting mischievously. They peered at each other with an intensity that unnerved her and emboldened him. They were no longer the prime entertainment, which was fine with her. A few were still lingering nearby, but mostly everyone had returned to their own undertakings.

She sighed softy, then began unpacking the meal and accessories. "How'd you know which basket was mine?"

He chuckled in a self-effacing way. "I no speak good, but I not stupid." Laughter was written all over his face. "I point you out to different people," he said, beginning to help her. "I ask who you were and other questions."

"Why?"

"When we met, I like you."

"Are you trying to charm me?"

"No. I wish to spark you."

"Spark me?" Her eyebrows scrunched, eyes drawing tight. "Mr. Weitzel, you should know I don't charm nor spark easily."

"I no want easily."

"What exactly do you want?" she asked frankly.

"You teacher, yaw?"

She nodded. "Yes."

"I want to learn good English."

She was flabbergasted; perturbed, even. "Mr. Weitzel! Are you telling me that you paid fifty dollars for my basket because you're looking for someone to teach you?"

Hans grinned disarmingly. "I say, what you call it? A lie? Having you teach me is bonus." He reached out and cupped her chin. She didn't pull back or resist. "I really look for a wife. I wish to court you to be my helpmate, my companion."

She stared at him. "Who are you, Hans Weitzel?"

He folded his hands in his lap. "I am blacksmith and tinker. I fix machines and things. I make different doodads and sell them. I here in Souderton to do a large job, but it won't last long, Eliza." He purposefully stopped, gauging her reaction.

She pursed her lips, putting on a pretense of anger. "Are you always this blockheaded stubborn?"

"Yaw, determined, I am."

"Yes," she said, correcting him. "If you want to learn proper English you can start with simple basics. Yes, not yaw."

He hesitated, squinting at her. He took a deep breath, and then precisely repeated her words, "Yes, not yaw."

"Very good." She had been busy setting up their meal as they conversed. She served him a plate of potato salad and fried chicken, then made ready one for herself. "When you finish the job here where will you go? What will you do?"

He took a hefty bite off a drumstick and spoke while he chewed. "I have a business opportunity in Gettysburg."

"Gettysburg?"

"Yes, not yaw." He wiped his mouth with the linen napkin she provided, smiling broadly. "You know the place?"

"Yes, it's a pretty area."

"That's good." He shamelessly patted her hand. "A beautiful lady like you deserves to live with lots of prettiness."

She blushed. Her face was crimson, her eyes gleaming.

Six months later, after a lightning quick courtship that was almost scandalous, the newlyweds packed up their belongings and relocated. Much to the chagrin of the bride's family, Hans and Eliza Weitzel set up housekeeping in Gettysburg, Pennsylvania.

In April 1854 Eliza Weitzel was in extreme duress. She had been in active labor for forty-eight hours. She was exhausted and dehydrated, but she stayed on task with tenacity and toughness. The doctor and a neighbor lady were in the bedroom with her, helping the process along as best they could.

The day was gray and dreary, with rain drizzling on the windowpanes. Hans Weitzel sat stoic and still at the kitchen table. He had a bad headache. He was thinking about fate and God and destiny, wondering if there was a bargain to be made to keep his wife and child safe. Helplessness was in him.

Until the first contraction, everything had been normal. There were no issues or problems to fret over. The pregnancy had been a heartwarming experience for them. They'd grown closer and closer, planning for all the days ahead. As her midriff swelled, they teased each other and laughingly looked forward to making another baby together, but not anymore; now all was iffy.

The doctor emerged, a capable man in his declining years who was altogether cognizant of his limitations to heal. He closed the door behind him, his face strained and grim. "Hans, if you have any special connection to the Almighty, now would be the time to call on his favor."

"We're not close, Doc," Hans said, blank-faced. "If the worse happens, we're going to be even farther apart." His voice was harsh and bitter, his English excellent. The accent was barely perceptible, his command of the language impeccable. He had put in long hours working with Eliza every evening.

Percy Nagle removed his spectacles. "The condition of your soul isn't my concern just now, sir. Your wife is in severe distress. She's lost a lot of blood. We may lose her and the baby. Praying for God's mercy can't hurt." He pulled out his shirttail to wipe his glasses. He put them back on. "I'm sorry I cannot do more." He abruptly returned to the bedroom.

Hans was dismayed and angry. His fists were clenched, his lips pinched into a straight line. He'd heard a doctor talk like this before. The words and prognosis, whether in German or English, were exactly the same.

It couldn't be happening again. He'd put an ocean between him and the tragic death of his first wife in childbirth. The baby, a girl, had survived for less than an hour. He had wept. He had gotten falling down drunk and sobbed some more.

He had stood at their graves and wordlessly, forcibly, vehemently cussed out the Maker of heaven and earth. He had decided then, even as the clergyman spoke of the eternal hope of the resurrection of the dead, that the Deity had no plan to ever look out for Hans Weitzel or his loved ones. He was on his own.

Now, as helplessness clawed away at his insides, he wanted to beseech God. He yearned to plead for Eliza and the baby to be drenched by tender mercies. He tried—over and over again he tried, but he couldn't, and that's what made him mad. He could gripe and grumble at the Almighty, and do so in colorful oaths, but he was unable to present a request.

Hans stood. The sounds from the other room told him that the crisis was coming to its final culmination. The doctor was earnestly commanding his wife to push. Her groaning in pain became a shrill shriek that filled the house. Hans winced and moved woodenly to a window. He stared at the rain. Moisture glistened in his eyes. He willed it away, teeth gritted.

Suddenly there was silence—horrible, awful, all-consuming silence. Hans stopped breathing. His fists were on his hips. The still quietness became so piercing that it hurt his ears and made the headache sink down his spine. Abruptly, the unremitting silence was shattered.

A cry came from the bedroom; a baby's cry. It wasn't the whimper of someone stealthily sneaking into the world, but the robust bawl of a child proclaiming his or her presence.

Hans wouldn't allow relief to brush up against him. He listened apprehensively, and waited. The baby wailed louder and louder, but he hadn't heard his wife's voice. A pounding throbbed in his chest. Then, ever so feeble, there was sweetness from Eliza—joyful giggles that gently touched him.

Hans Weitzel exhaled and gasped air into his stressed lungs. He went to his chair and collapsed on it. A release of emotion rushed out of him. He shivered. Hot, wet, salty teardrops slid down his cheeks, and he tolerated them. He was wiping his eyes, eliminating all evidence of sentiment, when the doctor came out and sat across the table from him.

"Hans." His tone was muted. "Your son is strong and healthy. Eliza says he looks like you. She may be the most courageous and resilient person I've ever met."

"How *is* Eliza, Doc?"

Percy Nagle let a whoosh of air hiss through his teeth. "I won't whitewash it. She almost died. She's going to recover, but your family is complete. I haven't told her that yet. It can wait until she recuperates." He paused, eyeing him. "She can never have another baby, Hans. It'd kill her. "

Weitzel puckered his mouth. "I understand."

Afterwards, when the doctor and neighbor were gone, he wished that he could ditch the diagnosis, knowing that he could not. To have only one child had never been in their discussions or projections. She expected to raise a plethora of offspring. For that not to be in their future would be a heartache they'd have to overcome together.

He sat at her bedside watching her sleep. Thick strands of straw-colored hair framed her face on the pillow. Her complexion was pale, yet she radiated a happy glow. Her beauty had never been so exquisite or captivating to him.

Caleb was a bundle cradled in the crook of his arm. There could be no denying it. The boy's face was a squished and wrinkly replica of him. As Hans rocked his son, there were reasons for him to be content, though he was unequivocally unfamiliar with that sensation. It tingled in him, and he mistook it for duty and responsibility. In every respect his desire to protect his family from meanness and hardships was overwhelming.

Eliza was an uncommon woman of strength and character, and Caleb had their love in his veins. Hans Weitzel resolved that he would forge and fashion a life with and for them.

The young slave woman was dead. He was finished with her. Blood trickled from a corner of her mouth, her head twisted at an absurd, grotesque angle. She had endured every abuse without whimpering or making a single sound, which infuriated him.

The man had viciously used her, hour after hour. There was no inkling of normalcy in anything he'd done to her. He had tied her spread-eagled on the bed, first face-down, then on her back. He beat her. He sodomized her. He had raped her back and front, repeatedly. Now he was satisfied.

He was at a swanky bordello in New Orleans, one of his favorite haunts in the city because of its anonymity, capacity to be clandestine, and unique amenities willingly provided. Here, he was Gerald Stevens, an up and coming go-getter from the west. He had no reservations or worries.

His only concern was to clean himself up because downstairs there was a poker game awaiting his arrival. The management of the brothel would see to the disposal of the body. That service was all covered by the pricey fee he had paid.

The water was cold. He didn't care. He washed himself head to toe, rinsed, wiped, then dried. He liberally splashed cologne on his chest and belly. He dressed standing in front of a full-length mirror, preening as he adjusted each article of clothing to his liking.

The final item was a bowler hat. It was his crowning brilliance. He perched it on his head at a variety of tilts until he settled on the attitude he wanted to project. He counted his hefty bankroll and tucked the ornate billfold into an inside pocket of his jacket. He departed without ever casting a glance at the dead woman on the brass bed.

A twelve-year-old had been hiding in the closet the whole while. The man's son had seen everything. On these kinds of trips, the boy was always left to his own devices, running free and doing as he wished.

The child was fond of this particular establishment because it was familiar. Father and son had come here several times. He knew the hallways and spots where he could disappear. There was even a lady here who would take him aside and bathe him, and under that guise, do secret things to his private parts.

Tommyboy had spied on his father at other places, but this was the first time he'd seen a killing. It fascinated him. He slipped out of the closet, creeping near the four-poster.

He examined the dead woman up close. He gingerly touched the fingerprint puncture marks and abrasions on her neck. He'd seen it happen and had felt powerful watching. He had witnessed his father straddling her chest as he shook and choked her with his bare hands. What strength, what majesty—he wanted to know those feelings; he wanted to *feel* them.

He thought about his mother. The memory of her was wrapped in a photograph and stories, and in the awful circumstances of her untimely passing. It happened on their way west.

A band of Kiowa painted up and on the prowl for glory had attacked their wagon train, catching them by surprise. The battle was a swift fury of chaos and confusion.

When the braves retreated and moved on, several of the travelers were dead. His mother was among those. She hadn't even managed to get out of their wagon. A daring redskin had snuck into it and brutishly killed her. She'd been strangled. His father wept; his eyes had been raw red for many days.

Now, staring at the scrapes and scratches on the Negro woman's neck, Tommyboy wondered. The suspicion vamoosed in the instant he heard a creak in the hallway. He scooted to his stowaway nest. While he listened as someone sanitized the scene, he made plans for what he was going to do next. As soon as he could, he intended to seek out the tiny-breasted lady who gave him special baths. He was going to help her fill a tub.

Gerald Stevens, a businessman in New Orleans for some high stakes gambling, was oblivious to all except appearances. He was obsessively compulsive about the façade presented to those around him. His given name was Thomas Lucas Thornton, and he was absolutely ignorant of his son's transgressions.

If he had been knowledgeable, a small part of him would be demoralized, but a much larger response would be blatant indifference. He would regard his child's behavior as mere coming of age peccadilloes.

The poker game wasn't what he'd hoped it'd be. There was little competition to challenge him or even hold his attention. After a half-dozen hands he was up over five hundred dollars without even concentrating.

He was good at cards. Plus, when necessity demanded, he had exceptionally deceptive skills at cheating. He wouldn't need to utilize those tricks at this table. He was disappointed.

This game had been arranged with the expectation that a certain wealthy land baron would be amongst the players, but the man canceled without explanation. The plan to gain a marker on him was gone, which was a setback to be rectified at the earliest possible opportunity.

For Gerald Stevens a.k.a. Thomas Thornton, a game of cards wasn't about money. It was give and take warfare around a table. Poker was where he did the groundwork for shady deals and sizable transactions, where he gained leverage that at the proper moment would be employed as blackmail or coercion. In all his maneuvering he was uncompromising and ruthless.

Now, without the prospect of putting hooks into a future business partner, he was bored. His mind drifted along with his eyes. There was a rough-and-ready man at the bar who appeared to be out of place. Always alert for new talent, Thornton measured him and decided it could be more profitable engaging him in conversation rather than staying in the game.

Thornton folded. He gathered his money. He casually moved across the room. When he stepped to the mahogany bar beside the stranger, he was counting and shuffling his winnings.

"Care to share in my good fortune, friend?" Thornton asked, offering his right hand. "Gerald Stevens."

The man chewed on the stub of a burnt-out cigar at a corner of his mouth. "Yance Rawlins." The handshake was firm, both eyeballing the other with undisguised wariness. A few moments later they were off by themselves in a corner with a bottle of the finest bourbon available on a table between them.

Thornton poured them each a shot. He sipped his while Rawlins snapped his back, then refilled his glass. "That certainly ain't rot-gut whiskey. Glad to benefit from your streak of luck, but whatever's on your mind, spill it."

"What business are you in, Mr. Rawlins?"

"Any kind that pays well."

Thomas Thornton pulled out a diamond-studded cigar case. He tapped one out. "What are you doing in New Orleans?" He fired it up, leaving the silver box beside his shot glass.

Rawlins laughed loudly. "I'm in a whorehouse. You think maybe I'm looking to get straight with a whore?"

"Ever kill anyone, Mr. Rawlins?"

"What are you, a lawman or a muttonhead?" Yance asked, dead serious. A sneer curled his lips. He tossed his cigar butt into the ashtray. He helped himself to a fresh one from the extravagant case. He gave it a lazy lick. He put a match to it and spoke around the puffs of smoke. "I won't say one way or the other, but I'll tell you this, mister. Another hairball question and I'll cheerfully slit your throat."

Thornton was undeterred. "I'd like to chat a bit about you hiring on with me. It'd be steady work," he said coolly.

Rawlins scratched his side as he thought it over. His hand came to rest on the handle of a custom made straight-razor hidden in an easy access pocket. He always carried it with him. It was honed to a fierce edge. A permanent straggle of beard sprouting on his chin like a fuzzy burr belied that fact.

"What's your answer going to be, Mr. Rawlins?"

Rawlins removed the cigar, rolling it between thumb and forefinger. "I prefer to freelance. Besides, I ain't sure a man who'd offer me a job out of nowhere has any sense whatsoever."

"I assure you that I'm not a man to make rash decisions or offers," Thornton said quietly. His demeanor was terse, his tone even and un-emotional. "Neither am I one to be trifled with, Mr. Rawlins." His voice remained unchanged, but there was coldness and a threat implied in it. His eyes were remote.

Rawlins smiled blandly. He tossed off two quick shots of bourbon. "I'm a jawbreaker and strong-arm artist, so those tactics, verbal or otherwise, don't even make me blink."

"Now we understand each other," Thornton said, puffing contentedly. "My operations are based in Santa Fe. I have investments in banking, lumber, land speculation, along with some mining interests.

I do alright. I intend to do much better, and for that, I'll need a trusted enforcer of my will. I thought your predecessor was going to fill that role, but he turned out to be inadequate, and I had to terminate him."

"Give me your best pitter-patter."

"Six month trial," Thornton came back hastily. "You sign on for a flat rate of a thousand dollars up front, plus expenses."

"I'm still listening."

"You're exclusive to me for that timeframe. Give me six months with no distractions or outside interests. Then, if there's mutual gratification, we can negotiate. At that point you hiring out as a freelancer will be taken into consideration."

"Santa Fe, huh?" Yance said, snuffing out the cigar. "I can be ready to travel in a couple days."

"Not so fast, Mr. Rawlins." Thornton leaned in close. "I hadn't finished. I have a situation that needs taken care of here in New Orleans. I was to meet a gentleman at the poker table this evening, but he stood me up."

Rawlins chuckled. "What do you want busted on him?"

"If only it was that easy a proposition," Thornton replied flatly. "This is a bit of a delicate matter. He owns a parcel of land in New Mexico that's important to me. I need his signature on a bill of sale for it. The document and $15,000 in cash await an interaction with him."

"Bloody hell, point me in the right direction."

"That's the spirit," Thornton said, nodding. "In a good faith gesture, here are my profits from the table, free and clear of your salary. Call it a start-up dividend in anticipation of a beneficial relationship."

Rawlins scooped up the stack of bills. "You get me that reprobate's location and your problem will be solved." He rose to his feet. "But first there's a cheeky whore around here who's just waiting for me to take my boots off." Grinning, he wiggled his eyebrows and was off to pursue carnal delights.

Two days later, Thomas Thornton had secured a signed bill of sale and legal deed to some land he coveted. Evidently when a man is gagged, stripped, bound, and terrorized he's susceptible to the power of suggestion; when a straight-razor is held against his genitals and he's assured that his choice is his signature or his gonads, his hand reaches for a pen.

The future judge was pleased with all the developments. It had been a productive trip. Accompanied by his new employee, he and his son were on their way home to Santa Fe.

All his life Jackson Scully wanted to be a soldier. It had consumed his childhood. He had attempted to gain entrance to West Point, but didn't have the political connections necessary to obtain an appointment. That setback stuck in his craw, where it continually festered.

Anticipating President Lincoln's call for volunteers, he'd been camped out in Washington for weeks when Fort Sumter was fired upon. Nothing was going to prevent him from signing on to be on the front-lines of the fight.

The drills and training thrilled him. He had jumped into the military exercises and distinguished himself. His enthusiasm for following orders was contagious. Others complained or grew tired of the long days and short nights, but not him. He'd been successful and flourished in every aspect of soldier life.

Now it was all gone. Jackson Scully was defeated. Sullen and full of rage, he lay in a hospital ward staring at the ceiling contemplating the unfairness of it all. The first battle of the war was over, and with it, his dreams of ribbons and medals. He was sidelined from the pageantry of armies clashing.

Bull Run had put a damper on his career and quite possibly destroyed it. He had performed with obstinate singleness of purpose, demonstrating dauntless bravery. The gunfire and artillery blasts hadn't startled or slowed him—if anything, the sulfuric scent of gunsmoke inspired and spurred him on.

He had followed commands and led the charge. When the lines broke in retreat, he held his ground. He aimed, fired, and reloaded his rifle with calm resolve. While companions turned tail and ran like frightened jackrabbits, he had fought honorably against the enemy until a blast stopped him.

His left thigh was fractured. Shrapnel ripped flesh apart and embedded itself in bone. Two procedures, one on the edge of the battlefield, the other in a makeshift surgical theater, had saved the leg from being amputated, at least for now. If infection set it, there remained a much better than average chance that some sawbones would have to chop it off just below the hip joint.

He would die rather than allow that to happen, and had vehemently made his wishes known to doctors and nurses. Misery engulfed him. In the depression he connived and made plans to keep his life-long aspirations alive. He filed papers to be transferred to the west.

Indian uprisings were disrupting the advance and flow of land-hungry sodbusters. As the country manifested its destiny there was a pressing need for troops to be dispatched for protection. There would be a unit and place for him to serve.

Jackson Scully's mind was determinedly set. He would be a soldier. By sheer force of will, no matter how impaired or deformed, he'd keep his leg. Then, instead of killing rebels, he'd go west to round up or slaughter savages.

In February 1864 the Weitzel family was sheltered in a barn halfway across Missouri. The owner of the farm had generously offered hospitality, which Hans couldn't graciously accept without strings. He contributed his strong back to the daily chores.

The rain had been coming down hard for almost a week. It was a freezing downpour, and presently, thunder and lightning were crackling the night sky. Bales of hay were arranged around the back of their Conestoga where they sat. The mules and oxen were bedded down. In one of the stalls at the back of the barn a hound was yapping and whimpering at sporadic intervals. The bitch was in labor and having a difficult time of it.

Caleb was fidgety. "How much farther is it to west, Pa?"

His parents exchanged a smile, then Hans said, "We've been traveling west since we left Gettysburg, son. Where we're going to build our home is probably another thousand miles."

"That's a long way."

"That it is." Hans stood and adjusted the wick of the oil lamp hanging on the wagon. "When the weather clears and warms we'll put miles behind us. We'll restock in Kansas City and maybe join others, though if we do, at some point we'll head off on our own." He stretched a kink out before sitting back down. "I do not want to go where everyone else goes."

"No, we don't want to do that," Eliza said, laughing easily.

"How come, Ma?"

"We're going to be the first settlers in some area of New Mexico, Caleb," she answered, pride in her voice. "We'll build a future in country that has to be tamed by our hands."

Hans nodded agreeably. "It'll be hard work that has no end. There'll be lots of sweat and aching muscles. We'll encounter danger and hardships from the land itself, but perseverance will reward us. When I close my eyes I can see it."

"Tell me about it, Pa," Caleb urged excitedly.

"You'll see it soon enough, son," Hans replied, giving him a sly grin. "We have to find our site by mid-summer to give us time to get a roof of some kind up before snow."

Eliza wagged a finger at him. "You'll have to do a good amount of hunting, too, Hans. We'll need meat."

A snapping splinter of lightning followed immediately by a booming roll of thunder startled them. Each reacted automatically. Caleb jumped to his feet; Eliza hitched in air, holding a hand over her mouth. Hans folded his arms over his chest. They relaxed and listened to the pounding storm. The hound let out a low-pitched, whining howl.

After a subdued lull in the conversation Caleb restarted it by raising a question. "Will there be Injuns?"

Hans arched an eyebrow. "Likely, yes."

"We may have Indians for neighbors," Eliza said softly. "It'll be good if we do for the land can be harsh and unforgiving. Indians have occupied it for centuries. We'll do well if we can acquire some of their wisdom."

Caleb stewed on that for a bit, then in pure innocence he asked, "Won't they want to kill us?"

Eliza assured him. "We'll be their friends, Caleb."

"Yes, but they're redskins!" he protested sharply.

Hans spoke up, his voice stern and weighty. "Son, we're whiteskins, and what does that mean?" He allowed the words to hang there as he kept his eyes intent on his son's face.

Caleb's forehead creased. "I guess I don't know, Pa."

"Skin color doesn't measure the heart," his father said with great emphasis. "Skin color can't determine character. People are people.

There are good and bad people in every race. I've known plenty blood-thirsty white savages, believe me."

Eliza took hold of her son's hand. "It's messed up more times than not, but our responsibility is well-defined. Everyone deserves the benefit of doubt and the right to prove by their character or actions whether they're our friends or not."

Caleb gave her a tiny but firm smile. Lightning flashed, thunder rumbled. The rain and wind was outrageously battering the barn. The dog yelped, obviously in tremendous pain.

"Now," she said, standing. "We need to see if there's anything we can do to help that poor dog." She got a lantern from a compartment of the wagon and lit it. In the pale lamplight mother and son were flickering shadows as they walked to the rear stall to provide comfort to a dumb animal.

Yance Rawlins was in a world of trouble. Flat on his back, he couldn't breathe. His lungs were on fire. His head hurt. It felt like a long needle was being jabbed back and forth through his ears. His mouth was full of dust. A patch of wet blood stained the collar of his shirt and was caking at the base of his neck. He couldn't see straight. The world was a spinning blur around him. His right ankle was broken.

The sun was burning high in a cornflower blue sky uninterrupted by even a wisp of cloud. Waves of heat shimmered. It was hot and getting hotter. The desert was a lonesome place.

Rawlins needed to find the shelter of shade. His horse whinnied and snorted. It was standing nearby. He attempted to sit up, but the surroundings distorted and closed in on him. He collapsed backwards. A fog blanketed his brain. There was a barbed wire of pain threading its way down his spine.

He tried to think, tried to remember what had happened. The events of the day were fuzzy. His short-term memory had been knocked for a loop by the wound at the back of his head. He was in a predicament, but what had caused it? Had someone taken a shot at him? Had he been dry-gulched?

The strained heat in his chest was easing. Air was hitching in and out in raspy gasps that sounded like notes made by an out of tune squeeze-box. The wind had been whacked out of him. He closed his eyes and consciously settled his breathing.

As his oxygen intake improved, his head cleared a bit. He had been lazing along, dozing in the saddle on an old familiar trail on his way back to Santa Fe after doing a dirty deed in Taos on behalf of Judge Thornton, but that was as far as his thinker would take him. There was nothing else for him to sort through. It was as though his mind was a blank slate.

His eyes squinted open. Sunlight hammered them shut with nails of pain. Piercing stabs went through his skull. He lay still. He wanted clarity, he wanted to grasp it and turn it over in his hands. It was nowhere to be found. If anything, the murkiness in his head was getting thicker, heavier.

There was a rustle close by. He stiffened. Another swishing hiss of sound in the sagebrush caused him to attempt to turn in that direction, but no go. Numbness spread across his shoulders and down his arms.

His horse stomped and blew loudly. The noise of dice shaking startled him, then the roar of a gunshot filled his ears. He jerked up, his right arm twitching spasmodically as he futilely reached for his holstered gun. The suddenness of movement set off a rush of vertigo. Stinging discomfort throbbed through him. He gulped a lungful of air.

Everything spun out of control. It was as though he was drowning in deep water. He sank lower and lower. The intensity of both the barbed wire agony in his spine and needle jabbing between his ears increased. A shadow covered him completely as a kaleidoscope of colors stretched and warped in front of his eyes. He blacked out.

The next thing he knew it was dusk. His eyes flickered open to gray skies above. His head felt swollen. His right leg below the knee had a splint on it. There was a pillow-like softness against the base of his skull. The sizzle of something cooking and wood smoke was teeming in his nostrils.

His vision focused decently. Tiny spots swirled, but then faded away. He looked around. A soldier in ragged army blues was at the fire tending to several chunks of meat on a spit. He knelt on a knee, his left leg stuck out peculiarly.

"Name's Rawlins. Yance Rawlins."

The trooper turned toward him. "Jackson Scully."

"What are you roasting?" Rawlins asked weakly.

"The rattlesnake that almost killed you," Scully answered, shifting his feet to a better balance. "A big granddaddy."

Rawlins was confused. "I never saw any rattler."

Scully gave a smart-alecky laugh. "Near as I can tell from reading the signs, it was likely snoozing and sunning itself when you disturbed it. When it came awake, the horse got spooked. You got bucked and tossed off. The back of your head struck a jagged rock. You got a helluva gash and bruise. I fixed a poultice when I got us settled in here." He stopped to examine the meat, and then continued, "Your brains were jarred so you probably got a concussion of some kind. You were out of it and the snake was coiled and ready to strike when I rode up. I put a bullet in its head, which splattered nicely." He smiled, an eyebrow rising.

Rawlins leaned on an elbow. "Thank you. All your figuring sounds about right. That rattler wasn't the only one taking a nap. I was nodding off in the saddle." He glanced around. The camp was a little clearing edged by a few pinyon trees. He was stretched out on his groundsheet beneath a stumpy cottonwood. The horses were picketed near a thicket of scrub grass. "How far are we from where you found me?"

"A couple hundred yards," Scully replied with a laid-back shrug. "You were in no shape for a long haul. I wanted to get the ankle set and bed you down as quickly as possible." He stood and went to his saddlebags in his unusual limp. He got out a couple battered tin plates, and returned to the campfire. He divided the rattlesnake into equal portions.

Rawlins picked tentatively at his food, taking nibbling bites. "How long you been in the army, Scully?"

"April 1861 until two weeks ago." Scully had settled on the ground. "I mustered out. I got papers saying as of the first of July 1867 I'm footloose and fancy free." He chewed each mouthful slowly, savoring the meal. "I had a good run, but it got to where there were too many nimrods giving orders."

"What are you going to do?"

"I'm doing it," Scully said flatly. "Drifting to and fro."

"Got any specific intention in mind?"

"There are a lot of saloons and ladies that await me."

Rawlins laughed, which momentarily became a wince. He pressed a hand against his forehead. "If I live long enough I'll take you to a high-end whorehouse in Santa Fe where the whiskey flows and the ladies can make your kidneys scream." He put his plate down. "I own a small interest in the joint. You got a few freebies coming to you. I owe you at least that much."

Scully gave a lopsided grin. "You'll live."

The moon appeared as a sun-scorched shard of bone in the darkening sky. Stars came out and sparkled as the men swapped embellished stories long into the cool night.

On an October day in 1868 Caleb Weitzel was well pleased. There were three wild horses turned loose in the corral, a steeldust stallion and two bay mares. He knew that he'd gotten extremely lucky in trapping them in a dead-end nook of Blanco Canyon.

He stood with a foot on the bottom rung watching them feed on hay he'd just put in place. The stallion was restless. It rose on its haunches and pawed the air, whinnying and snorting. It munched a mouthful, ran in a tight circle, then returned to feed some more. The mares merely ate contentedly.

The afternoon was turning in on itself. Slivery hues of twilight fingered the sky. Big fluffy snowflakes were floating down, gathering into a thin blanket as they hit the ground. Caleb opened his mouth and caught several flakes on his tongue. He heard footsteps squeaking on the snow and turned to see his father coming, a broad smile on his face.

"Capturing horses must not be any more difficult than catching snowflakes," Hans said, laughing.

"It was pure luck, Pa."

"Luck only comes to those who work hard, son."

"You'd know more about that than me, Pa."

Hans gave him a nudge. "You've learned it well."

Caleb made a gesture toward the horses. "I surprised them. They were feeding at the back edge of a narrow rock-walled draw that had only one exit. All I had to do was block them in."

"Did they stick their heads in your lasso, too?"

"Very funny, Pa." Caleb pushed his hat up his forehead. "The mares were easy, but the steeldust made me sweat some."

"I don't doubt it," Hans said, admiration in his voice. "That stallion is going to sire us a herd."

"Likely so, but I'm going to make it mine," Caleb reported confidently. "It's young, strong, and intelligent. I'll spend a lot of time gaining its trust and being its friend."

"You'll surely succeed," Hans said, touching his shoulder. "In all my days I've never seen anyone have a way with animals like you do. Look at Rainy standing over there watching the horses without making a sound. Every instinct a hound has is to be yapping, but you told it to keep its mouth shut. I swear there are times I think you taught that dog English."

"I wish I had taken Rainy with me." Caleb turned toward his father. "There was a man watching me, Pa. I first spotted him yesterday and he was still there this morning. He kept his distance. I'm pretty sure he had field glasses."

"He make any threatening moves?"

"No. He wasn't even making an attempt not to be seen."

"Well, it's a free country," Hans said, producing a wry smile. He gave his son a hearty clap on the shoulder. "Let's go get us some supper. You must be hungry."

In the house they shed their outerwear. They busied themselves with preparations for family mealtime. Caleb set the table while his father tended to the cast iron pot of venison stew. He stirred it with a big wooden spoon and also had himself a generous taste.

Eliza came in from outside, hung up her heavy shawl on a peg, and wondered, "Is the dog being punished?"

"Not at all," Caleb answered, frowning. "Why?"

Eliza cracked the door open. "Look at the lazy bones." Rainy was lying on the porch, its head resting on its paws, a sad-eyed sight. "Come on in, Rainy," she said softly. The hound merely shifted its head to the side and let out a low whine.

"Fine, be that way," Caleb said, closing the door. "Likely got its nose out of joint for one reason or another."

Hans lit a couple oil lamps. Then, he placed the pot in the center of the table. Eliza went to the cupboard and arranged a basket of biscuits left-over from breakfast. They sat down together. She said grace and served the stew.

"How's our patient?" Hans asked, breaking a biscuit.

"Not much change," she replied, spreading a linen napkin on her lap. "It's just shy of a week he's been with us and he's still sleeping eighteen to twenty hours a day. When he's awake, he's mystified and out of context. He talks gibberish. It's slurred and thick, but I think he speaks German."

Hans nodded thoughtfully. "A *Deutschlander*?"

"I don't know," she admitted candidly.

"Is he going to recover?"

"I don't know that either, Caleb." She smiled tightly. "He's making progress little by little, bit by bit. Early on I doubted he'd last this long." She took a small spoonful of stew, chewed slowly and swallowed. "He hasn't had any solid food yet, but he's taking more and more broth. I'll add a bit of rice to it tomorrow." She shook her head, her eyes wide and full of wonder. "All in all, he's doing well. He wobbles and appears dizzy, but he walks to the outhouse without assistance."

"He'll come around," Hans said, with certainty.

Eliza sighed quietly. "Physically, yes, he might come around as you say, but it's his head that worries me." She put her spoon down and folded her hands against the edge of the table. "His mind has suffered an extreme trauma. His symptoms of disorientation are the result of dehydration, the pounding he obviously took, or a combination of both. I'm afraid the insides of his head have been scrambled like eggs, and I never heard of anyone being able to unscramble eggs. His mental faculties, his ability to think and reason may never come back."

"We'll deal with whatever happens, Eliza."

"I know that, Hans." She looked at him a while, then spoke with hesitancy in her tone. "But we haven't even discussed what that man Yance Rawlins said regarding Coburn being a wanted man for crimes of a perverted nature."

Hans pursed his lips as he considered her words. He wanted to be clear and fair. "There's nothing to discuss until the patient gains strength enough to tell us his story. I'll not condemn a man I don't know based on the say so of another gentleman with whom I am unacquainted. If the time comes we decide his brains are permanently scrambled, we'll have to work through all this, but until that's the case, let's not waste energy borrowing against tomorrow's troubles."

Eliza exhaled a weary sounding sigh. "You and your pigheaded sensibilities are right again, Mr. Weitzel," she said, eyes easy and loving. "Can we please talk about something else?"

"Sure thing, Ma. Did you see the horses I brought in?"

"Enough to be able to tell you I told you so," she replied, laughter now showing in her eyes. "Didn't I say that corral would be put into use long before springtime? I'll have a closer look-see in the morning, but from where I stood, it appears you've gotten us excellent starter stock."

"It was almost accidental the way I got them."

"Accidental? Why not say Providential?"

Hans chuckled mirthfully. "Be mighty careful, son. Don't cross theological swords with your mother."

"Button it, Hans."

"We'll need more mares," Caleb said precisely. He'd long ago learned to ignore their teasing banter. "But that steeldust is a special stallion. You should've seen it fight and twist to stay free. It was bucking and kicking like a tornado."

"Did it hurt you?"

Caleb hunched his shoulders into an evasive shrug. "It surely tried and came close more than once. It was snapping and spitting, but I kept moving and talking." His eyes twinkled and there was a rosy shine of pride on his cheeks.

Just then Rainy barked twice and gave a drawn out howl. It was apparent that the dog was moving away from the house. The three of them got up as one, went to the door, then Caleb and Eliza went out onto the porch. When Hans joined them, his Henry rifle was cradled in his arm.

A chill was in the air. It had stopped snowing. An inch or so had accumulated, which created a pretty glow. Rainy was beneath the archway yelping in an erratic staccato. A rider was shadowed in the moonlight walking the horse at a leisurely pace.

Caleb stepped into the yard and spoke sternly to the redbone. It immediately became quiet, but stayed put. Father and son stood side by side near the hound. It pressed up against its master's leg, its body wiggling back and forth.

"Where's the preacher?" the man on horseback asked as the smallish pony stopped not more than ten feet from them. He wore a sheepskin coat and a flat-brimmed hat.

Hans kept an affable posture and tone. "No preacher around these parts, leastways none that I know about. I'm Hans Weitzel. If you're here on friendly terms, come join me and my family at the supper table. The stew's hearty and coffee's strong."

"Daniel Twosongs." He stepped out of the saddle. "I've been tracking a preacher friend of mine who stirred up a hornet's nest. If it hasn't already finished him off, I'd dearly like to find him. He had an appaloosa, but I came upon its carcass months ago. I lost his trail shortly thereafter. I've been crisscrossing territory searching for any hint of him." He squatted on his heels and chaffed his hands together. "The process of elimination blended in with desperation makes me figure that at some point he passed by this way."

Hans was suspicious. "Are you law?"

Daniel snorted a laugh. "Nope. Just an amigo."

Eliza was behind her husband. "Has your friend a name?"

"Deke Coburn."

Hans glanced over a shoulder at her. She sidled closer. "We were told he was a killer and molester of young girls."

"You were told wrong, ma'am," Twosongs said calmly. "I won't deny that he's killed men, plenty of them during the war, but the killing he's wanted for is a phony put up job. He shot the man who had been deflowering and murdering young girls."

"Why should we believe you?" Hans asked bluntly. "A man named Yance Rawlins told my wife that there was a warrant for Coburn's arrest from a judge in Santa Fe."

"Yance Rawlins is a two-bit thug who just happens to be in that so-called judge's pocket." Daniel bounced up and held his hands out in a conciliatory sign. "If that offer for a sit-down meal is still open, we can chinwag all this inside."

Hans and Eliza exchanged a nervous look, but before they gave any response, Caleb stepped forward and said, "I'll take care of your horse, Mr. Twosongs. I'll strip off its gear, give it a good rubdown and feed it a bait of oats."

"Thank you." Daniel handed the reins to Caleb. He led the horse to the barn, with Rainy scampering along beside him.

A few minutes later, the three adults were at the table. When a bowl of stew was placed before him, without hesitation, Daniel Twosongs removed his hat and lowered his head for a moment. Eliza took note and seemed to be impressed by his action, but obviously remained dubious. She openly and frankly studied his face to determine if he was trustworthy.

Twosongs spoke as he ate. He told them briefly about his journey with Deke Coburn and what he knew about him. He did so straightfor-wardly with an economy of words. His voice was tense and edgy when he came to the part about Sally, which led to the killer's journal. He was sensitive and appropriate, but even so, the information was shock-ing. He filled them in on what he had uncovered about the connections from his investigation.

When he had concluded his tale, he put his spoon down and asked, "Do you folks have any news about my friend?"

Hans took his elbows off the table. He'd been sitting rigidly as he listened. There was no longer any suspicion in him. He leaned back and said, "He's been here for almost a week. He was near death, but Eliza has been nursing him."

"He drifts in and out of a coma of sorts," Eliza reported directly. Her openness verified that she'd decided Twosongs was an upright and honorable man. "I'm doing everything I know how to do. There's been sluggish but steady progress."

"Has he said anything?"

Eliza shook her head slowly. "He tries, but all that comes out is mumbo jumbo that makes no sense. From time to time he gets fixated on a phrase. For example, does this mean anything to you: *She won't feed a dirty ragamuffin?*"

Twosongs puckered his mouth in a smile that wrinkled his eyes into slits. "I'm sorry, but I have no inkling at all about it."

Eliza stood. "Come see him with me. There's little chance that he'll be awake." She draped the shawl around her shoulders, picked up one of the oil lamps, and opened the door.

Hans shrugged into his coat. The sky was clear and pretty, the air brisk. Eliza and Daniel went into the one-room shack, but Hans contin-ued on to the barn.

The lamplight filled the room. The small potbelly stove had it snug and cozy. Eliza stepped to the side, expecting Daniel to sit on the stool beside the cot, but instead, he moved it out of the way and knelt. Deke Coburn was bundled beneath layers of blankets, breathing shallowly.

Daniel Twosongs tenderly touched Coburn's face. He placed one hand on a cheek, the other on his forehead, and prayed fervently. He addressed the Creator in an urgent, forthright manner that took Eliza by surprise. She joined him in agreement by bowing her head and closing her eyes.

When he said amen, he paused for a short beat of time. His voice rasped with emotion as he sang a song. It was in a dialect she'd heard once before. It sounded akin to the one the Navajo man Gray Eyes had chanted over her husband. She felt goosepimples on her arms. His voice was low and passionate, rising and falling in a rolling cadence that was mellow.

It ended by fading away. In the silence, Daniel Twosongs stayed in a kneeling position for a moment. He abruptly stood and spoke to her. "Mrs. Weitzel, thank you for answering the call to care for my friend. No coincidence or chance brought him here. It was destiny. Your lives are intersected together now." He stared intently at her. "Whatever comes, good or bad you're in the middle of it."

She felt wary and uncomfortable. "Let's hope for good."

"Hope is always good. Hope fixes us," Daniel said, giving her a warm smile. "Keep caring for him as you have been. He will mend or he will die; it's not for us to decide. His time ahead is in the hands of the One who is from forever to forever."

"What was the song you sang over him?" Eliza asked timidly.

Daniel Twosongs searched her face. He took hold of her shoulders with a firmness that startled her and spoke in a reverential tone. "You have much integrity and faith. It was my song of life and blessing, and it wasn't only for Deke Coburn. It was for this place and for the people that make it home. May the One whose storehouses are abundant provide the bounty of virtue and the grace of mercy for all tomorrows to come." He released his hold and stepped back, still focused on her.

"Thank you," she whispered, tears slipping down her cheeks.

"Do not cry," he said brusquely. "Now I must go."

"Not tonight," she replied, wiping her eyes. "I'm sure Hans and Caleb have prepared a bed for you in the hayloft."

Daniel bobbed his head once. "As the wind blows, I'll see you again, Eliza Weitzel." He left, and she held the door to watch until he entered the barn. She turned her attention to her patient. She adjusted his pillow, tucked the covers tight around him, swept his shaggy hair off his face and felt his forehead for fever. There was none.

She sat with him for a few minutes, considering all that she'd learned from Daniel Twosongs. It was much too much to process and put into perspective in one force-fed gulp. Disturbing thoughts mixed with expectant ones. She stoked the fire in the potbelly stove, banking it for the night. Then she went to the house anxious for the comfort of sleep.

Early the next morning, Daniel Twosongs was at the corral with Hans Weitzel. His sure-footed mustang was saddled and standing nearby. The day was dawning bright and blue. The men were enjoying it, admiring the horses. The steeldust paced back and forth, acting as protector of the mares.

"Those are a fine beginning," Daniel remarked, approvingly. "In a few years you'll have a superior herd."

"That's the way I see it, too."

"Your boy has a rare skill," Daniel said, turning slightly to face him. "It was from a far off perch and through field glasses, but I watched him capture these three. That stallion went after him. It was touch-and-go which one would win, but he stuck with it." He smiled, strolling to his horse.

Hans followed. "You sure you won't stay for breakfast?"

"Yes." He was firm. There was no doubt or wiggle room in his determination. "I must hurry home before nature decides to dump a load of snow." He mounted and settled in the saddle. He reached inside his coat and came out with a rawhide pouch.

"Last night I mixed this from herbs and medicines I carry in my saddlebags. Tell Eliza to dissolve a spoonful in a cup of boiling water and make the preacher drink it. One dose per day until it's gone. It'll cramp him up some, but also speed the healing." He tossed the bag to Hans, who caught it. "Give my thanks to your good wife and my best to your boy."

"Take care until we meet again."

"Never mind me," Daniel said adamantly. "You folks have stepped into a mess of manure here. It'll be real bad. Judge Thornton won't forget, and he has a way of papering over the illegal to make it look legal. He'll wait out the nasty weather, but come springtime be extra cautious."

"Thomas Thornton hasn't met Hans Weitzel."

Twosongs grinned. "Sit tight. Troubles are going to visit you because you helped Deke Coburn. Even so, stay hard and ready. Keep harboring him because he's a friend of mine."

"You have my word, Daniel. He'll be here when you return," Hans said, firm and adamant. "A preacher, you say?"

"He was kind of one once." Twosongs touched the brim of his hat. "Look for me when wintertime melts away." He whirled the horse around. It snorted and pranced a few steps, then trotted toward the sunrise.

Hans Weitzel stood with his hands in his pockets and his back against the corral. He watched until Daniel Twosongs dipped down a coulee and disappeared from sight. Then he went inside to fill up on a meal of fried taters, scrapple, and pancakes.

The man lay motionless. His breathing was quick and anxious. The air was chilly. His body was a relief map of goosebumps. A part of him wanted to make like a bandit and be elsewhere, but that wasn't going to happen; at least not yet, for there were feelings in him clamoring to be expressed. He wasn't alone.

He gazed at the pretty woman. She was tall and thin. Her hair was loose and bouncy as she moved about the room. She lit several candles. The flames danced in the darkness, creating shadows that played on the walls and ceiling.

She took her time. She was in no hurry. She had undressed him. She had silently stripped him bare, her hands deftly never touching his skin. There was no resistance in him. She had put him to bed, folding the blanket to just above his bellybutton. It had all been tender, slow, gentle.

She sat in front of a mirror and began brushing her hair in long, deliberate strokes. All the while she did so she kept an eye on his reflection. He was staring at her, and she wasn't unaware of her effect on him. The strength in him stirred her. She placed the brush on the dresser and stood facing him.

Her auburn hair was wavy and beautiful, shimmering in the candlelight. She wore a simple housedress with large buttons down the front. She released them from top to bottom, never allowing her attention to stray from the man in her bed. His eyes were wide, his smile sweet.

She eased her slender shoulders forward. The dress fell to her feet and she stepped out of it. She stood before him in a lacey white petticoat. She heard a tiny hitch of a gasp escape his lips. It was apparent that his respiration was speeding up. She tiptoed to his side of the bed. He stretched out an arm to hold her, but she leaned away from his reach.

"Before we go any farther," she said, "I need you to know something. I'm in love with you, Lawrence." She lifted the frilly undergarment over her head. She held it away from her. His eyes were riveted on her nakedness, which was lovely. She dropped the petticoat. As it wafted to the floor, she was gone, and Deke Coburn twitched awake.

The darkness surrounding him was total. He could hear himself breathing hugely, his chest rising and falling in rapid bursts. Despite the hot air, he shivered. Perspiration soaked him. He sat up. His head was woozy. He tossed back the quilts covering him. He swung his legs out to sit on the edge of the cot. Dizziness gripped him. He steadied himself.

"I'm sorry, Angela." There was emotional thickness in his scratchy voice. Moisture blurred his vision. He rested his elbows on his knees. Tears spilled out as he remembered. She had loved him without conditions. She had given herself to him, and he had spurned their passion; he had forsaken their love. A future that could have been was now a disconcerting if only.

He held his head in his hands. Confusion played havoc in him. The dream was so real, so vivid, so mesmerizing. Her face, her smile, her eyes, her body were all seemingly accessible to him. He wanted to talk to her. He wanted to hold her. He wanted to run to her and in doing so make the years go backwards.

When his eyes adjusted to the darkness, he looked around the small room. He was completely unfamiliar with everything he took in. He couldn't fathom where he was or the circumstances of his being here. Bewildered, he weighed the intense replay of the past, finding both comfort and the need for repentance in it.

The potbelly stove in a corner was throwing off plenty of heat. He was wearing a baggy pair of red long johns and heavy wool socks. He wondered where they had come from. The underwear obviously belonged to a larger man. It didn't fit, but even so, was comfy. There was much mystery for him to unravel and think over. He sat and did so, bleakly staring at the floor.

Four days after Daniel Twosongs had departed, Rainy was acting fretful and antsy. It was early morning. The dog was pacing and whining to go outside when Eliza stepped out of the bedroom. She spoke roughly to it, wrapped her shawl around her, and headed out to check on her patient.

The gray of dawn had a shiny yellow glimmer spreading across it. Rainy burst past her and began howling. She found it curious that the hound didn't even run off to the area where it usually did its business. Instead, Rainy raced directly to the hired hand's shack and plopped down on its buttocks.

Eliza Weitzel was put off by the dog's strange behavior. It distracted her. When she cracked the door open, Rainy pushed inside, its whole body wagging happily. Eliza stopped cold in the doorway. She watched in wide-eyed wonder.

Deke Coburn was sitting on the cot. He interacted with the dog, taking hold of the scruff of its neck to give it a gentle shake. Rainy responded with a sloppy grin. It whimpered happily and began licking the man's hands.

Eliza pulled the door shut. Coburn looked at her. He was pale. His eyes were red-rimmed and bloodshot, but appeared to be alert and responsive. They regarded each other. There was no tension between them, only questions.

Eliza broke the silence. "You must be a good man. Rainy is an excellent judge of character."

Coburn stared at her. Sadness poured out of him. "I want to be a good man, but I'm not," he replied, his voice croaky and dry. "I hurt people without even trying."

"Welcome to the human race," she said seriously.

He grunted. "*In my flesh dwelleth no good thing.*"

Her eyes narrowed at him. "Scripture? You're going to quote Scripture to me? You must be feeling much better."

Rainy barked in agreement. He smiled. "I'm alive, I guess. I ache all over. I'm hungry. I cannot tell you where I am or explain how messed up my head is just now."

"You're at the Weitzel homestead in New Mexico," Eliza told him. "A week and a half ago my son found you knocking on death's door in the desert. Actually, it was Rainy who sniffed you out."

"Did I have saddlebags with me?"

"No."

"A letter?"

"No. You had nothing but the rags you were wearing."

Coburn winced. He suddenly realized he was sitting in saggy underclothes talking to a woman. He grabbed one of the blankets and modestly pulled it over his lap. "Sorry, ma'am."

Eliza laughed breezily. "Don't waste your energy being sorry, Mr. Coburn. I've been washing you and tending to your wounds. You've got nothing I haven't seen before."

He eyed her. "You know who I am?"

"Sort of, I think," she said, shrugging. "I haven't quite figured out how Lawrence fits in."

He hung his head. When he lifted it, his expression was the epitome of sorrow. "He was an idiot stuck inside my skin."

"It doesn't matter now, does it?"

Coburn grew agitated. "It matters." Tears showed in his eyes. "There were no saddlebags with me?"

"I'm sorry, Mr. Coburn."

"Those Utes must've taken them."

"What do you need? Maybe I can get it for you."

"Can you reverse time? Can you fix the past?"

Eliza smiled. It was full and forceful; there was grace in it. She held it on him. "You really think that whatever you had in your saddlebags could do those things? The past is the past. It's gone. Wherever you find yourself now, in these moments and days, that's where you are, Mr. Coburn. Today is an opportunity that awaits you, so what's it going to be?"

He considered her words. "I apologize, ma'am. I am grateful for all you've done for me."

She repeated her question. "So what's it going to be?"

He felt his beard. It was overgrown and unkempt. "I'd like to get myself cleaned up some if I might, ma'am."

"Why? You don't think I'll feed a dirty ragamuffin."

Deke Coburn's head snapped back, his eyes gaping open as he gawked at her. It was as though someone had stuck a knife into his midsection and gave it a good twist. "How? What? Why'd you say that?" he stammered, fearful and apprehensive.

She was startled, shocked by his reaction. She took a shuffle step closer to him. "While unconscious, you repeatedly murmured those words. I meant no harm, Mr. Coburn. It's now my turn to apologize. I'm afraid I've scratched open a wound."

Coburn's head was slowly wagging back and forth. He let out a groaning sigh. "The wound you speak of is self-inflicted. I hope the pain I caused others has healed. I hope it no longer is even a memory. I hope I have been forgotten."

"A friend of yours recently told me that hope is always good. Hope fixes us," she said evenly. "I think he's right."

Incomprehension darkened his brow. "A friend of mine?"

Eliza beamed a smile at him. "Daniel Twosongs was here. He told us much. He wanted you to know that Sally is doing well, getting better and stronger every day." She couldn't miss the way his expression relaxed as his eyes moistened. "He also said that when you came around you were to stay with us. The troubles are still chasing you. He'll be back in springtime to help."

"I can't impose on your hospitality," Deke said, pensive and unsure. "My troubles are my troubles. Not yours."

"Mr. Coburn, this isn't open for discussion," she answered tersely. "My husband gave Daniel his word, which settles it. No matter what may come up against him, as long as Hans Weitzel is breathing, he'll fight to keep his word."

Coburn gave another groaning sigh. There was resignation in it. "I'm plum tuckered out, so I won't be fighting him anytime soon." He grinned. "I'd like to be rid of some crud, ma'am."

"That could be arranged," Eliza replied, nodding. "I'll have Hans and our son set up a tub and all necessary accessories in the barn." She opened the door. "First I'll bring you something easy on your stomach for breakfast."

Rainy yapped and scooted outside. She followed. Deke Coburn stood. He was weak and queasy. His legs were sore, his head foggy. He waited for equilibrium to come. When it did, he took several steps around the room. He felt safe.

That evening, Deke was bathed and shaven. He had left the moustache in place, though trimmed it back to the edge of his upper lip.

The whole process of washing away sweaty sickness had exhausted him. He'd slept for the entire afternoon.

Now at suppertime, he sat in the Weitzels' kitchen. He was picking at his food, merely moving it around his plate. He appeared particularly gaunt because he wore hastily adjusted clothes borrowed from Hans. Informality was developing as the family shared conversation around the table.

"I'm thankful to know you folks," Deke said sincerely. "I'll pull my weight around here as soon as I regain my strength."

Hans swallowed a bite of beef. "I have no doubt you will, but you'll do no such thing until Eliza gives her say so."

"Which won't be soon," she said quickly. "You have a long journey to recovery ahead which cannot be rushed."

"It'd be best to listen, Deke." Hans was smiling. "You don't want to cross Eliza. She can be a hard taskmaster."

"That's right, Mr. Coburn," Caleb chimed in, laughing.

Deke put his fork down. He felt weak and queasy. "I'll try my best to be a good patient." He gave a halfhearted shrug. He took a deep breath and asked, "Why *Freiheit*? Why freedom?"

Hans grinned broadly. "So you are a *Deutschlander.*"

"My people are, yes."

Leaning forward, Hans put his elbows on the table. "*Freiheit* is the blood that flows in my veins. I won't be beholden to any haughty landowner or potentate. I won't live by anyone's leave. I will do for me and mine, and we'll be free." His tone was sharp and edgy, his expression firm. "Or I will die."

Coburn thought it over for a lengthy moment. He recalled a seminal verse from the New Testament and shared it. "*Stand fast therefore in the liberty wherewith Christ hath made us free, and be not entangled again with the yoke of bondage.*"

"Sounds like church words to me." Hans picked up a linen napkin and wiped his mouth.

"Bible words," Deke said slowly.

Hans drew back. "Men easily change Bible words into church words so they can be used to keep others under their thumb. Sermonizers employ religion like a club to beat men down, but that's not enough for them. When their flocks are sufficiently subdued, the black-coated wonders pile on loads of impossible burdens."

Coburn gave a wince of a smile. "There's much truth in what you say, so you'll get no argument from me. What some have done in the name of religion sickens God."

Weitzel grunted. "Religion and freedom mixes about as well as oil and water. I want none of it." He placed his right hand on his chest. "Freedom resides in the heart."

Deke chuckled. When he spoke, it was in an uncompromising tone. "Freedom, like all good gifts, comes from God."

Hans had rigidity in his eyes. "Freedom must be seized and shaped."

Eliza joined in. "You're both right. Freedom is a gift from God. It's a yearning he places in our hearts, but each one must take hold of it to use for the common good."

"I like that," Deke said agreeably.

Caleb nodded. "Me, too, Ma."

Hans grew surly. It showed in the way his hands flexed as his eyes tensed up to the point of almost being closed. "It matters not." It surely wasn't his intention, but the gruff grimness of his mannerism put a damper on the conversation.

Eliza adeptly softened the mood with an easy expression of hospitality that encompassed everyone. She served generous helpings of apple crisp for dessert. As she did so, she related how the Weitzels came to be homesteaders in New Mexico. She then invited their guest to tell some part of his story.

Deke Coburn surprised himself, not only by how much detail he summoned to the forefront of his mind, but also because he spoke forthrightly. The words came at a tentative pace as he mulled over each segment he chose to share.

There were moments when his voice thickened, no such instance more so than as he articulated regret for abandoning a woman who had reached out to him in love.

That evening, in Ohio, not too many miles south of Xenia, Angela Langton rocked back and forth in her chair beside the fireplace. Blue-tinted flames were crackling, licking at maple logs. The rocker creaked with squeaky regularity.

Her face was pale, her expression downcast, her eyes red from crying and lack of sleep. It had been over a week since she'd had a decent night's rest. She stared off in the middle distance, distracted and out-of-focus.

She held a tri-folded sheet of paper in her hands. She had read the words on it a dozen times or more. They fired up anger in her in a way that didn't make sense. She wanted to crumple up the paper and toss it into the fire.

Denial nipped at her. Like starving wolves circling in for the kill, it had been harassing her relentlessly for over seven days and nights. Denial wouldn't leave her alone; what was on the page couldn't actually be true. It had to be a mistake or sick chicanery meant to deceive her.

If it was factual, if there was no course open to get her out from under it, her life had already been radically altered. The news changed everything. The future would be much different than any scenario she had ever visualized.

Abbey came in from her bedroom. She had a dime-store novel about fantastic episodes in the western lands in her hand. The tales of gunfights and wild excitement along the frontier thrilled her imagination. Collecting and devouring the paperback potboilers had become an almost obsession.

Angela was startled. Her lips winced into a thin smile as she slipped the paper under her apron. A leaden ache clenched in the pit of her stomach. Her discomfort was obvious.

"What's wrong?" Abbey asked, concerned. At fourteen she was already as tall and shapely as her mother, a girl inside the body of a young woman. Her hair was golden-brown spirals that swayed and bounced like a tumble of gathering waves. She settled on a braided rug with her back to the hearth.

"Nothing at all," Angela replied softly.

Abbey shifted a bit, crossed her legs, and swished her skirt around her. "What's in that letter? Who's it from?"

"It's not a letter."

"Whatever you call it, what's in it?"

"None of your business."

"That's not very polite."

"Maybe not, but it's true."

Abbey frowned at her. "You've been upset about something since you came home from town last week. You think I don't see you fretting over what you've got hidden in your lap?"

"You're such a smart one."

"I might be able to help."

"No," Angela said, firm and final.

Abbey knew that tone well. She sat in silence for a few minutes. She looked at her mother closely and asked, "Mom, do you ever wonder what happened to Mr. Lawrence?"

Angela visibly stiffened. "Abbey!" she snapped, her voice overtaken by disbelief. Streaks of red colored her cheeks. "What on earth made you ask that question?"

Abbey's eyes grew wide and expressive. "What's wrong, Mom?"

"Why'd you ask about Lawrence?"

Abbey shrugged easily. "I was cleaning my room when I came upon a stack of old tic-tac-toe scores. It made me think of that night we played with Mr. Lawrence. Do you remember?"

Angela smiled. "More than you can imagine."

"Why'd he leave?"

"Abbey, I don't want to talk about this now."

"You never want to talk about Mr. Lawrence."

Angela sighed. It was deep and sorrowful. "It still hurts."

"I know. Me, too."

Angela regarded her daughter tenderly. "I can't explain why he left us, especially the way he did. Sneaking off like a weasel . . ." She paused to get control of her emotions. Her voice was restrained as she continued, "Abbey, men are difficult to understand. Sometimes they get notions that make them unpredictable."

"But Mr. Lawrence was so nice," Abbey said insistently. "I thought we were becoming a family."

"So did I."

"What messed it up?"

"I suppose it just wasn't meant to be. I'm sorry."

Abbey wrinkled her nose. "For what?"

"For a lot of things, Abbey," Angela answered in a sad and weary voice. "For things you won't understand until you're a mother with a child of your own. I'm sorry your father died before you were born. I'm sorry he never got to see what a strong and beautiful lady you've become." She bit the inside of her bottom lip. Her mouth pinched into a tight grimace. "I'm sorry I took a chance and opened my heart up to Lawrence. I'm sorry that he's not here with us. Especially now."

Tears glistened in Abbey's eyes. "Why especially now?"

"No reason," Angela said quickly. "It'd just be good to have him here while we're both thinking about him."

Abbey tried to obscure the wetness in her eyes by turning her face downward. "I know it's silly, but I was fancying that one day he'd be kind of my Pa."

Angela swallowed dryly. "That's not silly."

"If I ever see him again, I'm going to give him a piece of my mind," Abbey declared, a fierceness in her tone. "Sometimes I hope he hurts as much as he hurt us."

Angela became stern. "That's wrong-headed, Abbey. Don't wish him ill. You'll become a bitter old prune. He was a decent man who had his own troubles." She stopped rocking. "Treasure the memories you have of him, as I do. If you ever see him again, treat him kindly, and by doing so you'll be letting him know what he missed out on by disappearing like he did."

Abbey nodded hesitantly. "I guess you're right."

"You know I am."

"What would you do if he showed up on our doorstep?"

"Put him to work," Angela quipped, with a light-heartedness that she didn't feel. "He did enjoy sweating up a storm."

Abbey laughed. Her eyes sparkled with it. That set-off back and forth tales about the man they'd known only as Lawrence. One yarn flowed naturally into the next recollection.

All during the storytelling, Angela Langton kept her anxious feelings at bay. Denial was chewing on her. The news couldn't possibly be real. She thought that she was being subtle, but her daughter took note of the number of times she fingered the letter or whatever it was secreted beneath her apron.

It was Christmas Day, 1868. Sally Twosongs had never known such a celebration. She was so excited, she didn't know what to do or how to act. She wanted to jump up and dance. That's what was happening inside her, but she kept it tamped down.

All this happiness and security was too much for her to understand. She was afraid that it would soon be gone, and she'd return to her former life, which had always been spartan and semi-nomadic. Passed from one relative to another, she'd known only difficulties and upsets. Then she'd been kidnapped and terrorized by the brutality of the monster-man.

The sun was rising bright and beautiful. She sat on a stool watching it through a swirled layer of frost on the thick window pane. The cinnamon-scented house was mostly dark. A single oil lamp flickered on the table, and logs crackled in the fireplace.

The only one out of bed, Sally was alone with her thoughts. Anticipation and mystery was racing side by side in her. She had hardly slept at all. The account of Jesus presented in the majesty of Midnight Mass had her imagination in upheaval.

The incense smoke had tickled her nostrils. It reminded her of the white sage smudge sticks burned by her people during religious ceremonies. She wondered if there was any connection between the similar traditions. Consuelo had quietly and kindly explained the meaning of the liturgy, but it wasn't easy for an eleven-year-old Navajo girl to understand.

That the Creator had become a baby was too much to grasp, but she held unto it with tenacity because of a visitation that had awakened her. She had many questions. The notion of grace was odd, and forgiveness seemed like an unsolvable puzzle.

There was the creak of a floorboard. She turned to see Daniel crouching at the hearth, stoking the fire. The scrape of steel on stone sounded loud and screechy in the peaceful house. He finished, returned the poker to its place, and gave her a look full of affection.

"Good morning, young lady."

She smiled gently. She liked when he called her that; his tone and manner made her feel warm and special. "Hiya."

"You're up awful early." He lit another oil lamp, moved a chair close to her and sat down.

She fidgeted and tugged on her long pigtails. "I've been thinking about the baby Jesus." There was a precise hesitation between each word, her voice soft and measured.

"How appropriate a topic for the day set aside to remember his birth," Daniel said, eyes lively and inviting. He eased to the edge of his seat. "Can I help your understanding?"

"Is the baby Jesus really God?"

Daniel chuckled dryly. "That's the question of the ages for seekers and skeptics alike, young lady." He watched her with careful eyes as he spoke firmly yet tenderly. "The answer is yes, whether one chooses to believe it or not. There is only one God. Countless stories, legends, myths, and folklore surround and shroud him. He is known by many different names, but he is the Creator of all peoples, nations, tribes, and languages. Jesus, the babe who was born in Bethlehem of Judea, was present at the creation of all that we know, and he is indeed God."

Sally nodded ever so slightly. "I dreamed about him." Her dark eyes were wide and filled with wonder.

Daniel's expression froze. His shoulders tightened as wariness or delight crept through him. He couldn't quite identify the sensation. "Dreams are often a gift requiring much wisdom to unwrap. To know the meaning is essential. A dream can be a blessing or curse, can thrill or frighten us."

"I wasn't scared."

"That's good."

"It was wonderful."

"I'd be pleased to listen."

There was urgency in her, yet Sally hesitated, a small smile forming. She took a deep breath, then said, "He was a man, but I knew he had been the baby Jesus in the manger. I saw his scars from the cross. He came to me and held my hand. He said I was Sally Twosongs, and I should always be Sally Twosongs." She paused to gain control of her voice, which was quivering. "He told me that he loved me and was sorry for what the bad man did to me. He placed his hand on my heart and promised to walk my path with me." Her cheeks were shiny with tears.

Daniel's throat was blocked by a sludge-like dryness. He felt compelled to put his arms around her, but a sense of what was right and wrong stopped him. So far in their journey together he had purposefully refrained from touching her in any way. He thought it best for her inner healing and restoration.

"Then I woke up and came out here," she said, sniffling. She slid off the stool and abruptly hugged his neck. Her arms locked so tight that it hurt. "I'm glad and thankful that Mr. Deke brought me to you and Consuelo. You're my family."

Daniel Twosongs exhaled a sob of breath. It echoed strangely and mixed with a flourish of movement behind him. Consuelo had been in the bedroom doorway. She'd heard everything. She cried joyfully as she rushed to them. It was apparent that her heart was full; her embrace fiercely enfolded them.

The free release of emotions was intense. After several moments, Daniel wiggled out of the arms knotted around him, wiped his eyes, then slipped away. He moved with quickness and purpose. He stepped outside. Misty white tendrils of cold eased through the door, but were soon swallowed by warmth.

When he returned, Consuelo and Sally were sitting at the table across from each other. They were holding hands and talking softly about plans for a special, sugary breakfast. He had a fringed deerskin stocking in his hand. It was narrow and had intricate beadwork along its sides.

Consuelo shot him an inquisitive stare. "Daniel, we're supposed to have something to eat before giving gifts."

"I can't always do what I'm supposed to do," he answered, smiling broadly. "It's what makes me so endearing."

Consuelo laughed easily. "I suppose so."

Daniel took his place at the head of the table. He cleared his throat. He had a whole speech prepared to convey to his daughter the value and importance he placed on her. He had thought through the ramifications of each word as he'd carefully crafted the distinctive present, but now, as he regarded the dark-eyed girl, all those words were gone.

He simply said, "This is for Sally Twosongs."

She took the velvety leather sock. She traced the beaded design. She peeked inside. Her breath caught in her throat as she removed a wooden flute. The detail and artistry were exquisite. It was aromatic cedar with pieces of turquoise embedded between the holes. Along each side, in a sweeping script, her name had been carved and burned. She fingered the letters. Her countenance radiated peace and contentment.

"Thank you," she whispered, happy tears flowing.

Later, after breakfast, Sally put her gift into action by presenting a mini-concert. She demonstrated that she had learned and applied the lessons Daniel had been meticulously giving on one of his flutes. She sat on the floor with her back to the fireplace, playing a low-pitched melody. Her parents were pleased and proud as they watched and listened.

When Yance Rawlins exited the rickety outhouse the sun was cresting above the treeline. He squinted as shimmering blades of light stabbed his eyes. He stretched and grunted loudly. He felt as fine as a bull elk in rut.

Several inches of snow had fallen during the night, but now the sky was high and clear blue. He trudged back to the cabin whistling a ditty remembered from childhood. The words were long forgotten, but the tune was stuck in his head. It was a haunting and dirge-like church-song that his mother had sang or hummed repeatedly at this time of year.

Yance had a streak of mischief in him. He gave into it as he entered the cabin. He hit the notes high and loud, then slammed the door hard and stomped his boots with gusto.

"Hey, half the day's gone," he roared, giving a raucous hoot. "Rise and shine, sleeping beauty. I put the coffee on before I went to the crapper. I figured you'd be up by now."

Jackson Scully cursed. He snuggled deeper into the feather mattress and wrapped a pillow around his head. "Leave me be," he said, punctuating it with a guttural swearword. The blistering hangover effects of the previous evening's alcohol consumption were discernible. His face was furrowed by pain, looking as though splinters of glass were being crushed inside his head.

"*Leave me be*," Rawlins mimicked, making his voice rise in a ridiculing manner. He thumped a well-used cast iron frying pan down on the stovetop. "Just so you know, I'll be rattling pots and pans here to make a stack of flapjacks for breakfast."

"You do that," Scully groused, sitting up. He tried to stand, but faltered in noticeable pain. "My left side is burning nonstop from my shoulders to my toes."

Rawlins clattered the frying pan, grinning wickedly. "Put a smile on that sour puss, you ornery geezer. It's Christmas!"

"Well, bless my soul and kiss my arse," Scully replied, making an obscene gesture. "Christmas is plain and simple crappola. Go pound salt with it for all I care."

Rawlins gave him an alarmed, wide-eyed stare. "Watch your mouth, muttonhead." His eyes tilted toward the ceiling as he swallowed and pursed his lips into a thin line. "You're going to bring a plague or disaster down on us."

"What?" Scully exclaimed, laughing. "Quit screwing around. You don't put stock in any of that religious crappola."

Yance Rawlins offered an evasive shrug. "I don't know if I believe in it or not, but I'll tell you this . . ." He paused to consider what was inside him. "I sure as hell *want* to believe it. I hope that baby in the manger was God's Son. My Mama believed it, and now she's walking streets of gold."

"Stop yanking my chains."

"I ain't. I'm dead serious."

Scully scoffed. "Ain't no heaven, ain't no hell, ain't no God, ain't no Sonny-boy Jesus. It's all a crock of crappola."

Rawlins poured himself a cup of coffee. It was as black as tar and, when he laced it with copious amounts of sugar, just about as gummy. He took a sip. Then, in an even and fierce tone, he said, "You don't want to be calling Christmas or any of it crappola around me ever again."

Scully glared at him. He was perched on the edge of the bed, elbows resting on his knees. "Well, bless my soul once more! Me in my cock-eyed good fortune done partnered up with a hard-ass gunner bucking for sainthood. What a lucky cripple I am."

"Are you busting my chops?" Yance asked sharply. "I'll beat you senseless just as soon as look at you this morning."

"Have at it," Scully replied, hands stretched wide. "Bust every frigging bone in my body to prove to me that God is real. That'll certainly set me straight." He stood and pulled his trousers on. He looped the suspenders up over his shoulders and adjusted the sleeves of his tattered long johns.

He took a step, teetering crookedly as his left leg gave out from under him. Scorching pain radiated from his hip joint and encompassed him. He did a wobbly crow-hop to catch his balance. He cussed with earsplitting zeal, making oaths and calling down damnation on himself.

Spittle filled the air as rage screamed out of him. When the spasm of agony passed, his bitterness ran its course, sputtering to teeth-clenched silence. He collapsed to the floor.

Yance Rawlins watched it all in awful helplessness. His mouth was gaped open. The wind and starch had been knocked out of him. He felt an emotion squeezing and clawing at his heart that he had a difficult time identifying. It was pity.

"Don't talk to me about God," Scully said, eyes raw and full of moisture. "If God is up there in the sky, then he's a mean-spirited mule who owes me. He kicked and trampled all over me. He robbed me of my future, my destiny. I was supposed to be a soldier. Look at me," he demanded, hands fisted. "I'm a circus freak hobbling along on a useless leg. If God did exist he'd do the right thing and put me out of my misery."

Yance frowned and scratched his wispy whiskers. He acted like he was going to respond, but then decided he had nothing to say. He finished off his coffee in one gulp, and turned his attention back to rustling up some grub. He got the canister of flour down and sifted some into a wooden mixing bowl.

Scully picked himself up. The whole left side of his body had a dull numbness that hurt. He moved in an unsteady shuffle, like an old man who'd been whipped into submission. He limped to the door, his face mottled and blotchy. He pulled his boots on, shouldered into his coat and went outside.

When he returned twenty minutes later he had an armload of firewood. The cabin smelled of bacon and coffee. His expression remained rigid and grim, his body stiff and strained. Even so, there was a perceptible shift in his attitude. He dumped the wood into the box beside the stove, shed his coat, then got his utensils and sat at the table.

"Dig in," Yance said, already working on his second helping. "Mighty tasty, if I do say so myself."

"Thanks." Scully forked and thumbed food onto his plate. He wrapped a flapjack around a couple hunks of bacon. "I've been thinking." He took a bite, nodded approval and poured a coffee. "If a thaw comes and lingers, we ought to make a trip over to visit those homesteaders. Catch them off guard."

Rawlins drew a breath, somewhat amused. He considered the idea for a moment. "That'd be one of those high risk, low reward deals, don't you think?"

"Maybe so."

"Damned straight, maybe so," Rawlins replied, a finger tapping the table. "We could surprise them, but we'd be taking a chance of getting trapped by bad weather. I don't fancy coming to the end of my days squatting in a snowstorm."

"I'm getting squirrelly holed up here, is all," Scully said flatly. "Plus, I figure by now Judge Thornton is probably expecting us back with answers as to Coburn's whereabouts."

"To hell with him."

Scully scowled, shaking his head slowly. "This is a mighty sweet deal money and benefit wise. I'd hate to screw it up."

"Don't be so dimwitted," Yance said, shoving his plate aside. "Who do you think keeps this sweet deal in place?" He chuckled and tilted back on his chair. "I'm the juice that greases the runners and makes everything run smoothly."

"The Judge gave you a direct order."

"That's army talk. I ain't no soldier; I'm a businessman."

Scully smirked. "A businessman who has a boss."

"What's he going to do, fire me?" Rawlins queried hotly. "I know every blackmail scheme, every dirty deal, every murder. I got a ribbon knotted around all his secrets. Thornton can talk tough, but when push comes to shove, he'd never cross me."

Jackson Scully raised an eyebrow and nodded, evidently in agreement, but not really. Ever ambitious, he saw an opening that at some point could be breached to his advantage. He had no intention of playing second fiddle forever. He'd been in command in the past; he would be in command again in the future.

For now he expected to be a good soldier and tough it out. He'd salute smartly and be a follower, while marking each opportunity and moment so that he'd be ready. Then, when the time was ripe, Yance Rawlins would be a dead man.

Abbey Langton woke up from an afternoon nap to the sound of her mother singing a Christmas carol. Curled up on the big braided rug in front of the fireplace, she had a flower-pattern comforter wrapped around her. She sat up and shifted, crumpling some newspaper clippings spread out beside her.

"Hey, sleepy-time girl, how was dreamland?"

Abbey pouted in an exaggerated way. She sighed as a sly smile tugged at the corners of her mouth. "I was just following my heart on a big adventure." She gathered the clippings she intended to add to a burgeoning scrapbook. Each article was about cattle drives and other goings-on in Texas and Kansas. "Do you ever dream of life someplace other than here, Mom?"

Angela sat in her rocking chair. There were dark circles under her eyes, making her appear tired and gaunt. She took a sip from a mug of herbal tea, her hands cupped around it. "Sure. I read books and newspapers too you know."

"What keeps us here?"

Angela was surprised by the serious longing evident in her daughter's voice. "It is home, Abbey," she said patiently.

Abbey displayed disapproval, pouting. "That's no answer."

"I'd like to see other lands, but this is home."

"That's not an honest answer, Mom."

"It'll have to do because it's all I got."

Abbey rolled her eyes. "Let's pretend that's not so."

"Okay." Angela gave her a large smile. "I'll play along. Where do you want us to move to, as if I couldn't guess?"

Abbey laughed and rolled her eyes again. "As far west of the Mississippi River as we could get because that's where all the excitement is happening."

"Really?" Angela teased brightly. "I doubt the west is anything at all like those dime-store novels you read." She altered her posture and tucked the cardigan sweater tighter around her. Lately she seemed unable to stay warm.

"All the more reason for us to go," Abbey countered, grinning. "If you're right, you can say you told me so."

"And vice versa, I suppose?"

Abbey stifled a giggle. "No, not at all."

"You expect me to believe that?" Angela asked, light sarcasm in her voice. "If there are bandits on stagecoaches and gun-play in the streets, you'll never stop telling me I was wrong."

"*If there are*—when are we going?*"

"Oh, stop being silly." Angela flinched as a sliver of pain stitched across the small of her back. It passed momentarily, but a knot of tension remained. She adjusted her position and began rocking slowly. "We can't just pick up and go."

"Why not? Others do and make out just fine."

"Others also have misfortunes on the trail."

"Misfortunes?" Abbey squealed, almost jumping on the word. "Those can happen anywhere and everywhere."

Angela was impressed. She kept that to herself and spoke in a level tone. "That's certainly true, dear daughter. I didn't intend to suggest otherwise. Difficulties or adversity can indeed crop up anywhere. We've had our share right here, haven't we?" Her expression was fixed and steady.

"Which is why I ask, what keeps us here?"

"It's a tie to who you are, Abbey—a connection to your father." Angela finished her tea. "Someday you'll travel far and wide, but you'll always take pieces of home with you."

"Someday . . ."

"Someday may come sooner than you imagine," Angela cut in, raising an eyebrow. "Wherever you go, just remember that, like misfortune, contentment can be found anywhere and everywhere."

Abbey tilted her head, regarding her mother closely. "I know that because I learned it from you, Mom."

"Thank you," Angela said softly. "Life has no guarantees wherever one lives it. I've always believed that choosing to be content is the best gift we can ever give ourselves."

Abbey nodded agreeably. "Being content here and now doesn't stop me from daydreaming about going west to experience those wide open spaces for myself."

"No, not at all. A girl has to have dreams." Angela felt a twinge in her lower abdomen and heard a discomforting rumble roll around inside her. "Get your scrapbook out on the table and we can work on it together."

Abbey leapt to her feet. "That's a grand idea."

Angela moved to the edge of the chair and stood. "First I have to pay a visit out back."

"Again?"

"Something I ate is disagreeing with me," Angela replied, giving her a sideways smile. "I thought some herbal tea would help, but it hasn't yet. Would you be so kind as to fix me another cup whilst I'm gone?" She got her coat and pulled it on. It felt much too big and heavy on her.

In the late-afternoon twilight she hurried along the well-trod path to the outhouse. The cramping urgency in her became greater with each step. She worried that she wasn't going to make it. Even so there was a song on her lips, a lyrical plea for the advent of Emmanuel. The notes, full and somber, followed along in foggy wisps of breath.

The outhouse door creaked shut behind her. She shed her coat, hitched up her dress, got her undergarments out of the way and sat down just in time. Her bowels evacuated in a watery, splattering rush accompanied by knife-like pain.

She was embarrassed and angry that her body was failing her. She reached for the candle on the shelf beside her. She lit it as another wave roiled noisily through her intestines. She leaned forward and hugged herself.

When the distress passed, she straightened up and dug around in the sweater's pockets until she found a dog-eared piece of paper. It had been folded and refolded so many times that the creases were beginning to split apart. The doctor had made his diagnosis just two months ago. He'd written out the details as to treatments and what she could expect.

She squinted hard and stared at the prognosis now for the umpteenth time. In the candlelight the words were difficult to discern, but it didn't matter. She had unconsciously memorized every one, and though she thought she was reading, she was actually reiterating it by rote.

There was a rapidly growing mass centered in her digestive tract. Based on the doctor's examination and tests, his best estimate was that she had less than a year to live.

She was no longer in denial—increasing weakness, steady weight loss, along with progressive bouts of bloody diarrhea, and intestinal anguish convinced her that she was marking her final Christmas.

Angela Langton wasn't afraid of being dead; there were no thieving sicknesses or boogeymen in eternity. It was the dying that rankled her senses, the letting go and losing more and more dignity. She'd made do in life as best she could and was mostly satisfied with her efforts, but now she was being robbed of the strength to persevere forward.

To have her independence stripped away from her bit by bit stirred up resentment which she determinedly kept stamping down. She refused to surrender. She would fight and remain upbeat until she could no longer summon the wherewithal to do so, which in her mind would be with her last gasp.

There were legal affairs to attend to and a prescription for laudanum to be filled, but neither of those matters agitated her much. What stole her sleep and had her pacing the floor in the middle of the night was the prospect of having a straightforward sit-down with her daughter.

Until now she'd managed to fib and make allowances or excuses to keep the ugly secret hidden, but it was obvious that Abbey suspected something was amiss. A bluntly transparent conversation was on the agenda for tomorrow. Angela had been praying for wisdom and mentally scripting it for weeks. It was currently a cumbersome yoke bearing down on her.

The cold seeped through cracks in the plank walls. Her hands were absently rubbing her midsection. When she was confident that the ruckus in her bowels was finished, she cleaned herself and carefully adjusted her clothes. Before snuffing out the candle, she took the doctor's letter and held it over the flame.

A triumphant gleam sparkled in her eyes as the fire devoured the dismal news. She dropped it into the open hole, laughing aloud when it was extinguished. On the way back to the house Angela Langton was singing joyfully.

In the dream the little boy was lost, but didn't know it. There were creepers and pitfalls everywhere, and so many wrong directions. He ran fiercely through dark woods, never looking back even though someone was behind him calling his name.

There was alarm in the voice, but it was muffled and ragged. The stress had a profound ring, but it came out thick and dead, sounding as though the bellowing cries originated beneath a pile of saturated leaves. Over and over, desperate shouts echoed insistently in the hot, humid air.

The boy ignored all the pleas and warnings. He raced past brambles and threats, darting nimbly across slippery moss covered rocks.

The topography was forever changing. Tall trees with gnarly branches, which appeared to be ominous claws clutching at him, were replaced by open fields littered by sinkholes and craters. The greenness of forests and pastures became barren desert surrounded by towering standing stones.

Clouds crashed overhead. Bombshells exploded, scattering a torrential rainfall of shrapnel, yet the boy never slowed. He ignored everything, fixated on whatever lay across the next valley or over the far mountain. The shifting landscape didn't faze him; he unwaveringly corkscrewed his way over, under or around every obstacle.

The man chasing him was tall and rangy, narrow hipped and broad shouldered. His arms and legs were pumping wildly, his chest heaving. His strides were long, but no matter how fast he ran he couldn't lessen the distance between him and the boy. Regardless of how stridently he strained, his calls bounced back at him and dissipated into nothingness.

Intrigues and dangers lurked ahead of the boy, but he was oblivious and unaware. The man could see a firestorm of violence swirling like a black tornado. Hungry and volatile, it hurtled toward the boy, threatening to swallow him whole.

A despairing scream scorched from the man's throat. Gunshots rang out. A dog bawled and yelped. Then, silence came in a deafening rush. There was blood and fire everywhere. The boy dove over the edge of a cliff, disappearing.

Amos Coburn lurched awake, rasping his firstborn's name. His body was lathered in sweat, his face wet with tears. Terror had him in its grip. He was pale and weak. His heart thumped hugely. He tried to lift his head, but couldn't muster the strength.

Rebecca was bent over him, one hand placed firmly on his chest, the other holding a damp cloth to his forehead. Her lips were moving, but only her Maker could hear that she was reciting the twenty-third Psalm as a prayer.

"Amos," she whispered softly.

There wasn't much hope or chance that he would be lucid and in command of his faculties. His mental condition was deteriorating even more swiftly than his physical. The threads connecting him to reality were frayed and unraveling, the past and present blended together in an unsettling mosaic.

White-haired and wrinkled, Amos would soon be acquainted with death. His sixtieth birthday was fast approaching, but the hour of his dying would come before that milestone. His health had been betraying him for several years and now, complications from influenza were piling on top of one another. He had brief respites and moments of clarity when he rallied, but mostly he was perplexed and frustrated by the downward slide.

"Amos," Rebecca repeated, giving his whiskers a tug.

His eyes fluttered open. "My son, my son . . ."

She pressed in close to plant a kiss on his feverish forehead. It was slick with perspiration. "We missed you, my dear. The children and grandchildren have all been here, but you slept through their visit. They each took turns sitting and reading the Bible to you. We had a lovely dinner together."

He stared vacantly at the ceiling. "The same dream . . ."

"I'm sorry. I know it grieves thee greatly."

"Three times," he slurred wetly. His lungs were full of fluid. "It's a message. It has to mean something."

"Of course it does."

Amos attempted to sit up, but was too feeble. His jaw clenched stubbornly. "There are chores awaiting me."

"You've been bedridden for more than a month, dear."

His expression flickered with disbelief. It was harsh and brittle judgment aimed at her. "What have you done to me?" he asked thickly. His eyes slammed shut. Torment and paranoia seemed to surge out of his pores to fill the room with raw tension for several bleak minutes.

She watched warily. Her heart ached in helpless resignation. She had prayed herself dry, yet now, from a lifetime of practice and pious submission, she offered up requests bathed in an all-encompassing acceptance of his final destiny. She begged for her husband's glorification, for him to be released from the travails of the flesh by being taken home.

When he opened his eyes again, they were moist. He blinked several times and looked lovingly at her. "Wife, where have you been? I am vexed and desire to speak with thee."

"I am listening."

"I want to see Deacon. I must make peace with him."

"I cannot be accommodating to those words."

"I must beseech my son's forgiveness."

"Leave it at the cross, Amos."

"Yes, yes . . . but I must speak to Deacon."

Rebecca's lips pursed grimly. "We've been over this, Amos. We have no way to contact Deacon, no idea where to look for him. Only the Almighty can intervene on our behalf, and all are diligently praying for our Master's favor."

"I was wrong. I seek to be forgiven."

"The Lord hears your repentance."

"I must reconcile with Deacon."

"Leave it in the Lord's care," Rebecca said pleasantly.

"I don't understand." His eyes spread wide. "Why will no one go tell Deacon I wish to see him? He cannot have gotten far. It was just yesterday we parted company on bad terms."

A sad moan slipped out of her. "Husband, it's been seven years since you refused Deacon the right hand of fellowship."

He raised his head off the pillow. It took tremendous effort. His breathing was shallow, his chest rattling with each quivering hitch. "Seven years? That's not possible." His eyes bulged, his mouth twisted, his body shook.

In a crisis-induced burst of vitality, he sat bolt upright as sorrow wailed out of him. His voice crackled and broke. A spasm trembled through his arms and shoulders. He collapsed. He sobbed in pants and wheezes of unfettered guilt and remorse. "My son, my son . . ." he slurred, twitching frightfully.

Rebecca held him until the convulsions passed. She was weeping. Unconsciousness took hold of him. Whether it was sleep or something more fateful, she didn't know. She was simply gratified that the terrible spell was over.

She carefully rearranged the blankets, wiped his face with much tenderness and fluffed the pillows. Before sitting, she moved the hard-backed chair even closer to the bed.

His breathing was spastic. She cried until there were no more tears. Sorrow was a knot that had tied itself around her heart, but she refused to be dismayed. As was her custom, she began praying snippets of Scripture, directing God to have his own way in the mournful grieving that worried her mind.

~~~

"Gallagher's Cove?"

On the evening of Christmas Day 1868, the Weitzel homestead was warm and cozy. Hot chocolate with peppermint sticks were being enjoyed around the table. Deke Coburn's question hung in the air surrounded by astonished laughter.

"What's so funny?" Hans asked, incredulous. He'd been telling of his arrival in Philadelphia.

"Not funny," Deke said, holding up a hand. "Interesting, ironic, quirky. I knew Blackjack Gallagher and his daughter Alice well. I had a room upstairs for several years."

Hans was speechless. His eyes narrowed suspiciously.

Eliza actually giggled. She covered her mouth for a moment. When she spoke there was a gleeful inflection in her voice. "I find it incredible. You two were destined to be friends."

"A fluky happenstance is all," Hans muttered gruffly.

"Says you." Eliza gave his ribs a jab.

"Says me."

Caleb tipped a knowing wink at his father.

Deke spotted it and did likewise. "Says you, Hans."

Caleb was grinning broadly as he stirred his cocoa and asked, "How did you come to know those folks, Mr. Coburn?"

"Deke. Please, for the hundredth time, call me Deke."

"Have you met my mother?"

Everyone laughed, Eliza no less than the others. "Lord, have mercy!" she quipped in mock crabbiness. "Look at me, getting older by the minute and having to deal with a passel of pigheaded men." She stared at her son in a meaningful way. Much pride and love became a pleasing bouquet in her eyes. Affection passed between them as she gave him a deliberate nod.

"Sure thing, Ma." He leaned forward, elbows on the table.

Deke cleared his throat. "Just like your father, I was hungry and looking for a meal. I cut a deal, struck up a friendship and worked with them in the abolitionist movement, what Alice referred to as the Cause."

"I'll say this," Hans interjected, "Gallagher's Cove sure set a fine table. The stew was stick to your ribs hearty; the ale was as sweet and satisfying as nectar."

"How'd Blackjack get his name, Deke?"

"I'm not allowed to tell you, Caleb," Coburn replied, remembering his promise. "Be assured that he earned it."

"Can we please get back on track?" Eliza said, shifting around so she could make eye contact with each one. She didn't intend it, but her manner and tone gave her the appearance of the school teacher she had once been.

When she was convinced of their undivided attention, she continued, "We're supposed to be sharing memories about Christmas from our childhood for Caleb's enrichment." Her eyebrows tented curiously. "I went first, Hans followed, and it was wonderful, but then somehow, he went down a rabbit trail and got from the old country all the way to America." She reached over to give her husband's shoulder a gentle squeeze. "Now I'd be interested to hear from Deke."

"Yes, ma'am." Coburn thumbed and fingered the sides of his bushy moustache as he mulled over what to say. His strength and weight were coming back, so much that Eliza had declared him fit and fine to do light-duty chores. He scratched his chin, dragged a hand through his unruly hair and offered an unconvincing shrug. "I don't rightly know where to begin."

"How about starting in the bright and early when the fire needed to be fed," Eliza said cheerfully. "Tell us what happened in the Coburn household on Christmas morning."

Deke's expression grew wistful. "There was always work to do, that's true enough; daily tasks for each one. We'd rotate responsibilities. Father would set the schedule and make the assignments on a weekly basis. I appreciated it when I was the one who had to keep the wood-box full and the fire stoked." He slouched back on the chair and folded his arms over his chest.

"Father was a fair man with a streak of sternness. He had no toleration for horseplay, which was rather funny because of Mother. She was a tease and instigator who was most happy surrounded by joy and laughter. Mother reveled in a funny prank or anecdote, and the more raucous, the better, whereas Father preferred and expected stoic merriment.

"On Christmas morning," Deke went on, "Mother would have the house smelling of cloves and cinnamon. After all the jobs and duties were complete, we'd gather around the table for a feast of a breakfast. There were five of us children, three boys and two girls. I was the oldest. While we ate, Father presided over a review of the previous year focusing on God's blessings to us. He'd call on all of us to participate. If we faltered, Mother would nudge or prompt us with a reminder or two.

"When the meal was finished and the table cleared, we'd sit back down, and Father prayed, long-winded and sincere. There wasn't a situation or occurrence that did not get included in his Christmas prayer. He'd pray around the world and back again. Oh my, that man could pray." Deke chuckled, eyes lively.

"Then the Christmas story would be told afresh and anew. Father wouldn't read the Scriptures; he'd relate the events of long ago in narrative. We'd all sit on the edge of our seats listening for a tidbit or insight." His eyes were focused on some faraway place that only he could see. "When I was eleven or twelve, as the eldest child, I was invited to tell the story. Evidently my rendition was fine because it became my annual contribution to our Christmas morning traditions."

Caleb gave a handclap. "I'd like to hear that, Deke."

"I, too," Eliza agreed quickly

Deke declined. His head wagged back and forth, slowly at first, then increased in speed. "No. It's been too many years."

Hans expressed intrigue with the idea. His lips formed a peculiar smile. "I'd be interested," he said quietly. His faith, puny and piddling at best, was always at odds with hostile undercurrents of doubt and reality, but the unpretentious assurance of the man across the table had produced a high level of respect in him.

Deke pondered the request for a hushed piece of time. "Father always began with a caveat. No interruptions allowed. Is that admonition acceptable to all?"

There was instantaneous consensus. Deke Coburn grinned at his friends as he bent forward to rest his forearms on his knees. His hands were clasped together. He spoke with authority, in a commanding tone that demanded attentiveness. There were few pauses, except those purposeful ones for dramatic effect.

"From the beginning, it must be understood that there was something extremely unique about the child born in a stable. Nothing will ever make sense until that fact is grasped.

"His parents, known to history as Joseph and Mary, were a peasant couple of no particular distinction. By decree of the Roman government they'd been uprooted from the obscure village of Nazareth and forced to travel to Joseph's ancestral hometown of Bethlehem. Perhaps that was best because there was upsetting innuendo about their relationship. Mary was expecting a baby, and it didn't take sophisticated mathematicians to figure out that the timeline was not kosher. There were even snide whispers that the soon-to-be-mother was batty. Busybodies gossiped and laughed that Mary claimed it was God's child in her womb.

"On the wondrous night Mary went into labor and gave birth, heavenly messengers visited shepherds on a hillside and told them to go and see for themselves. Amazed, they abruptly left their flocks and found the baby lying in a manger. Chattering about angels, they spread the news with much enthusiasm, proclaiming that this newborn was Christ the Lord.

"Everyone who heard the eyewitness reports from the shepherds were flabbergasted by the supernatural story, but the unusual circumstances surrounding this birth were not confined to the dusty roads and back streets of Palestine.

"Astrologers, likely from Persia or possibly as far off as India, observed a celestial event that, according to their charts, had great significance. They set out on a journey which lasted nearly two years and found Joseph, Mary, and the child at a house in Bethlehem.

"The response of the Magi was quite staggering; these wise and highly educated men bowed and worshiped the infant, honoring him with expensive gifts. King Herod, a local tin-plated monarch, clinging to worldly power, was so fearful of rumors regarding a foreshadowed Messiah's birth that he ordered the slaughter of any male two years old or under.

"An angel of the Lord warned Joseph in a dream. Joseph, Mary, and Jesus escaped and, after a sojourn in Egypt, the family settled in Nazareth. Jesus learned the carpentry trade of his earthly father, but he was also a conscientious student of the sacred scrolls, what we know as the Old Testament."

Coburn drew a decisive breath, then concluded, "Those miraculous events at Bethlehem of Judea all those years ago heralded the dawn of a new era for the human race. We now have an opportunity for redemption. Here endeth the story."

There was wonder and stillness in the room. It held steady for quite a long while, each alone with their thoughts. The looks that slid amongst them were tender and encouraging.

Hans hesitantly breached the silence. "You keep saying words like that, preacher . . ." He stopped, assessing what he was about to admit. "And I might be persuaded to believe."

"I'm no preacher, Hans," Deke replied mildly. "The saying is the easy part. It's the believing and living that's hard."

Hans grinned. "You're the only preacher who's ever broken bread with me." His eyes flinched. "And the only one to whom I'll ever give a fair listen," he added sincerely.

Deke Coburn exhaled a whoosh of air. Apprehension prickled his conscience. Falling short and letting others down preyed upon him. He carried past failures around like a funeral shroud draped over his heart. In his mind, the list of those he'd disappointed or caused grief was quite lengthy.

He stood. "I receive your kindness, Hans. Just don't put too much confidence in me." He stepped to the door and removed his coat from its peg. He pulled it on as he said, "It's been an excellent day. Goodness and grace, but that story reminded me of how truly difficult the living can be."

Eliza spoke up. "Telling of the birth of Jesus should also put you in the mood for hope. And never forget that Daniel Twosongs is right: *Hope is always good. Hope fixes us.*"

Deke bobbed his head, but a gloomy glint showed in his eyes. He turned up his collar as he went outside. Beneath a pristine canopy of starry vastness, he felt trivial. He strolled to his shack, considering an upsetting montage of yesterdays.

By the time he retired he squelched it by sheer willpower. The fervency of hope momentarily triumphed, but then, as he slept, images from the past returned as a nightmare crowded by sinister sorrows. He awakened, dispirited by uneasiness.

chapter four

Desperate Chances

"I returned, and saw under the sun, that the race is not to the swift, nor the battle to the strong, neither yet bread to the wise, nor yet riches to men of understanding, nor yet favour to men of skill; but time and chance happeneth to them all."

~SOLOMON~

WHEN JACKSON SCULLY RODE into Santa Fe, spring was blossoming all across the territory of New Mexico. The thawing had arrived early, which was just fine with most folks.

Cottonwoods were budding, bunchgrass was taking on a reddish-purple color, and yuccas were in the first stages of flowering. The air had a distinct freshness.

Scully sat on a white-face sorrel that had quickness and stamina. It was a fine, intelligent horse that had served him for years, but he treated it with casual disregard. He saw to its feed and watering without sentiment; he merely demanded that it do its job and nothing else. Despite being an ex-cavalryman, he'd never developed any respect for his mounts.

When Judge Thornton's palatial residence came into view, he gave the reins a snap and spurred the animal. It took several skittish steps before breaking into a trot.

A smile filled Scully's face, making his bulgy eyes even more pronounced. He was about as loose and content as he ever got. As far as he was concerned, he was in charge until proven otherwise. A natural gift for manipulation had been put to good use. His schemes were coming together just as he planned.

After stabling his horse, he went to the house. He was met at the door by a tall, impeccably dressed Negro butler. The man was old and rheumy-eyed, with a slight hunch in his shoulders and long, bony fingers that he wiggled incessantly as he went to announce the arrival. Scully waited in the foyer.

When ushered into Judge Thornton's office, Jackson Scully nodded greetings. Wordlessly, he walked straight to the sidebar. It was unmistakable that his left leg dragged even more so than usual. He poured himself a glass of bourbon and sat in an armchair across from the squat, solid man behind the desk.

"Help yourself, my good man," Thornton said, bemused. "A mite early in the day to be swilling my whiskey, isn't it?"

Scully swallowed a mouthful, holding it in his throat for several seconds. "The news I have might change that opinion."

Thornton eyed him narrowly. He glanced out the window, and folded his hands on the desk. "Where's Rawlins?"

"I'm in charge of the operation now."

Thornton's voice remained even. "Where's Rawlins?"

"Hell if I know."

Thornton stared at him, silent and forceful.

Scully shrugged evasively. "He could be dead . . ."

Thornton's brow creased. "Dead?"

Scully allowed the query to dangle. "Well, he *could* be dead in a ditch for all I know. I haven't seen him in almost a week. He's likely still at the cabin where we wintered. Or maybe he's headed west to visit those homesteaders."

"Visit those homesteaders?" Thornton asked, suspicion pealing low and loud in his voice. "What on earth would possess him to do that sort of thing without you tagging along?"

"To warn them," Scully said directly. "That'd be my best guess. Rawlins has gotten soft, Judge. I tried everything I could to follow your orders and go search the place long before now, but Rawlins put the kibosh on it."

"Did he now?"

"It was a bitter winter, I'll grant him that much," Scully allowed, "but we had opportunity to take care of business before now." He took a sip of bourbon. "The problem is that, along with being mushy on those homesteaders, he's gone rogue, Judge."

Thornton's jawline tightened ever so slightly. He kept his emotions under wraps and maintained composure. "Explain."

"He figures he's an independent businessman." Scully swirled the liquid around in the glass as he subtly observed the Judge in an effort to gage his reaction.

"The devil you say?"

"Indeed."

"Tell me more."

Scully finished off his drink. He rubbed his nose and said, "He claims that he has dirt on you, so he can do as he pleases."

"Blackmail?" Thornton breathed the word in a menacing manner, letting it drip off his tongue. "Is that misbegotten mongrel planning on blackmailing me?"

"He didn't put it in those terms, but that's definitely what he intimated," Scully said, rubbing a finger around the rim of the glass. "There was no mistaking his tone or meaning."

Fiery anger simmered in him, but outwardly, Judge Thornton was placid and controlled. "That could present an interesting personnel predicament for me." He stood and slackened his cravat. With both hands thrust in the pockets of his trousers, he began pacing back and forth behind the desk. "Why don't you humor me with your counsel, Mr. Scully?"

"Judge, I wouldn't presume . . ."

"Horse manure," Thornton sliced in, smiling. "Don't insult me with pretentious denials. I've got no use for a shrinking violet snitch. You're obviously a reasonably intelligent chap, so give me a reason not to dispose of the poison all at once. Why not terminate you along with Rawlins?"

"I ain't poison, Judge," Scully said coolly. "I'm a soldier who carries out orders. I'm here to report and make arrangements in preparation to get a rope around Deke Coburn's neck."

Thornton was pleased by that prospect. He paused in his slow, steady walk to scrutinize him. "What's the plan?"

"Recruit a crew," Scully answered quickly. "Get a wagonload of supplies and set up a base camp south of the San Juan River near where Coburn's trail went cold. It may get hairy, but if we turn that homestead upside-down, I suspect we'll have answers."

"How many men?"

"Six or eight capable roughnecks."

"Make it a dozen," Thornton said, resuming his seemingly leisurely to and fro movement. He was calm. There was no urgency in his body language or tone of voice. "Reliable men who won't get lily-livered or squeamish. No half-wit hooligans or goons. I pay top dollar, so don't skimp."

Scully smiled, satisfied and smug. "I'll handle it."

"Not quite, Mr. Scully." Thornton's eyes flickered icily. "Every hire goes through me because *I am* the one in charge of this operation. I'll be riding along for the duration."

"It'll be an honor serving under you, sir."

Thornton ignored the bald-faced flattery. "I only require one assurance, Scully. If Yance Rawlins has become a liability to be eliminated, do you have the *cojones* to take him out?"

Jackson Scully didn't hesitate. "I guarantee it," he stated tonelessly. There was no bravado or hyperbole in his voice.

"Fine," the Judge said, sounding cheerful and at ease. His head was popping with ideas. "As to supplies, here's a special order: Get a pair of the strongest bows available and a couple quivers of arrows, just in case we want to make a massacre look like an Indian attack."

Scully was excited. "That's an option to keep open."

"There could also be other uses for arrows." Thornton grinned. It was obvious that he was imminently delighted with the way his mind was cranking. "Also, purchase a Sharps rifle. That kind of long range accuracy may come in handy."

"Consider it purchased and sighted."

Thornton's grin encompassed his face. "This ought to be fun, Mr. Scully."

All matters were settled. Scully was dismissed with a list of instructions and details to be organized. He had exuberance bubbling in him. The sun was high. Scully filled his lungs with the newness of springtime. He moved determinedly, with a jaunty bounce in his hitching steps. The possibilities were opening up before him. He felt alive and ready to seize command.

~~~

"*That man!*"

On the outskirts of Taos, Consuelo Twosongs was angry and frustrated. She bustled around her kitchen setting the table for the evening meal. Mutton stew spiced liberally with red chili gave the house a spicy sweet aroma.

Sally was nearby ready to help when she could, but mostly she stayed out of the way. She was wary and on edge, worried and wide-eyed. She'd never seen the woman riled up; flustered, yes. Fuming, no.

"That man!" Consuelo repeated for perhaps the tenth time in the last five minutes. She doled out eating utensils and put a plate of fresh tortillas in place. In doing so, she spotted something that froze her inside. "Oh my," she sighed, sitting at her place. "I'm sorry, sweetie."

The anxiety sketched on the girl's face was palpable. She stood as rigid as a steel rail, her hands fisted, her lips a thin pale line. She wanted to hide; she urgently wanted to find a spot where all kinds of disturbances were banned.

Consuelo, her backbone straight and shoulders set, fiddled with her hands. She wondered what was going on inside her daughter's head and was terribly upset by the realization that she had caused distress. "Sally . . ."

Just then the door opened and Daniel came in from outside. He immediately sensed the tension. He removed his hat and shed his coat, then said, "I'll be leaving at first light."

Consuelo glared at him. "I figured as much."

Daniel appeared to be put off by her hostility. It was distinctly obvious she had a mad on over something. He fumbled around as though he was going to attempt a response, but then made an exasperated expression that said her anger didn't fit the parameters of his understanding.

"You think that's best?" Consuelo asked tartly.

Daniel roosted at the table across from her. "I do."

There were flinty sparks darting in Consuelo's eyes. "If you hadn't noticed, there have been changes around here."

Daniel gave her an odd smile. He glanced at the girl, who was easing away from them. The soft creak of the floorboards beneath her feet sounded loud, which accentuated the emotional pressure in the air. Sally backed up, taking tiny steps. With her eyes downcast, she quietly went to her bedroom. She remained close to the doorway, with her ears pricked.

Consuelo waited several minutes before leaning toward him. "It's not just the two of us anymore, Daniel. You can no longer come and go as you please," she said, her voice hushed, her manner adamant. "You've got that poor child tied up in knots."

Daniel was stumped. "Me? What?"

"Your leaving again has her worried."

"No. Your agitation is at fault."

Her lips pursed as though she was in pain. His remark struck her conscience. She knew there was truth in it, but wasn't yet willing to acquiesce. "Your leaving is at the root of it."

"Sally had no complaints when we talked a while ago."

"What would you know?" Consuelo shot back, eyes flaring.

Daniel slumped, exhaling audibly. "I'm at a loss here, Consuelo." His tone was calm and low, his eyes narrow slits surrounded by a web of deep creases. "This decision has been discussed many times over the winter. We were agreed."

"Listening to your plans doesn't constitute a discussion," Consuelo countered, "and resigned silence isn't agreement."

He put his hands behind his head, twining his fingers together. "This warm spell took me by surprise. I thought I had another week or so. I should've been prepared to leave at the first hint of spring. I have to do what I have to do."

She rose and took several hesitant steps, then returned to her chair. She was flushed and disconcerted, but her anger was dissipating. "Sally depends on you, Daniel. She draws comfort and stability from your strength. Much like me," she said evenly. The rock-hard cast of her expression was softening. Even so, her smile was tight and challenging.

Daniel wanted only peace between them. It wearied him to navigate the choppy currents of her temperament. "There's no other option. The trouble is real, and it'll play out perilously. I'm expected. Deke will need me."

"And you may need us."

His hands dropped from his head as he sat up, eyes spreading in surprise. The subtext of her words riveted his attention. He folded his arms over his chest. "No chance, Consuelo."

"Your wooden-headedness is misplaced."

"You cannot come. The dangers are too much."

"I can ride, shoot, cook on the trail, and tend wounds," she said straightforwardly. "If Deke Coburn needs help, I want to do my share. I owe the man as much as you do."

He considered that, but didn't say anything.

"He gave *us* a daughter, Daniel," she continued, sensing an opening. "He has troubles because he rescued *our* daughter."

"Thomas Thornton is known as a man without scruples," he pointed out. "No one will be safe from his fury."

"I'll not stand by and do nothing, Daniel."

He started to speak, but a swish of movement caused him to bite off the first word before it even formed. Sally stepped rapidly and with purpose. She went straightaway to the stove and stirred the mutton stew with a large ladle. Then, using a pair of potholders carried the cast iron crock to the table.

She sat at her place and held out her hands. She kept her eyes lowered and waited. The adults stared at her, then each other. Sally bowed her head. It took a moment for them to take her cue. When their hands were clasped together, Sally whispered a rhymed prayer of thanksgiving.

The *amen* was a mere murmur, but then was strongly echoed by Daniel and Consuelo. Awkward silence passed between them. It was pushed to the wayside when Consuelo served each a bowl, making small talk about the ingredients she'd used.

Sally passed the platter of tortillas. Setting her eyes on Daniel, she boldly declared, "If Mr. Deke is in trouble, I want to help. I'll not stand by and do nothing either."

Daniel squinted. His hands flexed. He forced a smile at her. He sent it in his wife's direction. He was outnumbered, and there was a certain amount of persuasion in their case, but he resisted. Range-wise wisdom and common sense dictated that he stick to his resolve to go alone to the Weitzel homestead.

He picked up his spoon and began eating. As he savored each morsel, he began bracing himself for the onslaught of protests that'd accompany the finality of his stand-pat position.

In the dream he was a lost little boy. The woods were deep and dark, with an overgrowth of stark bare tree branches hanging over him like scaffolding. He couldn't see the sky. If it was there, it was black and starless.

Somewhere above, an owl hooted. The low and mournful *who-who* was a ghostly sound that materialized from the thickness. It ricocheted all around him, making the nape of his neck prickle weirdly. He smiled. He thought that he should be afraid, but instead, a puzzling uncertainty dominated his mind.

He speeded up. There was no hesitancy in him. He was running faster and faster and faster. He had no identifiable goal in view; he couldn't see much in the inky darkness. He didn't even know which direction he was going, but kept at it. The terrain was uneven, littered with deadfalls here and there, but he raced with the sure-footed ease of a mountain goat.

Someone or something was behind him. He was being chased. He never slowed to ponder who or what it could be. Staying out front and on the move was all that mattered.

The air was still and empty. Every noise carried. He listened to his footfalls crunching sticks or rustling leaves. The loudness mesmerized him. He was inside the rhythm of his steps. Harder and harder he plunged forward.

A voice drifted past him. It was urgent and high-pitched, demanding his attention. He started to slow, but just then, the owl, almost on top of him, let loose a melancholy *who-who*. The nearness startled him. He jumped. His legs went all rubbery. His arms flailed wildly for balance. He got all twisted around and came crashing down on his buttocks.

The voice returned, louder and more insistent. He couldn't distinguish the words, but knew it was a woman crying out. She was behind him, coming closer and closer. He was being pursued by a woman, which bewildered him. The boy scrunched up his knees and sat staring at the darkness. It crept and slithered like a misshapen creature preparing to swallow him.

Above, the scaffold branches creaked and moaned. It was laughter, hideous mocking laughter that wailed stridently. Now a wave of fear swelled in him. It throbbed and pulsated in his temples and made his eyes watery.

"Lawrence . . ." the voice called, soft and tender.

He stood, turned a small circle and got his bearings. Something bizarre occurred. A gasp escaped his throat. He wasn't a little boy anymore; he was a tall man with broad shoulders.

Suddenly it was daylight, and she was standing there in an embroidered wedding dress, stunningly beautiful. Pretty pink flower petals decorated the auburn halo of her hair.

"Angela," he said, reaching for her. She was a mere ten feet away. Three giant steps was all that separated them, but his legs were immobilized, his feet anchored to the ground.

She flashed a smile. It melted him. Her eyes were lively and lovely, promising delightfulness. He was fascinated, absorbed, enthralled by her. His heart overflowed with love. His heartbeat was hummingbird wings fluttering madly.

Their concentration held steady, riveted on each other. There was a dove-tail quality in the way their eyes connected. He had no qualms, only affection swirling deep inside.

"Where have you been, Lawrence?"

"Everywhere . . . nowhere."

"I waited for you."

"I should have stayed."

"Yes. If only you had stayed."

"I was a mess, Angela."

"I looked for you."

"I should have come back."

"Yes. If only you had come back."

"I was a mess, Angela."

"We're all a mess, Lawrence."

"I failed you."

"There were dismal days when I needed a friend."

"I'm sorry. I was wrong."

Her eyes sparkled. "So many lonely nights when the lamp burned low and I wanted to hold you and be tender."

"I'm sorry, Angela."

"You missed out on a good life."

He hung his head. "We should have been married."

"Yes. If only we'd had a wedding day."

He felt the weight release from his feet. He made a move toward her. The freedom set off a surge of excitement. With his focus firmly on her, he ventured forth another step.

She backpedaled. "Should have, if only . . ."

He rushed at her. She rapidly retreated, but her legs were motionless. She was floating. He kept pace, stretching and straining to touch her, but she remained just out of reach. His knees pumped up and down as he high-stepped, but regardless of his efforts, he couldn't gain any ground on her. Terror clawed at him as she began a gut-wrenching transformation.

Her face embodied sadness. She spoke in a shriek that hissed out of her, "*Should have, if only . . . should have, if only . . . should have, if only . . . should have, if only . . .*"

Her beauty was annihilated as he helplessly clutched at her. Her shrill voice never stopped screeching the *should have, if only* refrain as she became a cadaverous wraith. The silky material of the intricately stitched dress yellowed and tattered into strips of soiled rags. Her skin turned charcoal-gray, her hair flamed, and her eyes sank into her skull.

A scream was bellowing from his lungs when he shuddered awake and tumbled off the cot. He hit the floor with a thud, banging his head. Disoriented and wheezing for air, he was almost instantly standing and flailing his arms as though he could ward off or punish the horrible nightmare.

Deke Coburn was crying. The tears pouring out of him were hot and salty droplets of remorse. He let the strangled emotions flow in choking spurts, making no attempt to stifle them. When the sobbing passed, he gradually gathered his senses.

He gingerly fingered the right side of his forehead. A large goose-egg had promptly grown where his head had collided with the floor. He lit an oil lamp, picked up a sealed envelope off the shelf, then perched on the cot.

His breathing had returned to normal. He felt as drained as a dry well. In the flickering lamplight he examined the grainy envelope containing what he'd invested much of the past three days hashing out, a heartfelt letter to Angela Langton. He turned it over and over staring at all sides of it.

He thought he liked the earlier version better, but that one had been lost in his unfortunate encounter with renegade Utes. After considering what he'd written and sweated over, Deke Coburn was satisfied that it was ready to be posted. He prayed that it would make it all the way to Xenia, Ohio.

Abbey Langton was mixed up. She felt scared. Or perhaps she was fighting, spitting mad. She couldn't say for sure one way or the other. All she was certain of was that she had a thing or two to tell God, but so far had kept her tongue tied.

She'd been awake most of the night, an almost fifteen year old girl caught up in the tempest of a spiraling, out of control meltdown. She sat at her mother's bedside, gripped by the darkness and an unrelenting confusion of thoughts.

The rocking chair had a rather annoying squeak so she kept perfectly still. Her mother was sleeping fitfully. Her health was declining, but most days she was still able to carry on as though nothing was wrong.

Abbey wanted to snuggle beside her to hold her close and not let go. All that was happening was so unfair; grossly unfair. Her hands were clamped together on her lap. Her heart ached, her belly was queasy with apprehension.

Her fear and anger were lashed to each other by questions formed in the deepest part of her. There were so many anxieties knotted up that unraveling them seemed to be an impossibility, but she expected answers, demanded them.

Where was God in this tragedy? There could be no possible explanation or excuse for his absence. He was supposed to be all powerful and all loving. He was supposed to have mercy. What was he doing off on a vacation when people needed him? How dare he allow this sickness to grow in her mother? What was he doing? Why was he being mean-spirited? Why was he silent?

Abbey stood. The chair creaked. She winced and waited for the noise to disappear. She stepped slowly, tentatively to the window. She leaned close, pressing against the glass. Its chill felt nice and comforting on her face.

That fragmented sensation swiftly dissolved. She stared at the night, longing for it to provide what she so desperately desired. Her mind was popping and jumping all over the place. There had to be some reason that would soothe her a bit, some rationalization that'd provide a measure of relief about the future. She could see the moon. It was high, white, and lonesome. Wispy feathers of clouds eased past it.

"What am I going to do?" she whispered, squeezing her eyes shut. Tears were forming, but she refused to cry. She was going to be strong and brave. In her assessment there was no other option available to her.

The pain in her heart and nervousness in her belly was intensifying—a pressure that craved release. It churned and gathered steam like water on the boil.

Through clenched teeth, she asked, "Why is God killing my mother?" It came out faintly. What followed was piercing and rancid in its animosity. "What is God trying to prove?" The keen loudness sent a shiver along her spine.

"He wants to teach us something," Angela said firmly.

Abbey jerked. "I didn't mean to wake you, Mom."

Angela pushed up on her elbows. "Don't worry, dear. I'm awake, then asleep. It comes and goes."

Abbey inched close to her. "Can I get you anything?"

"Light some candles and make the night pretty."

Abbey did so. Before she blew out the match, there were a dozen flames twinkling in a circular array on the dresser, reflecting in the mirror. She sat down and began rocking—squeak, squeak, squeak. "I don't know what to say or do. None of this makes any sense to me. It's not right, and it's not fair."

"Whoever told you life was fair? Not me."

"God doesn't have to be so mean."

Angela was inflexible. "He's not at all mean."

"You're only thirty-five years old . . ."

"I'm aware of my age," she said, laughing sadly. "Your father was only twenty-one. We live, we die, Abbey. There's nothing fair, unfair, or mean about it."

"Forgive me if I disagree."

"Of course. Just be careful."

Abbey eyed her, pensive and unsure. "Be careful?"

"No one gets to tell God what to do."

"He doesn't listen, so what difference does it make?"

"Oh, he listens, Abbey. You know he does," Angela said sharply. "He can take whatever you dish out, so go ahead, dump all your hurt and doubt on him. If you do, you'll come out the other side of this unpleasant reality wiser and stronger."

Abbey smiled grimly. "What does God want to teach us?"

"That it's the living that matters, not the dying," her mother replied, much confidence in her tone. "God doesn't have anything to prove. He's God, which is really the deal closer. Our lives are a gift from him. What we do and how we live is influenced by our acceptance or denial of that truth."

"I'm frightened, Mom."

"That's only natural."

"What's going to happen?"

Angela spoke gently. "I'm going to die, and you, dear daughter, are going to live. There's a great big wonderful world waiting for you to explore. Put my dying behind you. Walk away from my grave to go and do and see. Whatever days are ordained for you, cherish every moment. If you treasure the gift, your life will be colored by the brushstrokes of dreams."

"You're remarkable."

"Not remarkable," Angela quipped, "just dying." She scooted over, peeled the blankets back and patted the mattress. "Now crawl in here and let me hug you tight."

Abbey quickly accepted the invitation. She moved so fast that she created a breeze that caused the candles to flutter and dance crazily against the darkness. She slipped under the crook of her arm and sank into her mother's embrace. They squished around some to get the covers shared out equally.

"I pray you'll heed my counsel, Abbey."

"I'll try my best, Mom," she said, a tremble in her voice.

Angela gave her a squeeze. "It's alright to cry."

Abbey stiffened. A tiny, nearly smothered sob escaped her quivering lips. She gulped a deep breath, sucking air into her lungs in a bold attempt to remain dry-eyed. The resolve inside was wilting. Her chest heaved up and down. She burst into tears. Wrenching, anguished cries slashed out of her.

Angela fiercely encircled her. In a moment she was weeping, too. There were no more words to be said. Hours later, when early morning sunlight crept through the window, mother and daughter were sleeping soundly in each other's arms.

~~~

Hans Weitzel finished hitching the mules to the buckboard. He'd done the job with all the enthusiasm of a condemned man eating his last meal. He was out of sorts. Anxiety burned in him. There were so many variables in play outside his reach.

The chances he had no control over disturbed him this morning, which was unusual. He habitually took charge of those things he could affect or alter, and tended not to be bothered over what might happen, but not so just now. Lately the potential trails taken by others had him ill at ease.

"Are we ready?"

Hans looked up to see Eliza walking toward him as pretty as the day they'd met faraway and long ago. He was examining the harness. "I may need to switch this out for the spare one."

"I doubt it," she said, smiling. She nudged him out of the way to check the yoke and hitches. "Are there some bats loose in your belfry? You know darn well there's no problem with this rig." She stepped back, hands on her hips as she eyed him.

He ignored her. "I think it's best for me to talk to Caleb about taking you to town today."

"Do you now?"

He ran a hand over his close-cropped hair and nodded. "I do. I'm going to have a conversation with him right now."

"You'll do no such thing, Hans Weitzel," she snapped and moved quickly to get situated directly in front of him. "You listen to me, mister. One, we have business to take care of at the trading post. Two, we planned this trip together, and I for one have been looking forward to it. Three, Deke and Caleb are able to take care of matters here for a few days."

"First light's long gone. Why not wait on tomorrow?"

Eliza blanched. "What's your problem?"

"I don't know what you're talking about," he answered, sounding churlish. "Don't make a big thing here."

She put her hands on his shoulders. "Hans, what is it?" There was much concern in her eyes. "What's bothering you?"

"I'm stewing on that Judge Thornton," he admitted, eyebrows rising. "What if trouble jumps off while we're away?"

"Deke and Caleb are capable men."

"That they are, but from all we've learned, Judge Thornton is relentless and ruthless," he said, head wagging. "He'll be riding in here with a gang of cutthroats."

"All the more reason for us to go now so we can get back and be ready for whatever's coming," Eliza said sternly. "If we're going to make a stand and put up a defensive fight, we'll need much more ammunition than we have on hand."

"I know," he grunted, eyes tight and narrow.

She gave his upper arms a hard squeeze. "We'll be fine, Hans. This break in winter came early enough to surprise us. It surely did the same for those plotting in Santa Fe. I say we got a week or more before we see or hear from Judge Thornton."

"You could be right."

"Or maybe the man's forgotten all about Deke Coburn."

"That's wishful thinking, Eliza."

"Yes, unfortunately," she agreed grimly.

Caleb came out of the house and called to them. He was loaded down, lugging a large basket of food. There were also two over-sized canteens slung over his shoulders. He arranged the supplies in the back of the buckboard beside a groundsheet and tarp. There were also blankets and a haversack packed with extra outerwear in case of inclement weather.

"You're all set."

"Not quite, son," Eliza said, grinning. "Your father is in a rare dilly-dallying mood."

"I have no ideas at all about that," Caleb replied, hands slipping into his back pockets. "What I do know is that Deke has something for you, but he's dilly-dallying, too."

"You stay alert, Caleb. Trouble's coming."

"My eyes are wide open, Pa."

"Keep them that way. And keep your Spencer close."

"Always," Caleb said confidently. "Well, I have work to do. That steeldust figures it ain't going to happen, but by sunset I'll be stiff and sore, and it'll be saddle-wise."

"Be extra careful, Caleb."

"Sure thing, Ma."

Eliza watched him as he went into the house. A moment later he had his Spencer in hand and was headed toward the corral. Her mouth pinched into a wince that gave the impression of being uncomfortable. She forced a smile, but not rapidly enough.

Hans noted her expression. It pained him and stirred a flutter of emotion. He responded by wrapping her in a strong hug. "You raised a solid man, Eliza Weitzel. He'll stand up to every challenge with good sense and backbone."

"We did a fine job, didn't we, Hans?"

"You more than me," he said, without regret. He placed his hands on her hips and with little effort, lifted her up. She squealed and held onto her sunbonnet as he carried her. He softly settled her derriere on the seat of the buckboard. "Are we going to get on our way or what?"

Eliza laughed brightly. "Get on up here and let's go." She moved his Henry rifle to its spot to make room for him.

He swung up beside her. "Here's another delay," he said, mock grumbling as he motioned with a backhanded wave.

Deke Coburn ambled toward them. He had a blue bandanna tied around his neck and doeskin gloves on. He stopped at the side of the buckboard. "Eliza, will you please post this letter?" he asked, handing the envelope to her.

She took it, glanced at the name and address, then nodded knowingly and gave him an encouraging smile. "If we ever get on our way, it'll be the first thing I do at the trading post. Angela Langton must be an exceptional lady. I pray that writing and sending this provides some closure for you."

"She deserved better than me."

"Can the lonely hearts club meeting be over?" Hans queried, accompanied by a robust chuckle. "We got us a long ride ahead."

Eliza elbowed her husband. "*Now* you're in a hurry."

"Stay sharp, Deke," Hans urged, picking up the reins.

"Caleb and I have everything nailed down."

"Make sure it stays that way. We'll be back in a couple days." Hans made a loud click-click sound and spoke kindly to the mules. The beasts pulled away, ears twitching.

The wheels gave a groaning complaint at first, but then turned with well-greased efficiency. Rainy came running out of the barn. The hound circled the wagon once, yapped and howled a goodbye, then settled on the porch.

Deke stood watching as the buckboard went beneath the iron and wood *Freiheit* arch. He held up a hand in a grand sweeping gesture and headed for the corral at a lazy gait.

Physically, he was fully recovered from the ordeal that had almost ended his life. His weight and sinewy muscle mass had been restored. He was a long-limbed, rawboned man hardened by a steady diet of activity and labor.

The sun was in the east, halfway to its apex. He moved comfortably beneath the blue skies, enjoying the rising temperatures. The day was proving to be warm. He looked around at the miles and miles of sagebrush that stretched off in every direction as far as could be seen. A sense of peace and safety washed over him because of the isolated remoteness.

When he got to the corral, he was pleased to see that the mares were feeding on an oats and molasses mixture. It was a blended recipe he'd picked up from Big Bull Wallace in Texas. Coburn had tweaked it a bit by adding a generous amount of cornmeal. Both horses were in foal. By the end of summer there would be two colts scampering around the corral.

Deke stood by and observed Caleb working the steeldust. He had it saddled. It was chafing at the bit and snorting as he led it around by the bridle. There were three fifty pound bags of sand perched securely on the saddle.

He had put the animal through a progression of training, demonstrating patience and a natural affinity for the process. The stallion was free-spirited. At each stage it had rebelled in one way or another, but he was wearing it down. Ever so slowly, mutual trust and respect were developing.

"Coming along good, Caleb," Deke said, leaning on the top railing. "It's getting close to crunch time."

"Yep." Caleb put the reins back and looped them over the saddle horn, allowing the horse to do as it pleased. The steeldust didn't bolt; it merely wandered aimlessly.

"That stallion's stubborn and smart."

"Yep." Caleb sidled over to the shaggy-haired man who had freely shared much know-how about horses gleaned in his years on the range. "I'll likely get tossed a time or two, but there's no avoiding it. I have to put myself in the saddle."

"Have you named that horse yet?"

Caleb frowned at him, shaking his head. "I've been thinking on it, but I ain't ever named a horse before."

"Why not?"

"Just never have, Deke."

Coburn took his gloves off, folded them and tucked them into his belt. "Look at the way that horse is eyeballing you." He paused as the young man turned to see the stallion focused on him. "When you're around, it never lets you out of its sight. All the hours you've spent grooming and training, it has already formed an unbreakable bond."

"You think so?"

"I know so," Deke replied quickly. "When you're finished breaking it, that horse will smash through a flaming brick wall for you." He thumbed back the corners of his moustache.

"That animal will carry you until the day it dies. It'll take you over hills and hollows, and be a reliable companion." His tone was clearly respectful. "On those nights you're all alone in the wild, that horse will warn you if there's a bear, big cat, or outlaw on the prowl. Men have killed to have a horse of that caliber. It deserves a proper name, Caleb."

"Any ideas?"

Coburn mulled it over. "You got a favorite Bible story?"

Caleb hardly had a chance to hear the question. There was no hesitation as he answered, "Shadrach, Meshach, and Abednego."

"Why?"

Caleb drew in a deep breath. "Their refusal to bow and scrape before the golden idol even though the penalty of the fiery furnace was fully known inspires me. They boldly stood up against power because it was right to do so. They were men of principle, and that's the kind of man I want to be." He spoke with determination ringing in his voice. "It's like what Pa says about standing firm and being willing to pay the price."

"It certainly is," Deke said, clapping him on the back. "You ought not to think too hard to come up with a name for that fine horse. It's staring at you in that Old Testament story."

Caleb's lips cracked in a lopsided grin. His head bobbed as he eased over to the steeldust. It never moved an inch. He stood at its side, rubbing its neck for several minutes before gently taking hold of its head. "Shadrach is your name," he whispered, stroking its mane. "It means we stand together against whatever comes our way. You got that, Shadrach?"

The horse tilted its head at him and pawed the ground. Caleb patted its chest. He carefully removed the bags of sand one at a time. He took the reins, exhaling softly. He put his left foot in the stirrup and as smoothly and swiftly as possible, slipped into the saddle.

Shadrach immediately reared up on its haunches, violently twisting its body around. It lurched forward, tossing him head over heels. He hit the ground, somersaulted to his feet, and let loose a hearty yee-haw. Unhurt, he dusted himself off as he gingerly moved back and forth in front of the horse.

This was a test of wills—which one, man or beast, had the grit to out-stubborn the other. Shadrach snorted as it kept pace with the man, stepping lively. The horse blew, and Caleb detected a glimmering twinkle in its eyes.

"Are you laughing at me, Shadrach?"

The stallion shook its body and kicked its hind legs.

"Now see here," Caleb said, hands flexing. He got close and took the bridle, speaking in a hushed manner. The horse stood still, listening contentedly. "You and I are going to be friends, Shadrach. There's no two ways about it. So you may as well get that through your thick skull right now. Throw me if that pleases you, but I ain't quitting until we have an understanding." He pressed his forehead against its snout and draped his arms around its neck. "You got that, Shadrach?"

Coburn kept his attention riveted on the scene. A slight, sagebrush-scented breeze riffled the air. The hair on the nape of his neck stiffened. A funny feeling came over him. He ignored it, settling in to watch the man versus animal drama unfold. It was fascinating

Yance Rawlins saw the buckboard from a distance. He instantly sprang into action. He angled his mount, looking for a spot to get out of sight. The chestnut seemed to sense the flush of excitement in its rider and responded enthusiastically.

He kept the reins tight, carefully opting for a course that weaved its way through the endless sagebrush. He slipped in behind a thicket of scrub pines. Sixty yards or so off the crude trail he came upon a washed out arroyo. The horse stepped nimbly along the edge, picking its spot to dip down into the gully.

The sun was high and hot. Rawlins got out of the saddle and murmured a word of encouragement to the horse. He surveyed the hiding place and was fully satisfied. The steep-sided gulch was ten feet deep and better than twenty feet wide. He led the horse along the uneven bottom.

Sweat was beginning to trickle down his face. He kept moving steadily on the route he'd been riding, which was in the general direction of the oncoming wagon. His eyes were rapidly flitting to and fro. He saw a deep slash in the wall ahead that'd be perfect for his purposes. He picketed the horse in an area where it could munch on tufts of bunchgrass.

Rawlins checked his pistol and holstered it. He crept into the crease, edging his way to the top of the lip. He heard voices chatting nonchalantly before he actually spied the wagon. He listened closely, and though sound carried far in the high desert, he couldn't identify the words.

The fact that they were talking told him that his presence was unknown to them. He'd gotten out of their field of vision before his movement was detected. He smirked contentedly.

This was turning into a first-rate day indeed. He had an opportunity to make plenty of headway. He considered the odds. The smirk grew wicked and smarmy.

There was a possibility that he could have the whole matter settled before Jackson Scully arrived with the posse of ruffians he'd been sent to recruit. Rawlins decided that would be the best possible consequence of his actions.

The wagon was rolling at a relaxed speed. When it came abreast of him, it was less than fifty yards away. His breathing was shallow and deliberate. He pressed down even tighter into the furrow. He could see the homesteaders; it was evident that they were in no particular hurry. Husband and wife were sitting good-naturedly close to each other.

It was his first glimpse of the man, but he recognized the woman from last summer's encounter with her. She was speaking animatedly. She had loosened the ties of her sunbonnet. It hung down past her shoulder blades. Her straw-colored hair shimmered in the sunlight. A carnal thought about her leapt into his mind, but he squelched it before it could distract him.

There was business to do. As the buckboard passed his location they didn't even cast a glance toward him. He surmised their destination to be the trading post. He then did some time and distance calculations. He figured that at the earliest they would be returning home tomorrow afternoon.

This meant that he had plenty of leeway to give every inch of their ranch a thorough going-over. Every recess and niche of each building would be searched. With mother and father gone, he'd only have to deal with a pup of a schoolboy. It was going to be a rollicking lark with a degree of difficulty akin to sliding between a sassy whore's sheets.

Yance Rawlins hunkered down in his sandy crevice and waited. There was no rush. He wouldn't pull out until the buckboard was a mile or more away. He might even take a midday nap. He had no reason to hurry or be concerned. The targeted homestead could be no more than an hour or so ride. He reckoned that, by nightfall, when he kindled a campfire and spread his bedroll, Judge Thomas Thornton's problem of Deke Coburn would be hogtied.

Shadrach was running faster than any horse Caleb Weitzel had ever ridden. The steeldust stallion was in truth faster than any horse he'd ever even *seen*. It took gigantic loping strides that gobbled up ground at a spectacular swiftness.

He was bent low in the saddle, his body in sync with the fluid rhythm of the horse. One hand was on the reins while the other stretched down to continually rub Shadrach's chest. He was thrilled by the feel and temperament of the animal.

He spoke with authority in Shadrach's ear. Then, as he sat up straight, gave the reins a gentle tug. The horse went from a rip-roaring gallop to a trot. It cantered for several moments before slowing to a walk.

Caleb was grinning and chuckling when he rode up to the corral where Deke sat balanced on the top rail. "You never seen anything like it, Deke," Caleb said, jumping out of the saddle. "Look! Shadrach isn't even breathing hard. What a horse!"

"How far did you run?"

"We walked about a mile and raced back," Caleb replied, hands on his hips. "I doubt we hit top-speed." There was awe in his voice. "Not a bad exchange. I only got tossed and ate dirt twice, and now I've got the greatest horse in the territory."

Deke remarked, "Maybe the whole country."

Caleb smiled proudly. "I'm taking Shadrach to the barn for a good rubdown." He started to lead the horse that way, but abruptly halted and said, "Oh, I almost forgot. There's a fella coming this way riding a chestnut stallion."

Deke Coburn froze for a moment. "Was he alone?"

"I didn't see anyone else."

The past rushed at Coburn, leaving him cold. When his brain processed the information, he vaulted down. "That's my trouble coming to call."

"No. The guy's just lazing along."

Coburn's eyes were icy. "That matters not. It's trouble."

"If that's so, we're ready for it, Deke."

"Caleb, get your Spencer and make yourself scarce in the barn. Stay in the shadows, alert and ready. Keep me in sight, but don't use the rifle unless I go down." Deke stepped close to his young friend. "Even then, seek wisdom and caution because killing a man scars you forever. If I'm dead, nothing will be gained by you shooting him."

Caleb bristled. His expression darkened and took on the flinty texture of granite. "I haven't got much experience in these matters, but I can promise you this: I ain't going to wait for him to put a bullet in you, Deke." He gave him an assured nod and grabbed his Spencer. He led Shadrach to the barn.

Coburn was wary. There was too much blood on his hands, too many ruined lives in his wake. He didn't want his young friend to do murder to protect him. He went to the water trough, unknotted his bandanna, and soaked it. He wiped his eyes and face. The coolness felt good. It helped him think rationally.

He returned the bandana to his neck. He jogged to the house. Rainy was still lounging on the porch, unconcerned by all the happenings of the day. The hound cocked an eyebrow at him. He crouched to give it some attention.

When he rose to his full height he shaded his eyes and studied the horizon. The sun was at two o'clock and glaringly bright, but he definitely discerned an outline of movement approaching. Horse and rider were still a mile or more away, but were on track to arrive at the archway.

Coburn sat in a rocker and crossed his legs. "No matter what happens, you stick near me, Rainy. There's a rascal coming who intends me harm. I may need your help."

Rainy whined. It stood to nuzzle the man. He patted its head. It pushed against him, slobbering. He nudged it aside and told it to sit. It obeyed.

He began leisurely rocking as though he was merely taking a relaxing break. He kept silent vigil, watching and waiting as the silhouette took shape.

When the rider was still a long ways off, Deke Coburn stood and stretched. He stepped off the porch. He was armed only with his wits, experience, strength, and an unbending sense of rightness. He staked out a piece of real estate halfway between the house and the arch.

Rainy stayed at his side. The dog sensed the tension rising in the man. It barked and pranced anxiously. Coburn ordered it to behave and be quiet. It scrunched down and waited with him.

Yance Rawlins rode steadily forward. He could barely contain his glee when he realized his good fortune. As he closed in on the homestead he recognized the tall man loitering in the yard. He wanted to shout and celebrate. Luck had served him well.

The man whom he had vigorously pursued, the man who had given him fits and outfoxed him the previous summer was standing in plain sight. Rawlins kept his hands visible, the right one on the reins, the left held high. He was smiling in a sociable fashion when he came into the yard.

The chestnut whinnied. Rainy howled once and stayed put. The horse snapped and spat, straining at the bit. Rawlins fought it. He cussed and yanked back hard on the reins. The horse's head jerked and twitched, then it calmed down and took on a placid stance. The men measured each other.

"You be Deke Coburn?"

"You got me. You Rawlins?"

"All my life," he replied flippantly. He took some time to study the surroundings, eyes narrowed and suspicious. "Is the punk kid still out riding that steeldust I saw him on?"

"He's with the horse, yeah."

Rawlins held both hands up. "I'm going to reach back in my saddlebags to get something you need to see. I got no tricks, so let's not do anything stupid here."

"I'd be pleased to see whatever you got for me."

Rawlins scowled at him. He scrounged around for a few seconds. He came out with a yellowed broadsheet. It was folded, and it seemed to be stuck together because he had to fuss and fiddle with it a long while.

The air was still. From his alcove between bales of hay, Caleb Weitzel could see everything; he could hear the tone of their conversation. He vigilantly stayed out of the sunlight. He inched closer to the half-open loft door, every nerve coiled. He was flat on his belly, with the Spencer aimed.

He wondered if he had the courage and ability to pull the trigger when circumstance demanded it. Shooting pesky critters or meat for the smokehouse was far different than putting a bullet in a man. He worried on the consequences. He pushed those thoughts to the background. He concentrated on staying ready.

"You have to answer for Lucas Thornton," Yance said, holding up the paper. It was a copy of the wanted poster.

Deke remained unmoved. "I saw that bogus news in Taos."

"Says here, dead or alive."

"Lucas Thornton pulled and fired twice before I dispatched him to eternity," Deke said dryly. "By any reasonable standard it was a fair fight. No court on the frontier would see it otherwise. Besides, the man was a monster who got what was coming to him, and for doing justice I don't apologize."

Rawlins stiffened his shoulders. "I ain't going to argue the legal niceties with you. Or discuss Tommyboy's character. I have me a paper here that says dead or alive, and it's got your name on it." He refolded the poster and stuffed it back into his saddlebags. "What's it going to be?"

"Tommyboy kept a journal."

"What difference does that make?"

"He detailed every vile thing he ever done," Deke replied in a scratchy voice that was thick with sorrow. "Over the course of many years he kidnapped young Indian and Mexican girls and held them captive. Before brutally killing each one, he performed unspeakable acts on them."

Rawlins balked, chuckling dismissively. He removed his hat, wiped his brow and made a backhanded gesture. "Hellfire, you think that matters? Injuns and Mexicans?"

Coburn skewered him with a glare that swelled up from deep within. Righteousness was dancing fiercely in his cold eyes. "It matters to the Almighty. It mattered to me."

Rawlins squinted and squirmed in his saddle. The leather squeaked as he shifted his weight. He put his hat on, leaned his head back and took a deep breath. "Don't you love the smell of sagebrush in the springtime?" he asked wistfully. "Smells like that Almighty you speak of may actually produce new buds and second chances."

Deke Coburn appeared surprised; confused, even. When he spoke, he was serious and determined. "God is all about second chances. It's never too late for a new start. Jacob was a liar, Moses a murderer, David an adulterer. The Almighty gave each of them lots more than just one second chance."

"I heard all those stories from my Mama," Yance said softly. His eyes were hard, but there was evidence of tenderness in his voice. "I'd truly like to believe them; I wish to blazes that I could have faith in every bit of it, but I've seen too much cruelty and done too much wrong for any of it to apply to me."

"If you want to believe truth, then do so."

Rawlins scoffed. "Are you a preacher or something?" he demanded, but then didn't wait for a response. "I ain't sitting still for anymore of this bull session on religion. None of this yakking about pie in sky garbage changes what we have here. Dead or alive, what's it going to be, Coburn?"

"Neither."

"What's to stop me from shooting you here and now?"

Coburn gave him a matter-of-fact shrug. "That journal is as volatile and dangerous as nitroglycerin. Along with the gross depravity itemized, it gives a concise description that would lead the authorities to Tommyboy's lair where he disposed of the bodies," he explained, subdued and colorless. "Anything bad happens to me or my friends here by the order of Judge Thomas Thornton, and that journal will be delivered to the closest U.S. Marshal and the newspapers will be alerted."

Rawlins cursed. "Where is it? Where's the journal stashed?"

"In a safe deposit box faraway from here."

"To hell with the journal," Rawlins said, sneering angrily. "I should put hot-lead in your brain on sheer principle."

"You'd gun down an unarmed man?" Coburn stretched his arms out wide. "Do whatever you think's right and fair, Rawlins."

Yance Rawlins regarded him with disdain. He moistened his lips. His right hand flexed once. A gunshot exploded, rapidly followed by a second. Deke Coburn lurched in his footsteps. He instinctively clutched at himself.

Both roars boomed in the stillness. Rainy was up and scampering toward the barn. It howled and yapped as though it had been wounded. The chestnut stallion snorted repeatedly as it pranced around, skittish and irritable.

Rawlins was in a quandary. He struggled to stay in the saddle by desperately locking his thighs. He had his arms up in surrender, red-faced and sweating profusely. The first shot had sent his hat flying; the second one struck its brim and made it tumble crazily before it hit the ground.

"Have I got your attention, mister?" Caleb shouted, voice as sure and controlled as a tightly wound precision gear. He was standing in the doorway of the barn's loft. "That first shot hit the crown of your hat, which is exactly where I aimed. I figure I missed your skull by an inch or so. The next time I squeeze this trigger, the bullet will strike three inches lower. That'd put it right between your eyes."

Coburn picked up the hat and fingered the charred holes. He tossed it to its owner. "You'd best be on your way."

Rawlins swore at him, savagely. He returned his hat to his head. "I'm by myself now, but a day's coming when I won't be."

"I'll be here for a spell." Deke pushed a stern smile at him. "Just make sure Judge Thornton knows about the journal."

"Screw the journal," Rawlins snapped snidely.

"Really? That's the tact you're going to take?"

"Why the hell not?"

"I suppose the Judge could get practiced up to hang me by stringing you up for dereliction of duty," Deke said wittily.

"Screw the journal. And screw you."

Coburn brushed back the sides of his moustache. "Your employer should have the information. If he chooses to say screw the journal, that's his decision. A respectable law firm is involved and it's already a done deal."

Yance Rawlins eyed him, somewhat glibly. "I'll deliver the message, but it won't save your skin." He tipped his hat to him, then took it off and waved it at Caleb, who was still in the loft's doorway with the rifle fixed on him. "I'll be seeing you again, Coburn," he said, baring his teeth in a grimace.

With that, the beefy man twisted the horse's head around and dug his heels into its sides. The stallion made an awful yelping noise as it bolted beneath the archway. Soon all that remained was a thin trail of dust disappearing in the air.

Sally Twosongs was as sick as the proverbial dog. Feverish and nauseous, the illness had come out of her at both ends. She was bundled beneath blankets in a hastily erected lean-to. It'd been twenty-four hours since the first eruption of vomit.

The family was camped near a creek that was usually a trickle or dry-bed, but was now full because of snow melting in the mountains. Consuelo was caring for her daughter, sitting by her side to periodically wash her face with a cool cloth. A canteen of icy water was stationed within her reach.

The sun was slinking close to its nighttime resting place. The western sky looked like it was bleeding. Daniel was on his haunches near the cook-fire, absently whittling on a short length of willow he intended to shape into a whistle. He had a pair of jackrabbits on a spit. Dripping grease sizzled, making the flames crackle and hiss. He tended to the meal by and by.

A bull elk bellowed. Daniel listened to its trumpet call. It was moving through the woods not far from the campsite. He felt an old familiar yearning constrict in the pit of his stomach. On another occasion he'd be inclined to get his rifle and have some fun harvesting a supply of meat, but not today. They were supposed to be traveling light and fast.

The delay was unavoidable. The little one's discomfort disturbed him, but he was anxious to be back on the trail. He had staunchly stood his ground against Consuelo and Sally coming on the trip for as long as feasibly possible, but their bold teamwork arguments defeated him.

As far as it depended on him, there were neither repercussions nor regrets. The child's well-being weighed heavy on his mind. He had to recalibrate his timetable, but that wasn't upsetting. He wanted to get to the Weitzel homestead, but was confident that they would do so soon enough.

He stood, slid the knife into its sheaf on his hip and pocketed the half-finished project. He went to attend to the stock. There were two horses and a donkey to be watered. He led them to a shallow section of the stream. As they drank, he spotted a bald eagle gliding just above a line of tall aspens. The sight soothed a deep cranny in his soul.

When the animals were finished drinking, he picketed each one on a grassy patch for the night. Like the night before, he intended to guard against any four-legged predators by sleeping nearby in the open air with his rifle at his side. He took a round-about route back to the fire to check the perimeter.

He moved through the sparse forest on cat's feet, quiet and careful with each step. The soft-soled moccasins allowed him to feel the terrain to avoid the crack of a fallen branch or the crunch of dried leaves.

When he came up alongside the lean-to, he found Consuelo bent over as she served chunky strips of roasted rabbit on tin plates. The firelight sparkled in her eyes. He paused and remained perfectly still to enjoy watching her. He did so for a full minute before she saw him smiling in the shadows.

"There you are," she said, standing. "Supper's ready."

He went to her and accepted the plate she'd prepared for him. It had two hardtack biscuits together with the meat. He gave her an appreciative nod as he squatted on his heels.

She rolled out a mat across the fire pit from him. She did a survey of the area, urgently on the lookout for creepers or crawlers. She sat down, her plate on her lap. He waited until she was settled before making a request at the throne of grace for protection couched in words of thanksgiving.

After his amen, she said, "Lord, hear our prayer."

"We're genuinely blessed."

She agreed. "The tonic you made for Sally seems to be the right medicine. She's sleeping deeply."

The lines around his eyes crinkled. "Pleasing to hear."

"The fever broke. She's on the mend," Consuelo said, nibbling on a biscuit. "She'll be weak, but we should be able to travel the day after tomorrow."

"That'll be fine," Daniel replied flatly. "All signs point to this warm weather holding for many days."

"How much farther?"

"Two solid days riding briskly."

"I'm sorry we're holding you back."

He sighed. It sounded sad and weary. "No reason to be. A man makes his plans, but the Creator guides each step. You and Sally are with me for a purpose, Consuelo. This slowdown happened for a reason. Let us value the chances and whims of the trail."

Her cheeks flushed. She smiled happily. "Until that bug got hold of Sally, it had been good for us to be with you."

"It still is," he said, adamantly cheerful. "We'll nurse our young lady back to health, then be on our way."

They polished off their meal cocooned in the snug silence that comes from an unconditional acceptance of each other. The rest of the evening found them busily occupied with necessary tasks. By nightfall, clean-up chores were completed, the fire banked, and a stack of wood piled next to the lean-to.

Three days later, as dusk draped its curtains across the sky, the family's destination was in hailing distance. Daniel Twosongs was feeling impish. He reached into an inside pocket and dug out the wood whistle he'd carved on the journey. He gave it a long and hard blow.

The pitch was ear-splittingly shrill. Sally clutched her hands over her ears; Consuelo plugged hers. In this case, Daniel had no mercy in him, only merriment. He blew the hollowed willow stick again even harder and longer. As the strident sound dwindled into an echo, he erupted in laughter.

In the gathering gloom he heard the redbone hound barking wildly. He called its name at the top of his lungs. There was an instant of stifled puzzlement that gave way to understanding, and then the dog howled a full-throated welcome.

Hans Weitzel was on the porch with his Henry rifle in hand. Rainy's baying had alerted him. He shouldered the firearm when he recognized the squat rider by his flat-brimmed hat. He thundered his own jovial greeting, which brought the others running. There was much good cheer as they waited together.

When the three travelers rode under the arch, excitement and relief prospered in the air. The reunion and introductions took place in a whirlwind of motion. Caleb took charge, volunteering to stow their gear and care for their animals.

In mere moments the visitors were ushered into the house. Everyone was seated at the table while Eliza hustled around the kitchen and began preparing generous helpings of food.

"It's good to see you folks," Deke said earnestly.

Daniel scrutinized him. "The last time I saw you I thought your time of dying had come. You had the look of death." He sat back, arms folded over his chest. "What's the situation?"

"About what we supposed," Hans answered quickly.

"Yance Rawlins paid us a visit a few days ago," Deke said, "and we had a rather pleasant exchange of information. He knows where we stand, and what we got, which didn't set well with him. Caleb had to dissuade him and was quite convincing."

Hans cracked a broad smile. "That's how we must proceed. Caleb set the example for us. We can't appease nor show weakness of any kind." His manner and tone was unyielding. "We need to prepare for the worst. This Judge Thornton is bent. I've dealt with his kind more times than I care to say. Nothing he plans, nothing he attempts against us would surprise me."

Deke exhaled lowly. "Any ideas on what to expect?"

"He may try honey at first, but it'll be pretense," Hans replied, hands fisted. "While he talks, the hired gorillas and apparatus for an assault or siege will be in place."

"An assault or siege?" Consuelo exclaimed in a gasp.

Daniel took one of her hands. "I warned you of the danger, Consuelo. I don't disagree with Hans. His assessment is accurate." He stared at Weitzel. "What provisions are in place?"

Hans nodded as he leaned forward. "This is a defensible location. We've got stores of food, a stable water supply and now, enough ammunition to hold off a small army . . ."

"Excuse me," Eliza interrupted sharply. She placed a platter of cold cuts of ham on the table along with a woven basket of bread and a stack of plates. "This war council ends right now." Her voice had a bitter inflection in it. "For future reference, it isn't necessary to have these types of discussions when there are little ears in the cornfield."

Each of the men shot glances at the pigtailed girl.

"I came to help Mr. Deke," Sally piped up strongly.

Coburn's face filled with emotion that made his bottom lip quiver and eyes misty. "Sally, you just being here is all the help Mr. Deke is ever going to need." He reached across the table to touch her, but she slipped off the chair and went to him. She put her arms around his neck in a fierce hug. He squeezed her as he melted. Tears trickled down his cheeks.

Suddenly the air was thick and heavy. The other adults all seemed to be holding their collective breath. There wasn't an eye in the room that wasn't moisture-laden. A choked, nearly stifled sob escaped Consuelo's lips. Eliza rushed to her side and leaned over to give her a comforting embrace.

"We can learn much from Sally Twosongs," Daniel said, his voice wavering. "Survival, love, toughness, bravery."

Coburn thumbed his eyes. Then, soberly and with much emphasis, spoke words from the prophet Isaiah: "*The wolf also shall dwell with the lamb, and the leopard shall lie down with the kid; and the calf and the young lion and the fatling together; and a little child shall lead them.*"

Just then Caleb came in with Rainy at his heels. Sally jumped and scooted back to her chair. The hound followed her, its body wagging as it kept bumping up against her. She giggled.

Eliza and Consuelo wiped the wetness off each other's cheeks. Caleb took note of the dishes on the kitchen counter to be delivered to the table—butter, mustard, pickles, apple jelly. He placed them where they belonged. As the adults began passing around the plates, he got glasses for everyone.

"I was thinking," Caleb said, fixing a sandwich while still standing. "Daniel and I could arrange our bedding in the barn so Mrs. Twosongs and Sally can use my room."

Consuelo shook her head in protest. "No, no."

"Thank you, son," Eliza said, "that's a swell idea."

Daniel was in agreement. The issue was put to rest.

The remainder of the evening had tenderness entwined around it. There was cheery banter, questions asked and answered, and funny stories told. Conversation buzzed, and a game of charades descended into gales of shouting laughter rife with exaggerated pantomimes. By the time candles and oil lamps were snuffed out, an easy familiarity had been established amongst them.

Early the next morning, Sally Twosongs discovered that she had made a friend. She was outside using a well-chewed stick to play fetch with Rainy. There was a tight heart connection forming between the child and dog.

The sunrise had been magnificent, flaming tongues of orange that disintegrated the darkness. Caleb Weitzel had given it some attention as he worked his daily routine. Now, with the sun up and daybreak chores done, he sat on the chopping block watching his dog playing with the girl. He wondered about her. There was something in her looks and bearing that intrigued him.

"Rainy, come!" he called. The redbone stopped, dropped the stick and bounded toward its master. Caleb energetically waved and motioned for Sally to join them. She followed the dog to the side of the barn where stacks of wood were piled.

"Rainy likes you," he told her when she was close enough to converse. "I want to show you some tricks the scamp knows." He stood and gestured for her to take a seat on the chopping block. She did so, scrunching her legs up under her skirt.

Caleb positioned himself in front of her. "Rainy, sit." The hound plopped down on its buttocks. "Rainy, play dead." He cocked a finger at it and mimicked the sound of a gunshot. The dog whimpered and fell sideways to the ground.

Sally clapped gleefully.

"Wait, wait," Caleb said, raising a hand to end the applause. "One more." He held steady for a long moment, and the dog didn't move a muscle. "Rainy, hide," he ordered as he pushed a palm at it. Rainy swiftly rolled onto its belly, flattened out, then covered its muzzle with its paws.

Sally's dark eyes were lit up brightly. "Can I try?"

"Sure," Caleb answered, stepping aside. Rainy sprang up. He took hold of both sides of the scruff of its neck. "Rainy, you listen to Sally. Understand?" The dog tilted its head, sad-eyed and grinning wetly. He turned to Sally and said, "Just say its name and give each command in a firm voice."

Sally followed the instructions to a tee. She demonstrated patience and a knack for the task. The dog responded perfectly. When it hid, paws over snout, it even whined. She was giggly.

"Good job, Rainy," Caleb said, which was its cue to get to its feet, wagging its tail madly. He gave it a rough rubdown.

Sally crouched on the edge of the chopping block. "Rainy is so smart, but that's kind of a dumb name for a dog."

Caleb demurred. "Not for this one."

"Why not?"

Poking around the woodpile, he selected a suitable log to be used as a stool. He grabbed it, set it in place near her and hunkered down. "For starters, my parents told me that when I came hollering into the world it was drizzling rain all day long. Of course, I don't remember that," he said, laughing.

He thought for moment, quickly doing arithmetic in his head. "Five years ago, this hound-dog was born on a rainy night in Missouri, the only one of the litter to survive. Shortly after its birth, the bitch that bore it died. Ma and I hand-fed it like a baby. I raised it up and did all the training myself."

"Rainy *is not* a dumb name," Sally said, locking her hands around her knees. "You had no other choice."

"It could've been *Thunder* or *Lightning*, actually," Caleb allowed, "because Rainy was born during an awful storm."

"Rainy is much better."

"I think so, too." He saw his mother step onto the porch. "It looks like we have to go. I hope you're hungry. Ma always sets out a bounty of food, especially for breakfast."

Caleb Weitzel and Sally Twosongs walked to the house side by side as Rainy ran circles around them the entire way. There was an idyllic contentment emerging in their relationship. In a few short days, unbeknownst to anyone, a bullet would shatter that serenity, and a grave would have to be dug.

Judge Thornton was raging mad and, for once, was making no effort to conceal or disguise his anger. "You warned them?" he screamed, lumbering back and forth in front of the tent that would serve as his headquarters.

There was acid swirling in his stomach and an inflammation burning his backside. Along with all the frustrations of the operation, he had a large seeping carbuncle on his right butt cheek. The ride from Santa Fe had been harder on him than he'd ever imagined. It'd been twenty or more years since he'd spent that much time in the saddle.

"Warn them?" Rawlins queried, skeptical and guarded. "I went there to search the place for clues as to Coburn's whereabouts. I happened onto the mother lode and found him."

Thornton studied him suspiciously. "Scully says you've gone rogue. I hear that you're an independent businessman."

Yance Rawlins almost lost it. His eyes bugged open. He took a step toward Scully, hands balling into fists. He wanted to pulverize him, to tear him apart limb by limb and not stop until there was nothing left of him, but then reason prevailed. He stopped cold and forced calmness to the forefront of his mind. Even so, he glowered at the former bluecoat.

Jackson Scully lowered his eyes and looked away. The three men were near a patchy grove of cottonwoods, supposedly formulating a plan, but that had been side-railed for now. Their combative discussion was taking place amidst the noise and bustle of the hired crew laboring to set up camp.

"Scully ought to say his piece with me standing here."

"No," Thornton snapped, slowing his pace. "You've heard all you're going to hear, Rawlins."

"That may be," Yance countered, "but *you* ain't heard nothing yet. I got information that's going to hurt your ears."

Thornton stopped to squarely face him. "You've botched this entire operation from the beginning. It's fouled up because of your piss poor handling of it. Coburn should've been dead or captured in Taos."

"Is that so?"

"It is indeed so."

Rawlins laughed derisively. "I'm all broke up over your assessment of my work, boss." He turned toward Scully, grinning wildly. "Just so you know; I'm going to carve out your guts and ram them down your throat." He turned his attention back to the Judge, his round face still a mask of mockery. "All those rumors about Tommyboy's misbehavior with little girls were true. Your son was the loopy twitch, not Coburn."

Thornton wasn't fazed at all. For the briefest of moments a glint of awareness glimmered in his eyes. It had much to say, but then as swiftly as it appeared, it melted away.

Rawlins flinched, stepping backwards. His face reddened. "You knew," he whispered incredulously. "All along, you knew."

"How dare you!"

"How dare I what, Judge? Tell the truth?"

Thomas Thornton grimaced, cold and calculating. "Where is the evidence for this truth of which you speak?"

"I saw it in your eyes and my belly hurts," Yance answered evenly. "Plus, Tommyboy kept a journal. It has particulars and is in the possession of some hotshot lawyer."

The news struck like an icepick, but Thornton never blinked. Suspicions had lingered in him because of Sanchez's inference about written evidence, but mostly those possibilities had been repudiated. He looked off in the distance, apparently watching clouds scrape across the sky, which was getting stretched into streaky shades of gray as twilight gathered.

He pursed his lips tightly. His inner workings locked down as he evaluated all angles. "Tomorrow's another day."

"We'll handle it, Judge," Scully said confidently.

Rawlins scowled. A chuckle rumbled in his throat as he spoke, "It ain't going to be an easy proposition."

"Lawyers can die. Journals can disappear," the Judge said, shrugging. His venting was finished. His naked emotions were now entirely enshrouded. "Every truth has its price, Mr. Rawlins."

Jackson Scully took a limping step forward. "Give me the order, Judge. It won't be that difficult."

"What about you, Rawlins?"

"Me? What about you, Judge?"

Thornton ignored the question. "There are circumstances we have to muck our way through, Mr. Rawlins. Are you going to come along and follow orders or what?"

"I'll do your bidding until I decide otherwise."

"I liked Scully's expression of loyalty much better."

"Loyalty cuts two ways," Yance said fiercely. "I sent Scully to Santa Fe to report to you and sign up a crew. I have no idea what falsehoods this bottom-feeding deviant told you, but it's obvious you were swayed by them."

"Nothing's obvious."

"He buffaloed you," Rawlins stated with conviction. "After all the altercations and calamities we've been through together, I deserved the benefit of doubt. You owed me that much, boss."

Thornton slowly moved close to him. "My apologies, but you're too thin skinned," he said persuasively. His voice took on a formidable smoothness. "When this is over you and Scully can part company. You can have it out with him any way you call it; knives, guns, or bare knuckles. It matters not to me."

Rawlins nodded. "That fight can't come soon enough."

The Judge took a hasty side-step so he could eyeball the two of them. "Until this job is done, I need both of you. The tasks ahead require a unified front. Can you delinquents cooperate and function as a team for a bit longer?"

"All in, Judge," Scully vowed, displaying an attitude that suggested he might snap off a stiff-bodied salute.

Rawlins sneered and remained silent. He gave a terse bob of his head, which would have to suffice for his answer. He stared at his employer, refusing to back down or give an inch.

Thornton analyzed all that had transpired. When he was satisfied that their longstanding business arrangement still had juice, he smiled and asked, "How far is it to the homestead?"

Rawlins was less than cordial. "Five miles tops."

"My arse isn't going to survive this debacle," Thornton said, grimacing. "Tomorrow we'll ride over and pay our respects. I want to check out the lay of the land and evaluate what we're up against. Perhaps I can be done with it by making an appeal to greed, which is the common failing of humanity."

"Not likely," Scully chimed in. "They're do-gooders."

Rawlins walked away. There was no chewing the fat left in him. He'd heard and said enough. He would check on specifics and oversee what still needed to be done to secure the camp.

As noontime arrived the next day, Hans Weitzel, his son, Deke Coburn, and Daniel Twosongs exited the barn just at the right moment. They had been making plans and considering the desperate chances that lay ahead, the various scenarios as to how Judge Thornton would proceed.

Their confab settled on the most probable tactic to expect first. It would be a straight-up approach, accompanied by lots of chatter. Now it was clear that their assessment was accurate. Three riders were coming from the north, a half-mile or so away. The horses were loafing along lazily.

"Here comes the honey," Hans said sarcastically. "Caleb, get in place in the loft. Daniel, take your spot in the house. Keep the women folk inside away from the windows."

Caleb and Daniel moved swiftly. Hans and Deke stood waiting in the middle of the yard. Both were unarmed. Deke felt strange. Rainy came running, but Hans shooed the hound back to the porch.

The riders never varied their tempo. They came under the arch with a casual ease, stopping side by side, with the Judge in the middle. The five men scrutinized each other, those on horseback also surveying the house and barn. Tension mounted with each passing second; the air prickled with its intensity.

"Coburn," Yance said, nodding.

Deke returned the nod. "Rawlins."

Yance Rawlins made formal introductions as though this was a meeting of diplomatic dignitaries. Then, eyeing the barn, he chided, "I suppose there's a rifle in the loft aimed at us."

Weitzel said, "There's more than one gun on you."

"Guns?" Thornton leaned back in the saddle, hands spread wide. "Gentlemen, gentlemen, there's no need for guns. Can we get down and have a polite conversation?"

Weitzel had his hands on his hips. He gave his head a rigorous shake. "No, you can't get down. I don't want my land contaminated. Stay put and spit out what you came to say."

Thornton never gave a visible response. "If that's the way you want it, that's the way it'll be. After all, we're guests on your land, are we not?"

"Uninvited guests," Hans pointed out, all smiles.

Thornton reflected that same brashness back at him, but it was taxing all the strength he could rally. He had a couple problems. The carbuncle on his keister had salve on it and was padded with layers of cloth but it was irritated. He could feel the wetness of bloody pus dribbling on his backside. Added to that discomfort, his bowels were in a cramping uproar. He'd been hoping for an opportunity to use their outhouse.

"I was mistaken," the Judge began, carefully adjusting his posture. "When word came to me of my son's death, I was crushed. The investigation led us to you, Mr. Coburn. Then there were rumors about debauchery involving my son with young girls. It shocked and appalled me. As a father I couldn't believe it of my son, flesh of my flesh." His voice cracked as he sniffed and wiped the corners of his eyes.

Yance Rawlins lowered his head to hide the smirk curling his lips. He had witnessed the Judge in action enough over the years to be aware that the demonstration of emotions was phony, a performance worthy of an accomplished stage actor.

"Mr. Coburn," Thornton continued, "as you can imagine, it was natural for me to connect you, the one responsible for my son's death, to the depravity . . ." His voice drifted off as he pushed up on the saddle horn and shifted his weight. "I now know that I was wrong. I understand that my son Lucas kept a journal. How can one know the madness another has in him?"

Deke Coburn stared at him and gave an answer from the prophet Jeremiah, "*The heart is deceitful above all things, and desperately wicked: who can know it?*"

Thomas Thornton produced a widespread smile and spoke amiably, "Of course, the Good Book addresses these matters."

"What are you here for, Thornton?" Hans asked roughly.

"I'm here as a father," the Judge replied, his voice stoked with meekness. "I want to preserve my son's legacy. To that end I have a lucrative proposal for you folks."

"Let's hear your honey," Hans said impassively. "I can't speak on Deke's behalf, but I must warn you before you babble on and on. I never do business with the criminal kind."

Jackson Scully abruptly leaned forward. The saddle squeaked eerily. "Be careful with your mouth, Weitzel."

Hans roared belly laughter. "I told you a long time ago that teaching you some manners man to man would gratify me. Get off that horse without your gun and let the lesson begin."

"No!" Thornton held a hand up in Scully's direction. "There will be no violence. I'll not stand for it. I'm a law-abiding businessman here to offer a deal."

Yance Rawlins was amused big time. He could barely contain the hilarity tickling his sensibilities. He prodded the cranky chestnut to take a couple steps. In a restrained tone that obscured the smarmy pitch in his voice, he said, "You'd be wise to give the Judge a fair hearing."

Thornton frowned at him, dubious and uneasy. "It's really a simple proposition." A wince darkened his expression as spasms clutched at his belly. He pressed and struggled to maintain composure. "When my lawyer has the name and contact information for the firm that guards the journal, $10,000 will be deposited in whatever banking institution you designate. When the journal is in my possession, another $10,000 will be put on deposit."

"No," Deke said, anger in him.

"You got your answer, boss," Yance said, jerking the reins to wheel the stallion around. His back was to the barn. There was a flash of movement and without anyone truly seeing it happen, his pistol was out and leveled at Jackson Scully.

"Are you insane?" Thornton asked, eyes gaping.

"No, he's not," Deke said soberly. "He's figured out that all the money in the world won't sanitize filth."

Rawlins screwed his face into a frown. "I wouldn't put it in those grandiose terms, Coburn. I got my own reasons to be done jumping to the Judge's tune." He kept the gun aimed at Scully as he conveyed terms to Thornton. "I'm throwing in with these folks. You ride out and be gone. Leave them be. If any harm comes to anyone here, by all that's in me I swear . . ." He stopped, grinning frigidly. His eyes were reptilian, cold and hooded into slits. The unspecified threat dangled ominously.

Judge Thomas Thornton made an instructive gesture to Jackson Scully. His teeth were clenched as his stomach cartwheeled in a sickly fashion. They cautiously spun their horses around. Scully cast a barrage of slurred curses over his shoulder as they rode off. A hundred yards separated them from the homestead before Rawlins holstered his pistol and stepped out of the saddle.

"This ain't over," Yance said softly.

Hans eyeballed him. "No chance of that."

Daniel and the women were huddled on the porch. Caleb came running from the barn, his Spencer in hand. Everyone kept their focus on Yance Rawlins, wary and worried. He seemed sheepish and remorseful. His attention was stuck on the ground.

Deke Coburn stepped toward him with his right hand thrust forward. Their eyes connected, and Rawlins received unspoken acceptance. He grabbed Coburn's hand and pumped it forcefully.

Judge Thornton was suffering. When they had covered just over a mile, a groan ripped out as noise rattled through his lower abdomen. He slowed the horse. His eyes bent crazily around the area, seeking a spot for an emergency call of nature, but it was too late. He bit the inside of his bottom lip, fisted his hands, and squeezed his buttocks as taut as possible.

Scully turned his horse around and came up beside him. The white-faced sorrel sniffed and snorted. "We aren't done, Judge."

"No, we're not," Thornton said, seething. The rolling waves of constrictions in his belly were relaxing. "I want them dead, but before that I want to terrorize them. You hear me? Put that military brain to work and together we'll come up with a plan."

Scully grinned proudly. His eyes were full of excitement.

Thornton aggressively spurred his mount. He cussed because the remainder of the ride to the campsite would be uncomfortable and messy. The bloody pus staining the inside seat of his pants now had a squishy layer of sticky brown sauce for company.

Jackson Scully had been in place since long before sunrise. With a Sharps rifle loaded and double-checked, it was time to implement the initial stage of the strategy. He was hidden in a shallow indentation on a slight ridge within striking distance of the Weitzel homestead.

Stealthy scouting, in the three days since the confrontation in which Yance Rawlins switched allegiances, had uncovered the nearly flawless sniper's nest. Encompassed by endless hedges of sagebrush, he could remain unseen and still sustain a clear angle on the porch and a portion of the yard.

The conspiring had been methodical and coldblooded, with the Judge fully engaged. Scully was in awe of Thornton's scheming brilliance. His meticulous cunning had proposed and approved every aspect of the plan. All preparations for the second phase were already in motion, but first Scully had to do his job.

His nerves were calm, his senses alert. He was merely waiting for conditions to be perfect. In a few more minutes the sun would be high enough to not affect his vision.

He took a gander through the big rifle's scope and smiled at what he saw. Rawlins sat on the steps of the porch cleaning his guns. Coburn was behind him in a rocking chair, immersed in a black leather book that appeared to be a Bible.

Jackson Scully took a deep breath and held it, practicing. He lined them up in the crosshairs—first Rawlins, then Coburn. He knew he only had one shot. His getaway horse was picketed far enough behind that he'd have to hustle in his hop-skip gait to be on it and gone before any pursuers got close.

The redbone hound came into view, scampering onto the porch. It nuzzled Coburn, who took some time to roughly tease it. When the dog became bored with that, it went over to poke its nose into what Rawlins was doing.

Yance put down the oily cloth he'd been using, holstered his pistol, set aside his rifle, then stood. He stepped into the yard, picked up a stick, and started tossing it for the dog to merrily chase.

Scully watched, amused. He kept focused and on edge. Shortly a girl in pigtails appeared in his range, followed by the boy who had a stiff-shouldered motion in his assured stroll. He was absently juggling a patchwork rag-ball from hand to hand. Rawlins and the two youngsters spread out a bit and began a game of three-corner keep-away with the hound.

Their voices and the sounds of the redbone's yapping howls carried to him. Jackson Scully emptied his lungs, beginning the process of intentionally slowing his breathing. He was no longer practicing. It would be just a few more heartbeats.

He put the crosshairs on the sturdy looking teenage boy. He held it there until the whelp threw the ball. He monitored the running dog in the scope. He aimed the rifle at the girl as the hound jumped around her. His conscience felt fine enough to end her life, but then he followed the throw to Rawlins.

He zeroed in on his erstwhile partner's throat, grinning. It wouldn't bother him at all to blow his brains out. He elevated the rifle a tad to get it in alignment with Coburn's heart. He held it there for a spell before shifting again.

Back and forth he eased the rifle, placing the crosshairs alternately on Caleb, Rainy, Sally, Rawlins, and Coburn. He repeated the pattern four times. His breathing had become so shallow as to be nonexistent. He finally established his target and in a fraction of a second gently pressured the trigger.

The firearm roared and bucked in his hands. He held steady. The scent of gunpowder filled his nostrils, thrilling him. He inhaled an open mouthed gulp of air. He fixated on the scene, wanting to be sure that the bullet had realized its purpose. When he was thoroughly satisfied that the kill was complete, he hightailed it.

In the yard, shouts and cries scorched the air. Eliza and Consuelo came sprinting out the front door, almost tripping each other in their haste. Hans and Daniel had been in the blacksmith shop at the rear of the barn repairing a farming implement. What assaulted their eyes when they raced out of the barn caused Hans to momentarily lose his balance and stumble.

Deke and Yance towered over Caleb; both were struggling with Sally to hold her back. Consuelo was trying to help as the girl kicked and thrashed to escape. Eliza had crouched down and was kneeling beside her son. She wanted to reach out to him. Her heart ached; her senses were enraged.

Caleb sat in the dirt. He was holding Rainy in his lap, his one hand clamped over a ghastly hole in the back of its skull, the other stroking its side. Its body was limp, lifeless. Its warmth was already dissipating. There was blood all over him. His expression was stoical, blank-eyed and straight-lipped.

Sally wrestled free. She draped herself over his back. She was weeping as she furiously hugged him around his shoulders. He clamped a bloody hand around her clenched hands. Their slashed open emotions twined together wordlessly.

After a long while, Caleb said, "I have a grave to dig." He nudged Sally and she took a shaky step back. He looked around at the blotchy faces and reddened eyes fixed on him.

Deke touched him. "We'll all help."

"No," Caleb replied strongly. "I have to do it myself." He struggled to his feet, straining to keep Rainy in his arms. "Pa, will you please make a marker for my friend?"

Hans Weitzel had tears streaming down his face. "I'll have it ready, Caleb." He moved aside to allow his son to pass.

"Caleb," Eliza called, starting after him.

Hans stopped her. "Leave him to it," he said, clinging to her. They peered into each other's eyes, revealing mutual hurt and helplessness. They embraced, arms tightening. They held onto each other as frantically as in those weeks and months following their son's birth when they fought to accept the fact that they could never have another child.

Sally broke away from the group and ran into the house. Both Daniel and Consuelo followed, dismay and concern written on their faces. They discovered her sorting through the few belongings that had been brought along.

When she found what she was looking for, Daniel's uneasy expression relaxed a bit. He gave Consuelo's shoulder an encouraging squeeze. Their daughter rushed past them and back outside carrying her fringed deerskin stocking.

Caleb had selected a location behind the vegetable garden for Rainy's final resting place. He'd laid the dog's body nearby and was already busy digging. There was dismal sadness in the sound of the shovel breaking up the sod.

Sally Twosongs watched him. She kept well away from him, sitting cross-legged, her skirt billowing around her. She shook her flute from its sheaf, then bowed her head and closed her eyes to pray and listen to the music whispering in her soul.

When she started playing the song, Caleb stopped and leaned on the shovel. He listened for several minutes, allowing the notes to push into grief-stricken recesses within to provide consolation. He cast an expressive nod in her direction before getting back to work. The whole while he dug, she accompanied him with a mournful tune.

Eliza came carrying a bucket of water, Deke with her. He had a piece of canvas. They both paused to appreciate the evocative melody before getting to their tasks. She took a rag from the bucket and carefully washed the redbone hound. There was affection in her touch and tears in her eyes.

When she was finished, Deke stretched out the coarse material. He lifted the dog onto it. He folded it over, arranging it just so. Eliza took out a dangerous looking darning needle and a spool of heavy thread. They took turns stitching the burial shroud shut. Caleb never once slowed in his labors.

Late that afternoon everyone had cleaned up and were gathered at the graveside. Daniel and Yance were on guard duty, armed with rifles as they vigilantly kept alert. Consuelo and Sally stood stiffly beside each other. Deke said some tender words. Hans, Eliza, and Caleb lowered the canvas-wrapped corpse to the bottom of the grave.

Caleb immediately scooped up the shovel and started filling the pit. Each clod clumped noisily. Once again in his young life, the finality of death impressed itself upon him. Sally inched away from her mother and took a position at the edge of the pile of dirt. Her eyes kept darting from Caleb to the hole as it inevitably disappeared.

Hans brought the marker he'd hastily designed and built. There was a pair of foot-long sharpened steel prongs on its bottom to secure it in the ground. He situated it, and using a sledgehammer, drove it into place.

It was a single two-inch thick plank board framed in angle iron that had been heated and forged into shape. He had sweated longest over the wording. When he decided on the phrases to be used, he diligently burned the epitaph into the wood:

Rainy
1864 – 1869
Rainy served us as a good
friend and faithful companion.

All remarked about it being entirely appropriate. Caleb studied it approvingly. He was dragging as he walked away from the grave. It had been an emotionally draining day. Everyone was exhausted, and looking forward to a good night's sleep.

A flaming arrow lit the darkness in an arc, followed by another and another and another. Daniel Twosongs was immediately in full action mode, running and yelling an alarm. All four arrows struck the roof of the barn and stuck.

It was the middle of the night. The surprise attack came from so far away and was so swift there was nothing Daniel could do to stop it. He fired his rifle toward the sky three times and kept shouting warnings as he ran to the barn.

Daniel had been on the porch, wide awake and on watch. He had completed a long circular check around the property less than a half hour ago and intended to begin another tour soon. He was due to be relieved by Deke Coburn shortly. That had all changed in an instant. Chaos was everywhere.

"Lord, have mercy!" Eliza shrieked. Fear and anger competed in her. She was barefoot and in her bed clothes. Reason rose up in her. She quickly took a look around. Everyone was present and accounted for—Consuelo and Sally were right beside her.

Hans was waving his arms and barking orders. Flames were rapidly crawling across the roof, consuming it. The dryness of the high desert contributed to the fire's feeding frenzy.

Caleb, Deke, Daniel, and Yance were seeing to the safety of the livestock. The stalls were opened to release the mules and few milk cows. The sheep and goats were set free from the pens alongside the barn. The animals scattered as Caleb attempted to herd them.

It was an impossible effort. He gave up and ran to check on the horses. The corral was brightened by dancing yellow hues from the firelight. Yance's chestnut was bucking and jumping as though it was possessed by a demon. The two mountain bred ponies belonging to Daniel were milling around, scared and out of sorts. The donkey was kicking and hee-hawing constantly.

Caleb was pleased to see that Shadrach had the mares against the rails at the farthest point away from the barn. He raced back to the fire. The tumult was an outraged commotion.

The entire roof was engulfed in roaring flames and showing signs of collapsing. Beams were groaning. There would be no preventing it from burning to the ground. Neither the means nor apparatus was available to them. The possibility of mounting a bucket brigade had passed in the first moments after the arrows hit their mark.

All energy and focus was centered on retrieving valuable tackle, gear, equipment, and ammunition before the crossbeams came crashing down. Every hand was at work. Caleb almost slammed into his mother as he rushed into the barn.

She had a saddle in her arms. Her face was smudged with sweat, tears, and grime. In the blistering heat of the fire, mother and son shared a frozen moment that communicated much resolve and determination. There was inflexible iron in her expression that spurred him on. A split-second later he heard her screech a word he had never heard her utter.

"*You bastards!*"

The exclamation rang above the bedlam. The sheer velocity and shrillness of her voice galvanized everyone. The saddle had been discarded at her feet in the doorway of the barn. Her eyes bulged in disbelief. She took several stutter steps toward the object of her attention.

The inside of their house was in flames, and from all appearances the fire was out of control. A couple torches had also been tossed onto the roof. The sight repulsed her. She had witnessed several fleeting shadows speeding away, which had elicited her use of vulgar language. Even in the urgency of the crisis she already regretted expressing that epithet.

The stench of kerosene was adrift and thick in the air. It was evident that the interior of the house had been soaked with the accelerant. Now oil lamps were popping and exploding like incendiary bombshells, increasing the voracious hunger of the flames devouring their shelter and belongings.

It had been a well-coordinated assault, executed impeccably. Hans cussed once. Then, with stark reality glaring in his face, he simply put an arm around his wife. The barn was gone. Whatever could be recovered from it had been. The house and all its contents were beyond hope. Nothing else could be done.

That bleak realization crept through the group. Everyone except Yance Rawlins was clustering together in the middle of the yard, wide-eyed and overwrought. He stayed by himself near the inferno that had been the barn. He acted like an interloper, an intruder who bore responsibility for this atrocity.

Hans, Eliza, Caleb, Deke, Daniel, Consuelo, and Sally moved woodenly. Shock, with its numbness and detached denial, was coming upon them in various degrees. Each face was strained and reddened, streaked by lines of dirt. Shoulders sagged and fists clenched as defeat endeavored to knock them out.

The reverberating noise of the firestorm was loud and overpowering. Conversations were brief. Consuelo bustled from person to person to quickly determine that there were no burns or injuries of any kind. Everyone was safe.

The night grew long and weary. Tiredness came to no one. Excitement, frustration, anxiety, anger had been set loose along with a host of unspoken questions. Each had thoughts that would be almost impossible to express in words.

A large chunk of the past was disintegrating in the flames. The future was a knotted rope twisted with the promise of hardships and unknown variables. The fire raged on, crackling and snapping as sparks and cinders darted heavenward.

When an orange line showed on the eastern horizon, Caleb and Sally sat on the ground side by side. From time to time they leaned against each other. The women were the first to join them, then Hans and Daniel eased down beside their wives. Deke stepped close to them, but remained standing.

When what remained of the walls of the house came down in a hissing crash, Caleb broke the silence. "They burned us out."

"No," Eliza said, staring at her husband.

"No," Hans repeated inflexibly.

Eliza rubbed his shoulder, with steely encouragement in her touch. "We aren't deadbeats or quitters."

Hans stood. "They burned us down, not out."

Consuelo looked up at him. "What's the difference?"

"We're not getting out, leaving," Hans answered calmly. He squinted at the damaged jewel he had christened *Freiheit*. The sight of the archway, unharmed and unmoved, made his backbone go rigid. In the grayness of daybreak, optimism and gutsy fortitude framed his evaluation of the situation. "We came here with much less than what we recovered. We got livestock that needs rounded up." He pointed to the cows and mules moseying around far behind where the barn had been. The sheep and goats were out of sight, but he presumed all the animals had to be nearby.

Hans stepped lightly. "In the corral there are the beginnings of a herd of horses. The butchering shed and smokehouse are still intact, as is Deke's shack. The root cellar will be in good shape." His face, bright red from getting too close to the fire, was full of chuckles. "Look at that essential still standing," he said, making a gesture at the outhouse.

Laughter fluttered like a fragile ribbon in a breeze. Eliza got to her feet. "We'll clean up and rebuild. This is a rare land. We came here to spend the rest of our lives," she said, putting her arms around her husband's waist. "There are some clothes in storage in the root cellar, which is good. I cannot go through my remaining days in a flannel nightgown."

Hans smiled. "We'll need to take an inventory."

"Yes," Eliza said, almost cheerfully. "Consuelo and I can start that now and figure on what's available for breakfast."

Daniel was up and moving slowly. "Where's Rawlins?"

A collective frown passed between them. As everyone took a cursory look around the surroundings, Caleb jumped up and ran toward the corral. He quickly returned. "His stallion is gone."

Deke shook his head. "He shouldn't have slipped away."

"Feeling guilty, he is," Daniel said dryly.

Hans scowled. He had no tolerance for that opinion. "Rawlins has no reason to be feeling guilty. He may have done some plotting, but when it mattered most he stood strong with us." He took a step toward the smoldering heap of the barn. Blue tongues of fire were still lapping at the rubble. "None of us are shirkers. We've squandered enough of the day."

With that admonition, all found tasks to do.

Yance Rawlins spent most of the day sleeping. After riding away from the flaming ruins, he found a hiding place in the shadow of a rock formation. He picketed the horse at one end of the ravine, then crept into a crevice and curled up.

The sun was dipped low in the west when he awoke. There was a chill in the air. Swaths of thick gray clouds scudded along in a slipshod fashion. He was cold and hungry—he didn't care. He'd been cold and hungry plenty of times. He had a plan and he intended to carry it out without regard for his needs.

There was a job that needed doing. He relieved his bladder. When finished, he went to saddle the chestnut. The stallion was prancing and preening in a splash of late afternoon sunshine. Rawlins rummaged through his saddlebags to find a couple old hunks of jerky. It was tough and stale, but it'd do. He would give it a thorough gnawing as he rode.

His mind was set in stone. There would be no diverting him. He walked the horse at a careful pace. His head appeared to be on a swivel. It never stopped moving from side to side, his eyes alert for any sign of movement anywhere.

Dusk grew into full darkness as he effortlessly stayed off the beaten trail and picked his way to his destination. He took a circuitous route, not at all in a rush because he was cocksure of the sleeping habits of the man he was tracking down.

It was after midnight when he got off the horse. He put a hand on his rifle in its saddle scabbard, but decided against carrying it. He also removed his gunbelt and secured it on the saddle horn. The premeditated act he intended had to deliver a message that promised further reprisals against any who would dare to come against him, which according to his code, meant that this payback had to be extremely personal.

The sky was overcast, pitchy black and starless. He set the picket pin, gave the horse a loose tether, and began the mile or so hike to his objective. The orangey glow of a campfire acted as a beacon leading him onward. His footfalls were purposeful and soundless.

As he closed the gap, he began to hear the low chatter of voices. He paused to give a serious listen, attempting to discern all he could about the conditions in the Thornton camp. By the sounds of it, most of the men were around the fire drinking and swapping tall tales.

He came to the skimpy stand of cottonwoods. Twenty yards separated him from the backside of the tent. Caution had been adjusted to the highest levels in him. He patiently waited, listening. Every sound provided important information. His ears were particularly attuned to the slightest change in the voices cracking wise at the campfire.

He crept through the trees, stopping and waiting with each step taken. His listening skills were getting a comprehensive workout. It took him over ten tensely wrapped minutes to make it past the trees.

Despite the nippy night air, perspiration was dampening his bulky underclothes. He knelt at the tent, smiling at what he heard through the canvas. Thomas Thornton was snoring, which was what Rawlins had expected to come upon.

Rawlins surmised that the success of the attack on the homestead guaranteed that Thornton would be on his customary timetable. Unless a nighttime meeting was required due to a disconcerting circumstance, the Judge would have retired precisely at eleven, with slumber aided by sleeping powders supplemented by a couple shots of bourbon.

Those around the fire were getting even more raucous and off-color. The loudest voice belonged to Jackson Scully. His words were slurred and sloppy, a sure indication that whiskey bottles were being emptied in celebration of the previous night's effective foray.

Yance Rawlins readied himself. He slid his right hand under his coat to the modified pocket that contained the only weapon he had with him. He withdrew the finely-edged straight-razor. In all the years it had never failed to serve him well. He opened it. He rapidly sliced a large L-shaped slit in the tent. The cutting was a quiet scratch. He gritted his teeth.

He watched and waited. The snorts of Thornton's heavy breathing continued unabated. Nothing had changed in the noise or mood at the campfire. Rawlins lifted the flap created and entered the tent as slyly as a bobcat.

The Judge was flat on his back, with blankets wrapped and tucked around him. Rawlins wasted no time or motion. With one hand he plugged Thornton's nostrils and clamped his mouth shut, laying the cold steel blade in place.

Thornton tried to gasp, struggling mightily. Yance Rawlins leaned close to make sure there was recognition flickering in the Judge's bugged open eyes. It was then that Rawlins applied ferocity to the straight-razor and drew it across his throat as he whispered, "You ought not to have killed the dog."

A gusher of blood spurted from the carotid artery. The man shuddered and convulsed. Rawlins didn't release the grip on his nostrils and mouth until all signs of life ebbed away.

Judge Thomas Thornton was dead. The pus swollen carbuncle on his right buttocks pestered him no more. It would be noonday before Jackson Scully discovered the body. By then, Yance Rawlins had returned to his hiding place and slept blissfully for several hours.

In the aftermath of the attack on the Weitzel homestead, everyone took to whatever tasks available to them. Defeat had come nowhere near to knocking them out. Instead, there was a single-minded sense of hope and purpose that united them.

Eliza and Consuelo had categorized the foodstuffs and all that was in the root cellar, and were gratified. A fair amount of basics were available, along with a diverse smattering of raw materials to provide for necessities. Now the ladies were sewing old dresses, and when finished making alterations, they would get busy stitching together elk hide moccasins.

While Daniel Twosongs was off hunting game for the table or smokehouse, Hans and Deke were poking around the skeletal remains of the house. It was a hot and smoky pile which wouldn't allow much access as they attempted to determine what could be salvaged. The stone chimney and foundation, though sooty and still generating lots of heat, appeared solid.

Caleb was on a mission birthed in his heart. He knew that if he could complete his scheme as he saw it in his imagination, it would be an enormous encouragement, especially to his mother. His hands were filthy, his face smudged and greasy with sweat.

Sally had listened to his idea and was helping him. He had a pitchfork over his shoulder as they searched for a tall timber to be reclaimed from the ashes of the barn. They had been wholly preoccupied with the project for several hours and already had one piece of suitable lumber, but needed another.

"Look there," Sally said, pointing to a portion of a beam sticking out of the debris. "Can you get to it?"

Caleb studied a possible pathway. He put the pitchfork to work to move fragments of wreckage out of the way. He scraped and shoveled until he could get close enough to the charred joist. He gave it a shove, glad to see that it wasn't jammed tight. It was buried in loose ashes. He stabbed the prongs of the fork into it and began dragging it out. Dusty smoke wafted all around him, and the soles of his boots were getting hot, but he persisted until he had the girder free.

"Whew." He cooled his feet by hop-stepping. He grinned as he examined the timber. "It'll do. I'll make it do."

Sally watched him closely. "Now what?"

"Now the fun begins." Caleb shouldered the pitchfork. He carried it over to the buckboard parked near where the pens for the sheep and goats had been. Now all the livestock were in the corral, coexisting with the horses.

The wagon had become the repository for the tools rescued from the fire, a kind of toolshed on wheels. He put the pitchfork back where it had been, poked around some, then picked up the double-edged axe.

Sally stuck by his side. Soon he had both timbers situated as he needed them to be. He did a thorough eyeball measurement. When sure about where the notches needed to be made, he began chopping. The sound of steel taking bites out of wood was loud in the afternoon stillness.

Hans looked up at the noise. "What's he doing?"

Deke gave a quick look-see. "I couldn't say."

The men were crouched side by side behind the spot where the back porch had been. They were returning to their inspection of the house's foundation when a feathering of dust rising in the northwest caught their attention.

They stood together and walked around to the front yard. By then they could distinguish a horse being ridden hard and fast. They watched. The rider waved and hailed them from a ways off. Hans and Deke recognized him and relaxed.

Yance Rawlins rode up, slowed the chestnut stallion, and walked it to a stop beneath the archway. "Your troubles are over," he reported casually. He pushed his hat up his forehead and mopped his brow with the back of his hand. "The Judge got the comeuppance he deserved. He's dead."

Deke winced. His mouth tightened as though he'd been kicked in the stomach. Cold sorrow flared in his eyes. "I wish you wouldn't have done that."

Hans regarded him kindly. "It's not on you, Deke."

"No, it ain't," Rawlins said, leaning forward. "Thornton only listened to the language of blackmail or murder. I merely straightened out my accounts with him. I pray to God it's the last killing I ever do . . ." His voice trailed off.

Deke gave him a sympathetic smile.

Yance received it with an uncertain shrug. "Well, I wanted to give you that news, but I got to ride. The rest of the gang will scatter, but Scully will be coming after me with bloody vengeance in mind. I got business at a bank in Santa Fe. After that, I'm disappearing." He adjusted his hat, pulling it low.

"May our paths cross again," Deke said warmly.

Yance nodded and touched the rim of his hat. "Just so you know; there's an old Injun riding a broken down mule heading this way." He turned the horse, gave it the reins, and galloped away to the southeast. Plumes of dust rose up in his wake.

Meanwhile, a mile or so away, Daniel Twosongs felt like he was being visited by a ghost. A weathered, white-haired man was riding a swaybacked mule, moving along slowly. The years could be deceptive liars, but it appeared to be a Navajo elder he had become acquainted with more miles ago than he could number.

The sight struck him with the force of a blow from a hammer. He almost fell backwards. He had a good-sized mule deer balanced precariously halfway on his saddle, so he was sitting far back on the rump of his horse. He eased up alongside the lone rider.

A pleasant glimmer flickered in the old man's distinctly colored eyes. "Where have you been traveling, Daniel Twosongs?"

Twosongs dipped his head in respect. "To and fro to see much of the wonder that the Creator has given us, Gray Eyes."

"There is wisdom in your words."

"What of you?"

Gray Eyes tilted his head and showed a broken-toothed smile. "I have tasted good and been visited by evil. The winters come and go. Each spring the earth is reborn and I still draw breath," he said, sounding brisk and lighthearted. "The soldiers let us leave Fort Sumner. I have walked and ridden many miles. I came to check if my old friend Weitzel found his place. I did not expect to meet up with a learner I knew long ago."

"Weitzel?" It wheezed out, awe and confusion bursting in the query. Twosongs could manage nothing more. He was befuddled. What currents had shifted and were at work? How was it possible that his mentor knew Hans Weitzel? He stared at Gray Eyes, anxious for an explanation. No response was forthcoming. The two men continued on in silence.

Early the next morning, when the sky was hazy, Hans Weitzel crept out from under the buckboard. The first thing his eyes focused on tugged at his heart. So much that tears formed as a lump crawled up his throat.

Without disturbing the other men still sleeping behind him he hurried to the root cellar to get his wife. He rapped at the door, waited to hear her, and lifted it. She came up the rungs of the ladder with a shawl wrapped around her shoulders.

A frown creased her forehead. When she started to say something, he hushed her with a finger pressed to his lips. He simply pulled her into the side yard and pointed. An emotional whimper whirled in a rush from her lips.

There, not far from the *Freiheit* archway was the blackened timbers of a heavy cross. Caleb was on his hands and knees busy packing dirt around its base. He had sunk it three feet down. Even so, it was a tiny bit taller than the arch.

Eliza grabbed her husband's hand. They ran to their son, startling him because he was so engrossed in finishing the job. She hauled him up in an intense embrace. She was sobbing happy tears. Hans put his powerful arms around the two of them. Hands entwined. Each drew strength from the other.

Hans was the first to release his grip. He stepped back to appreciate what had been redeemed from the incinerated remnants of their lives. The seared and singed wood was ordinary, but its shape spoke unexpected peace to him. "It's a fine thing you have done here, Caleb," he murmured, thumbing moisture away from the corners of his eyes. "I do not fully understand, but in humility, I'm grateful for this gift."

"We're meant to be here," Eliza said firmly. "When Gray Eyes showed up as he did, my heart leapt, then there was calmness in me, and I knew that everything has happened for a reason. We must simply accept that and press on."

Hans nodded. "I want to make a place for Gray Eyes here."

"Yes." Eliza was beaming brightly. "Go get everyone, Hans. I want us to start this day . . ." She caught herself and stopped. Her eyes were dreamy and full of enthusiasm. "No, not just this day; I want us to begin the rebuilding of our home seeking God's favor. Tell Deke I'd like him to say some words."

Ten minutes later the whole group was gathered together, hushed and reverent. The grayness of dawn had vanished inside the crystalline promise of a new day. The cloudless sky was high and blue, the sun low. There was anticipation in the air.

The shaggy-haired man from Conoy Creek, schooled in the ways of the River Brethren, strolled to a fitting spot. He stood in front of the cross with the sunrise in his eyes. His throat was dry and itchy. His heart was thudding loudly.

Just two days earlier he had sat on the porch mining the Psalms in Eliza's Bible. He excavated a handful of verses that he then committed to memory. He recalled them now with passion and plain-spoken eloquence: "*O magnify the Lord with me, and let us exalt his name together. I sought the Lord, and he heard me, and delivered me from all my fears. They looked unto him, and were lightened: and their faces were not ashamed. This poor man cried, and the Lord heard him, and saved him out of all his troubles. The angel of the Lord encampeth round about them that fear him, and delivereth them.*" He then bowed his head and prayed a profound blessing that asked for God's grace to flourish in the lives of these people.

When Deacon Coburn opened his eyes, there was tranquility in his soul. He was at ease inside his skin. He searched the faces of each one in his congregation—Hans, Eliza, Caleb, Daniel, Consuelo, Sally, Gray Eyes. A thought slipped through his mind, and he smiled in agreement, knowing that at least for now, and for these friends, the long days of purgatory had passed.

Angela Langton sat stooped over at her kitchen table. She had a blanket draped and bundled around her. The house was warm, but she was shivering. She was weeping. Her sunken eyes were glassy, her hands shaky. She was reading a letter that her daughter had just brought home from town.

> *Dear Angela: I don't know if you still live in the same place or if you have moved on. I trust this will reach you, and that you and Abbey are doing well.*
>
> *I have never stopped thinking about you, Angela. Your love saved me and gave me hope. I know I can never go back and fix mistakes, but I write you now seeking your forbearance and forgiveness. I am sorry for treating you so badly.*
>
> *You knew me as Lawrence, but my real name is Deacon Coburn. My brain was addled by the war, but that's no excuse. I am responsible for my actions. It was wrong of me to leave you as I did. Not a day goes by that I do not regret my stupidity.*
>
> *When I regained my senses and realized what I had done to you, I was ashamed of my behavior. Still am, actually. I should have returned. I cannot explain why I did not do so. I was running away from past wrongdoings and shame was eating me alive. I continually grieve because of my choices.*
>
> *I worked on a ranch in Texas for Big Bull Wallace. It's in my mind that I'll return there for a time. I'll likely hook on with a cattle drive going north to the railhead.*
>
> *If it's in your heart to forgive me, you can send any correspondence in my name to Abilene, Kansas. Sooner rather than later I pray that it will catch up with me there.*
>
> *Sincerely,*
> *Deacon Coburn*

Abbey was nearby, watching her mother and crying. Angela released a half-choked sob. She asked for pen and paper so she could reply. Her feelings were numb, her heartbeat thumping. Weak and undone, she took a moment to collect her disjointed thoughts and gather emotions into words. When she wrote, it was in a scribbled scrawl.

She would not live long enough to see the letter delivered.

~The End~

www.ingramcontent.com/pod-product-compliance
Lightning Source LLC
Chambersburg PA
CBHW070838030726
47504CB00005B/1140